Praise for Conni ✍ SO-AKJ-534

Reinventing Romeo

"Truly a delightful read that will leave you with a smile on your face."

—ARomanceReview.com

"The story is a fireworks decathlon . . . technical details, romance, and opportunities for sabotage should light readers' fuses."

—*The Akron Beacon Journal*

"One of those rare novels that manages to combine suspense, humor, and romance believably in one package. Not many new authors can pull off this feat, but Connie Lane does it successfully. . . . *Reinventing Romeo* balances suspense with sexual tension to create a page-turning tale of adventure and romance. It's an engaging ride well worth the price of admission."

—*Milwaukee Journal Sentinel*

Romancing Riley

"Sassy and stylish. . . . With its fresh, feisty characters and diverse settings, this past-meets-present tale will help Lane win over a younger generation of romance readers."

—*Publishers Weekly*

"Lane's fast-paced story is a lot of fun, and the electricity between Riley and Zap crackles."

—*Booklist*

CONNIE LANE

The Viscount's Bawdy Bargain

POCKET STAR BOOKS

New York   London   Toronto   Sydney   Singapore

This book is a work of fiction. Names, characters, places and incidents are products of the author's imagination or are used fictitiously. Any resemblance to actual events or locales or persons, living or dead, is entirely coincidental.

An *Original* Publication of POCKET BOOKS

A Pocket Star Book published by
POCKET BOOKS, a division of Simon & Schuster Inc.
1230 Avenue of the Americas, New York, NY 10020

ISBN: 0-7434-6286-6

First Pocket Books printing June 2003

10 9 8 7 6 5 4 3 2 1

POCKET STAR BOOKS and colophon are registered trademarks of Simon & Schuster Inc.

For information regarding special discounts for bulk purchases, please contact Simon & Schuster Special Sales at 1-800-456-6798 or business@simonandschuster.com

Front cover illustration of locket by Alan Ayers; front cover illustration of couple by Pam Wall

Printed in the U.S.A.

THE Viscount's Bawdy Bargain

❧ 1 ❧

....

"**W**hat we really need is a virgin."

Nicholas Pryce, Viscount Somerton, tossed out the comment as easily as he discarded the seven of clubs in his hand. Through a haze of alcohol fumes, he watched the card skid across the perfectly polished surface of the mahogany table that had been delivered from G. and R. Gillow & Co. only that morning, so intent on his game, he did not notice the sudden silence that fell over the small but fashionable assembly.

Nick took another drink and waited for Arthur Hexam, who was seated next to him, to play a card. Only when Hexam failed to do so did Nick bother to look up.

He found Hexam staring at him, his eyes red, his gaze slightly out of focus, his mouth agape. A quick look around told him Hexam wasn't the only fellow struck speechless by the offhand remark.

Across the room, the billiards game came to an

abrupt and unceremonious halt. Roger Palliston, whose turn it was to shoot, missed the ivory cue ball completely. His stick scraped the wool table covering and Nick heard the ominous sound of tearing cloth.

"Damn!" Palliston swore under his breath and slapped his stick against the table, but there was no sign of annoyance in his expression, and certainly no trace of guilt. When he spun toward Nick, Palliston's bleary eyes were lit with unabashed admiration.

Near the tall French windows that overlooked the gardens of Somerton House, Deware Clifton, the young Duke of Latimer, had been part and parcel of a raucous discussion of the problem at hand. How he'd managed to hear Nick over the din was quite as much a mystery as how he was able to keep on his feet after the quantity of spirits he'd consumed. Latimer raised one unsteady hand, signaling for silence, and even before the echo of Nick's suggestion faded against the crystal chandeliers and the damask draperies, he turned his gaze in Nick's direction.

So did every other fellow in the room.

Nick was as surprised as they were by the words that had tumbled from his mouth, but he wasn't about to admit it. He was foxed enough to think himself quite the genius, and canny enough to take full credit for the notion even though he had no idea where it might have come from. As pleased with himself as he was with the turn of events, he finished the claret in his glass and signaled to Newbury for another. He looked from Latimer to Palliston, and from Palliston to Hexam, and from

Hexam to the other stylish and in-the-altitudes young bucks who lounged around the room, and if his own hospitality had not been so generous and his own cellar not so well stocked, the scene might not have spun before his eyes quite as much as it did.

"Well, what do you think?" Nick looked from man to man. "It seems a simple enough solution."

"Simple?" Palliston, whose visage was usually florid, was so little able to contain himself that he was more flushed than ever. He hurried across the room to clap Nick on the shoulder. "It's positively marvelous! Better than marvelous. It's bloody brilliant!"

"They won't be expecting it, that's for certain," Hexam added on the end of a loud hiccup.

"A virgin?" Bracing himself against the wall, Latimer repeated the word as if he wasn't quite sure what it meant, and from what Nick knew of the lad, he could well imagine that he did not. "It's an interesting suggestion, to be sure." Latimer burped. "But does it qualify? What I mean is, we have to through this think . . . think this through. We wouldn't want to be disqualified on a techi . . . techni . . . cality. Will it satisfy the Blades?"

Nick raked his fingers through his close-cropped, honey-colored hair. "Damn the Blades!" he said. "I refuse to let them best us."

"Not like last time."

Nick wasn't sure who'd ventured the comment, but when every other man in the room chuckled, he could hardly help himself. He had to laugh, too. It was a fault he had. He had the singular ability to remember his humiliations better than most and along with the rest of the ton, he had the capacity to laugh at them.

Even if he didn't, he knew these fellows, who called themselves the Dashers, would hardly let him forget. At the time of the incident, the Dashers were in the midst of a long and delightful house party at the country home of the Duke of Weyne. They weren't the only guests, of course. Also present were members of the Blades, a group of friendly but determined rivals. Not one, but any number of them—men of impeccable character and incontestable honesty—assured Nick that a particularly appealing and eager young widow would be spending the night in a certain room. Her window, they told him, would be unlocked.

As far as Nick could remember—and thankfully, he was too cup-shot, now and then, to remember too much—he was as anxious to deepen his acquaintance with the lady as she was to encourage his attentions. She had told him as much with a fluttering look before din-ner and a casual comment or two afterward. She had more than hinted at it later in the evening when she re-tired for the night, brushing so close to him on her way out of the room that he could feel every delicious curve of her body against his.

Damn him for an idiot, but he never questioned her motives.

When he climbed through the window of said lady's room, buck naked and as randy as a rabbit, it was only to find every last member of the Blades there waiting for him, laughing like loons at the success of their ruse.

The Dashers and the Blades were sworn to secrecy as to the identity of the unfortunate wretch who'd made such an extraordinary gudgeon of himself that night, of course. But as it always did, word of the escapade traveled through the Society in seven league boots. More often than not these days when Nick walked into a room, the men looked at him with a mixture of pity and awe and the women twittered behind their fans and blushed mightily.

Setting aside the stinging memory, Nick slapped the arms of his chair and stood, and when the room tipped slightly, he leaned against the table to steady it. "You may laugh, gentlemen, but I will not let the Blades get the better of us. Not this time. Newbury!" He looked toward his butler who, having anticipated his master's wishes, stood at his elbow, a silver tray in his hands. There was a single folded piece of paper on the tray and nodding his thanks, Nick reached for it.

He shook open the paper. "Shall I read the challenge again?" Nick forced his eyes to focus and read through the dispatch that had been delivered to his home no more than two hours earlier.

"It bears today's date, March 28, 1816, and is signed . . ." Holding the message at arm's length, he squinted. "It is signed, 'Respectfully, the Blades.' "

"We know all that!" Latimer waved away the formalities. "Get to the meat of the thing, man. Exactly what does the challenge say? Will this idea of yours satisfy their requirements?"

Nick cleared his throat. "It says . . . 'To those who call

themselves the Dashers, Gentlemen: You are hereby issued a challenge to commence upon receipt of this message and to be fulfilled at midnight this night.' "

Instinctively, Nick checked the tall floor clock that stood in one corner of the room. It was only a bit after eight and reassured, he went on. " 'Knowing that it is your custom to meet at Somerton House on Thursday of each week and this being Thursday, we challenge the Dashers to produce at said meeting place and at exactly midnight, something so singular and extraordinary as to astound and amaze us. We will be bringing something particularly remarkable ourselves, gentlemen, and we invite you—if you are able and clever enough to do it—to eclipse our offering. Upon producing such object, you do hereby agree that the group that presents the most unique and surprising item will receive from the other one thousand pounds to be paid immediately.' "

Reading so much made a man's throat remarkably dry, and while the import of the message settled in, Nick took another drink and glanced around the room. "I think you'll agree, my initial proposal is not only suitable but deucedly clever. They challenge us to produce something unique. Something odd and unusual. Something the likes of which neither the Dashers nor the Blades have seen in a good long while. Gentlemen, I do believe there is only one solution. What we really need is a virgin."

A cheer went up. Nick's back was thumped, his hand,

shaken. He accepted the accolades in stride, smiling and nodding. After all, it was a hell of a plan. Nick knew it and so did the other Dashers. It was a scheme that was certain to confound the Blades no end, and as such, it deserved to be toasted.

Nick called for drinks all around and once Newbury had refilled the glasses, he raised his own glass and waited for silence.

"Then it is settled." He looked from each of his chums to the other, his chest puffed with pride inside his white waistcoat. "Tonight, finally, we shall have our revenge."

"If we can find a virgin."

His glass halfway to his mouth, Nick paused. It was Hexam who had spoken and Nick looked at him in wonder. Hexam was hardly older than Nick's thirty years, but his hair was nearly gone. He rubbed one pudgy hand across his balding pate. "Do you know one?" he asked Nick before he looked at their companions. "Do any of you? For I can tell you, I am certain I do not."

The reality of the situation dawned and the mood in the room plummeted. Young gentlemen of their station and fortune were not supposed to know virgins, at least not until they were willing to go shopping at the marriage mart.

They knew the ladies of the Polite World who married for money, provided their husbands with heirs, then went through a series of lovers to amuse themselves and while away the boring hours between social calls.

They knew the Cyprians who plied their trade in the better houses near Regent Street.

They knew the charming actresses at Covent Garden and Drury Lane and the delightful and quite accommodating opera dancers. They knew the prettiest of the orange girls who sold their fruit—and sometimes themselves—out in the streets, and any number of lady-birds.

Not one of them knew a virgin.

It was a singularly devilish problem.

"There has to be someone." Nick's voice was tinged with exasperation. "Palliston, what about that pretty housemaid at your mother's home on Great Stanhope Street? Not the dark-haired one with the hearty smile. The other one. You know, the yellow-haired beauty with that little skip to her step that makes her hips sway so delectably."

"Too late for that one." Palliston hardly looked contrite, but he did, at least, have the decency to look embarrassed. His cheeks shot through with color. "Too late for both of them, I'm afraid."

"But the Blades don't have to know that."

The unlikely proposition came from Julius Monteford, a young fellow new to the Dashers. The man came highly recommended by Latimer and it was only that connection that kept Nick from crossing the room to dislodge the smug grin from Monteford's face.

Every man in the room saw the danger. Except for Monteford. Monteford went on smiling broadly, remarkably pleased with himself for having thought of so clever a scheme.

At Nick's right, Hexam held his breath. At his left, Palliston locked his knees and curled his hands into fists, ready to come to Nick's aid if the need should arise, even though he recognized as surely as Nick did, that no man in the room was unscrupulous enough to give the plan a second thought.

No man but Monteford.

Holding on to the thought as surely as he held tight to his temper, Nick strolled over to where Monteford stood. "That would hardly be honorable," he reminded the fellow, his teeth clenched around a smile that would have been warning enough had Monteford known him better. "We may be a high-spirited bunch, Monteford. We may even be a bit mad. But we are not dishonorable, and if you think we are, or if you yourself are, I would suggest that you find someone else's claret to drink and someone else's fire to warm your arse."

His warning delivered, Nick spun around and raised his voice, his anger skillfully concealed behind his usual good humor. "No. We need a woman whose virtue is unquestionable. I know you all agree." He tossed Monteford a final look. "There's my cousin, Lynnette, of course. She's always in for a lark. But she is off in Bath and damn!" Nick grumbled, slapping one hand against his buff-colored, doeskin trousers. "I cannot think of another one."

He did a turn around the room, sipping his drink while he pondered the problem with a clarity that could only be attributed to the excellence and the amount of the spirits he'd ingested. After a full five minutes, he had to admit that he was completely flummoxed. As were his companions. Just when it seemed all hope was gone, Latimer spoke up.

"There is my sister, Beatrice," the young duke said, his nose twitching the way it always did when he thought himself decidedly resourceful. "We could ask her. She's a bit bird-witted, but she is a good sort and may be willing to go along with the plan."

Nick was nothing if not tactful. It was inbred. Tact. Diplomacy. Discretion. They were qualities the English valued in their aristocracy, and along with Greek, Latin and a smattering of fashionable French, they had been drilled into him all the while he was growing up. They were qualities that had served him well any number of times in any number of situations. Qualities that had charmed his betters, delighted his peers and sometimes astonished his friends.

But even he was not adept enough to listen to Latimer's suggestion and not react. He gagged on his drink. "Beatrice!" Nick coughed out the name and, try as he might to be circumspect, he could not help but notice that he was not the only man in the room who met the suggestion with raised eyebrows. Even if Latimer did not realize the truth about his sister, the rest of them knew about Beatrice. If not from gossip, then surely from experience.

Nick scrambled to salvage the moment as well as the young lady's reputation. At least in the eyes of her brother. "Beatrice is a diamond of the first water, but surely we cannot bother her with so foolish a scheme."

"That's right," Palliston chimed in, coming to Nick's aid. "Besides, she is off to some concert or another with my younger brother tonight," and when he added "Lucky devil" under his breath, it was for Nick's ears alone.

"Then it seems we have no choice." Sighing, Latimer slumped against the wall. "We shall simply have to park ourselves here until we come up with another idea. That, or pay the Blades a mountain of guineas."

"Park." The word sparked something inside Nick's brain but, damn him, he could not think what it might be. He mumbled it, trying to put together the pieces of the curious puzzle, and it wasn't until he'd said the word a dozen or more times that the significance of it hit him full force.

"Park!" Nick laughed. "That's it. Park. Hyde Park!"

The other Dashers looked at him as if he were mad, and Nick could hardly blame them. Reining in his excitement, he tried his best to explain.

"I crossed Hyde Park this afternoon," he said, so pleased with himself, he could not keep from toasting his own cleverness. "And I came upon a crowd gathered around a preacher. Hannibal Something-or-Another. Culligan . . . Culter . . . Cul—"

"Culpepper!" Palliston stepped forward, beaming. "That's the fellow's name. Reverend Hannibal Culpepper. Famous in his own way. One of those bombastic old goats who believes no one is right unless they think the way he does. He's taken it upon himself to convert the world from its wicked ways!" As if to prove those ways were alive and well, at least in the confines of Somerton House, Palliston raised his glass in silent salute to the aforementioned man of the cloth. "He operates missions, or so I'm told. In India or some such place. My aunt Agatha is enamored of the man. Says he'll lead us all to salvation, of which I say, I most assuredly hope not."

"You're not suggesting that we ask the good Reverend Culpepper to provide us with a virgin, are you?" Latimer asked, his tone of voice as droll as the roll of his eyes. "I for one hardly think he'd be of much help."

"More help than you imagine." Warming to the idea, Nick went on. "When I came upon him, Culpepper was preaching to a sizable crowd and what's more to the point, he had his entire family with him. He introduced them one by one. A whole flock of Culpeppers, large and small."

"That leaves out Mrs. Culpepper!" Hexam observed with a laugh.

"It does, indeed," Nick agreed. "Though now that you mention it, I did not see a Mrs. Culpepper. Nonetheless, it does not leave out the reverend's daughter."

He had the interest of the Dashers now, even Latimer, and Nick knew it. They gathered around him, eager to hear more.

"From what I could tell, the daughter is the oldest of the lot," he explained, casting his mind back to the afternoon. "Her name is Wilhelmina, if memory serves me right, and she stood behind her father like one of those gargoyles you might see atop a church. Stone-faced and as somber as hell. Stiff as a poker and as righteous-looking as any three country curates. She was dressed as if for a funeral. All black and dreary. Sleeves down to here." Nick indicated the middle of his hand. "Neckline up to here." He tapped one finger against a neckcloth he could have sworn had not hung so loose earlier in the evening.

"It was gloomy, you remember, but even if the sun had been shining like a sovereign, she would have looked like a thundercloud." Recalling the young lady's expression, Nick shivered.

"She was a pretty enough bit of baggage," he admitted, realizing for the first time that he'd thought as much the moment he saw her. "Ginger-haired, if the bit of a curl that escaped from her plain-as-ashes poke bonnet meant anything. Gray-eyed. All the right curves in all the right places, it seems, though it took some imagination to picture them beneath the shapeless mantle she wore." He quirked his eyebrows, confessing with a look that just as they all would have done when confronted with a woman of even limited appeal, he had done his level best to picture what might lie beneath the yards of black cloth.

"But curves or no curves, eyes like starlight or not, she was a perfect Devil's daughter, I can tell you that much. Icy as the Thames two winters past. Unbending as the stoutest willow. Surely there isn't a man who could get within ten feet of her and live to tell the story." Nick thumped his fist against the table. "I'm certain of it! If ever there was a virgin in all of London, it is Wilhelmina Culpepper!"

The Dashers cheered and might have gone on saluting Nick's brilliance had not Monteford waved his hands, calling for silence.

"That's all well and good," the newest of the Dashers proclaimed. "But I don't see how it helps us."

The others were obviously not so lackwitted. Already, they were heading for the door. As was his habit, Newbury appeared as if by magic and started handing around gloves and capes and tall top hats. Hexam stowed the appropriate supplies, one bottle of claret in each of his pockets. Palliston tucked in reinforcements.

"Monteford, Monteford, Monteford." Sympathetic both to the man's naïveté and the fact that he was so new to the Dashers as to be oblivious to the lengths they would go to top the Blades in any and all mischief, Nick clapped him on the shoulder and wound one arm through his, hauling him toward the door.

"The answer is simple," Nick told him. "We will go around to this church of the Reverend Culpepper's and collect the pious miss. We'll bring her back here and when they arrive, we will present her to the Blades. After which we will collect the one thousand pounds."

"But . . . but . . ." Monteford spluttered. "But if she is anything like you say she is, I cannot believe she would participate. What if she doesn't want to come with us?"

Naïveté was too kind a word.

Nick threw back his head and laughed, grabbing for a wine bottle on his way out the door.

"Of course she won't want to come with us," he said matter-of-factly. "And that leaves us only one choice, doesn't it? We will simply have to abduct her!"

❧ 2 ❧

························

$\mathcal{W}$ ilhelmina Culpepper did not much enjoy the choir of the Church of Divine and Imperishable Justice.

Ebenezer Miller, who served the congregation as choirmaster, pounded the keys of the hand-pumped organ until they screamed for mercy. He had a voice that was every bit as mellifluous as his musical touch was deft, and as if that wasn't bad enough, he had persuaded his tone-deaf wife to join him in his musical quest for redemption.

Try as she might to find it in her heart to be thankful for the Millers' talents as well as their enthusiasm, Wilhelmina had to admit that their combined voices did little to enhance the overall effect produced by the other members of the choir: faithful, devoted, inharmonious all.

Officially, of course, it was Ebenezer Miller who chose the hymns, Ebenezer Miller who inspired the choir to practice long hours in the unlikely hopes of reaching heavenly perfection.

But it was Hannibal Culpepper who was the true driving force behind the music. They all knew that. Hannibal Culpepper was the driving force behind everything that had to do with the Church of Divine and Imperishable Justice, from how many lamps were lit within its walls to which prayers were recited and how loudly they must be said.

The thought made Wilhelmina uncomfortable. Raising her eyes from her hymnal, she dared a glance at her father.

Eyes closed with zealous concentration, high forehead beaded with sweat, the Reverend Culpepper sang the words of the old familiar hymn with far more gusto than Wilhelmina supposed even its composer had ever intended. His bass voice boomed through the barren and cheerless church, emphasizing those words he wanted his congregation to remember: the verse that sang of the perils of eternal damnation, the line that spoke of fire and sword, the tuneful chorus that reminded the reasonably well-fed, well-scrubbed tradesman-class folk huddled there against the spring chill that it was their responsibility—nay, their divinely ordained duty—to convert the heathen throngs.

Heathen throngs were another thing Wilhelmina did not want to think about. If she dared, her mind would start racing and she knew exactly where it would lead: to the fate that awaited her the next morning. Even listening to the singing was far more agreeable than thinking about the journey to India and what would happen once they got there and her father put into motion the plans he had for her future.

The thought was too painful and eager to be rid of it, Wilhelmina brushed aside her black mantle so that she might check the small round watch attached with a golden pin to the bosom of her black dress.

It was nearly nine o'clock.

She didn't have much time.

Once the hymn was finished and her father started preaching, she knew he would not be finished for at least another hour.

And in another hour, Madame Brenard would be here and gone. It was now or never.

Steeling her resolve and holding her breath, Wilhelmina slipped out of the pew. Her youngest brother, Isaac, looked up from his hymnal with a question in his eyes, and she signaled him for silence, one finger to her lips. When she pulled open the door, it creaked dreadfully and Wilhelmina cringed.

Fortunately, at that moment Mr. Miller raised his voice to an impossibly high pitch over an even more impossibly long note. Reverend Culpepper heard neither creak nor groan but remained as engrossed as ever in his devotion.

The strident sounds of salvation still ringing in her ears, Wilhelmina stepped out into the street.

It was chilly for a spring evening, and she clutched her mantle closer around herself. In the meager light that spilled from the open doorway of a house across the street, she made her way toward the deep shadows that shrouded the back of the church. She was almost there when she heard the sounds of footsteps behind her.

It was too soon for Madame Brenard.

Tipping her head, Wilhelmina listened carefully and when she heard no other sounds, she scolded herself for her childish fears. Pulling back her shoulders and raising her head, she continued on her way.

She might have made it if someone hadn't clutched her by the arm.

Wilhelmina's heart leaped into her throat. She spun around. "Madame Brenard!" The name whooshed out of Wilhelmina along with every last vestige of anxiety. "You startled me!"

"Sorry, *chère amie*." Coloring from her massive and recklessly exposed bosom to the roots of hair the color of which God had never intended on mortal woman, Madame Brenard dropped her hand from Wilhelmina's sleeve.

Madame was an immense woman with beefy hands and a face that, no matter how much paint she daubed on it, always looked far too florid. In spite of her enormous size, she had the smallest feet Wilhelmina had ever seen. She stepped from foot to foot on the tips of her red satin slippers, struggling to keep them out of the puddles left by a fleeting afternoon rain. The effect was not unlike that of a sailing ship listing in stormy seas.

"I didn't mean to frighten you," Madame said. "I only

thought I might get 'ere a bit early-like so you wouldn't 'ave to be gone too long from the service." She poked her chin in the direction of the church and even in the dim light, Wilhelmina could not help but notice the look that crossed her face, as if she'd just bitten into a lemon.

" 'E's going on right well this evenin', ain't 'e? Like a regular Hapostle." She clicked her tongue and tossed her head. " 'E'd 'ave apoplexy right enough if 'e knew you was out 'ere with the likes of me."

Wilhelmina knew Madame Brenard was absolutely right, and regardless of the fact that she also knew it was as sinful as it was uncharitable, she could not control the anger that rose inside her at the realization. In spite of her name (which she claimed was legitimate) and the French accent she sometimes affected (to add a certain Continental ambience to the house of comfort she ran over near the river), Madame Brenard was as English as the sky above and as generous and warmhearted a woman as any Wilhelmina had ever known. The fact that her father chose to ignore the woman's kindly nature and focus instead on her dubious profession had always been something of a sore spot with Wilhelmina.

"Papa means well." She was not so much a perfect block to believe it, but Wilhelmina said the words nevertheless, both to cheer Madame and to appease her own conscience. "He is simply more interested in—"

"More interested in savin' them what don't need it than in 'elping them what do." Madame shook her head in disgust. "What 'e needs is more of your kind of charity and less of 'is own high and mighty—"

"Pay it no mind." Wilhelmina cut Madame off before she could get any further. It was one thing to think such thoughts herself about her father. It was another to allow someone else to give them voice. Especially when they both knew Madame's assessment of the Reverend Mister Culpepper's character was true.

Reaching behind a rain barrel that was tucked up against the back wall of the church, Wilhelmina retrieved a bulky bundle. "Here." She handed the parcel to Madame. "Here are the clothes I promised you for your girls. They are not all the crack, I'm afraid, but they are warm and serviceable and with your skills as a seamstress—"

"Don't you think another thing of it." Madame accepted the bundle and tucked it up under her arm. "*Haut ton* or not, the girls, they'll be grateful for whatever you've collected. You can be sure of that. We've got some new young things just in from the country. All of them orphans. They 'aven't a decent stitch among them."

Wilhelmina did not need to tell Madame that she understood and that she sympathized. There might be nothing Wilhelmina could say to help, but she tried to do as much as she was able.

"There you go." Madame darted a glance toward the church, as the last strains of the hymn lumbered into the night air. "You'd best get yourself back inside. Before 'e finds you're gone." She didn't move an inch but looked at the ground and if the light had been better, Wilhelmina would have sworn Madame's eyes were misty. She hugged the bundle of clothing to her bosom.

"We'll miss you, lamb," Madame said. "It's a crying shame 'e 'as you goin' off to India with 'im in the mornin'. And sadder still that 'e insists you marry once you get there."

"I'll be fine." Wilhelmina spoke the words she'd been practicing ever since her father announced that he had arranged a suitable marriage for her with the suitable, like-minded and perfectly odious Reverend Childress Smithe.

Odd, her speech had sounded convincing when she said it to herself in front of her mirror. Now, it sounded as hollow as the feeling that gnawed at her insides.

"India is quite beautiful," she said, steering the conversation away from the topic she knew she could not broach without losing all that was left of her self-possession. "You know we spent a number of years there when I was a girl and even though it is where my mother died, I do have good memories. Brilliant blue skies. Generous people. A culture I find fascinating."

"Even though 'e thinks it ain't fit for you to be fascinated."

Wilhelmina managed a bittersweet smile. "The journey is long and it will give me a chance to practice my sketching and catch up on my reading and—"

"And when you get there?"

Madame's question hung in the air, as real and as chilling as the wisps of fog that floated by.

Wilhelmina braced herself. "Reverend Smithe will be following us out when he is done with the business he is undertaking now in Glasgow. He should arrive a month or so after we are settled and then . . ." She swallowed down her disgust. "Papa says it is the perfect match."

"And what do you say?" The question burst out of Madame along with an exasperated "Harrumph!" She shifted the bundle of clothing up under her left arm. "A girl like you shouldn't be condemned to life with a man as 'ard as that. And don't you go sayin' it ain't true. I seen 'im, you remember. When 'e visited 'ere last month to toady up to your father and check you out as if you were a 'orse to be 'aggled over at the Weydon Fair. I seen that Reverend Smithe and I'll tell you somethin', my girl, 'e's a stub-faced, self-righteous son of a sow who will get 'is children on you, work you near to death, bore you until you're want-witted and in the process, miss nary an occasion to offer you the Turkish treatment and re-mind you that you are a cabbage head and not nearly as saved for all eternity as 'is damned, bloody self is."

"I know all that." The words stopped against the knot wedged in Wilhelmina's throat. "But as Papa likes to remind me, I am twenty-eight and not getting any younger. Perhaps if I had some means of my own . . ."

There was nothing more she could say.

In spite of the fact that she knew it would embarrass her quite as effectively as it would put an end to their disagreement, she gave Madame a peck on the cheek. "I hope to return someday and when I do, I promise I will see you again."

"But I—"

"Take care of yourself." Wilhelmina shooed Madame toward the street. "Make sure you keep up with your rent. You know Mr. Murtaugh promises to send you packing into the street if you do not!"

She heard Madame sniff. The subject of her landlord was one sure to make Madame indignant. With any luck at all, it would help to take Madame's thoughts off Wilhelmina's troubles and put them squarely on her own. "I'd like to see the bastard try," Madame grumbled.

Wilhelmina watched Madame disappear into the foggy night. "I'll miss you, too," she whispered, and she turned to head to the church door.

She never got there.

Before she could move another step, someone grabbed her around the waist. Before she could make a sound, a hand—a man's hand—clamped over her mouth.

Reason fled and instinct took over. Wilhelmina struggled with all her might. Writhing and kicking, she ground her heel into the top of her attacker's foot.

To her wonder, when the man spoke, she heard an edge of laughter in his voice. "You were wrong about this one, Somerton." The man grunted from the strain of holding on to Wilhelmina. "She's a lively little fish and no mistake!"

Summoning all of her strength, Wilhelmina twisted in such a way that she was able to sink her teeth into the man's pudgy hand.

"Damn!" The man loosened his hold and Wilhelmina slipped from his grasp. She whirled around, ready to dart into the street, and ran smack into something that felt like a brick wall.

The *something* in question was the person of the fellow called Somerton, and he quickly fitted his hands around her waist.

Trapped, Wilhelmina looked up into a face that was as handsome as any she'd ever seen: lips that were neither too thin or too fleshy, a chin that looked to be chipped from stone. Peeking out from a tall top hat was hair that might have been honey-colored in the light of day but now, looked more the color of old brass, rich and warm and touched with gold.

He may have had the face of an angel, but he had the eyes of the devil himself.

They were blue. As cold as ice. As hot as sin.

At the same moment the realization caused a flutter of awareness to streak through her, Wilhelmina realized his mistake. She breathed a sigh of relief at the same time she tamped her wild imaginings firmly into place. "Surely, sir, you have confused me with someone else. Some other type of woman. It's Covent Garden you want if it's a canary bird you're looking for."

Somerton's face crinkled into a smile. "And if it's not?"

"If it's not—"

Wilhelmina frowned. If it was not a woman of easy virtue he was looking for, then what?

Never one to settle for less than the whole accounting, she raised her chin and pinned Somerton with a look. "Explain yourself, sir. Now! You simply cannot think to accost a woman and—"

"But I can!" Somerton tightened his grip. He was a

tall man, and larger by far than Wilhelmina. The night was chilly. His body was warm. "I can accost her, I can even waylay her. If she is pretty enough, I might even try to steal a kiss." His mouth was as dangerously close to Wilhelmina as she was to giving in to the temptation that shimmered around him like the heat from a candle flame. He leaned nearer and quite suddenly, she was all too aware of another, less-polite-to-mention portion of his anatomy as well. One an unmarried lady such as herself might not have known about at all if she did not have brothers and a friend like Madame who had always been generous enough to share her vast knowledge.

Somerton's motives might be a mystery, but there was suddenly no secret as to what his body was urging—and all too ready to accomplish. Wilhelmina's confusion dissolved in an instant, drowned beneath a pulse-pounding wave of fear.

She flailed her arms and kicked her feet but as if he knew all along that it was a useless show at best, all Somerton did was laugh.

"Settle down!" He sidestepped a kick that would surely have damaged more than just his pride and though he looked at Wilhelmina with new respect, he did not relax his grip. He back-stepped her against the door of the church and slid one hand over her mouth to assure her silence. At the same time, he pressed himself close against her to hold her in place.

Wilhelmina's breath caught.

Except for the Reverend Mister Smithe who had once forced a kiss on her that she had neither encouraged nor enjoyed, she had never been so near a man. Even so, she needed neither experience nor the memory of Madame's bawdy tales to know she was in danger.

Surely it must be dangerous to breathe in the heady scent of spirits that wrapped this gentleman like a cloud. It was, no doubt, the reason her head suddenly spun like a child's top.

It had to be dangerous to allow him to hold her so, his body fitted tight against hers. It must certainly be hindering her ability to breathe because she heard herself laboring to do just that, each of her breaths as quick and as shallow as Somerton's.

"You have my word as a gentleman. No one's going to hurt you, Miss Culpepper."

Somerton's assurance might have been far more heartening had he not hiccupped at the end of it. Wilhelmina twisted beneath his weight but he would have none of it.

"We don't need a crowd," he said, darting a look around. For the first time, she realized there were other men there as well; not just the one she'd bitten, who was standing nearby watching the whole thing with a foolish and quite fuddled look on his chubby face, but others as well. Three, four, five or more of them as far as she could tell. Her hopes of flight faded and for one panic-stricken moment, she gave in to her fear and screamed.

An act of defiance that might have been far more effective if Somerton's hand wasn't over her mouth.

"Oh, bother!" Somerton mumbled a curse. "Let's not turn this into a commotion. "If you'll simply come along quietly . . ." As if he did not expect that she would, he spun her around and one of the others tied a cloth over her eyes. A second later, Wilhelmina felt herself lifted off her feet.

"Blackguard!" Wilhelmina cried out. She flailed like a windmill and kicked for all she was worth. It mattered little. With her father booming inside the church with the voice of salvation, no one heard. Somerton carried her to the street and deposited her into a waiting closed carriage. He settled himself beside her and before she could move, a number of the others staggered in to join them.

The horses took off at a furious pace and Wilhelmina pitched forward. She might have taken a tumble if it wasn't for Somerton's arm around her shoulders.

"Nothing to worry about, m'dear," he said, and she heard him uncork a bottle and take a long drink. "You'll be right back where you belong soon enough, the Dashers will be one thousand pounds richer, and I . . ." He chuckled, his voice heavy with spirits and the sound of pure satisfaction. "I will finally have my revenge!"

❧ 3 ❧

....

Wilhelmina wasn't sure when her fear melted into anger.

It may have been when she attempted to remove the cloth over her eyes and Somerton stopped her. Without reproach, without warning and certainly without dropping a single word of the conversation in which he was engaged, he slipped one of his hands neatly around both her wrists and held them in her lap.

Then again, her anger may have blossomed when the other gentlemen in the luxurious carriage began a boisterous recounting of their night's adventure. They congratulated themselves mightily—though Wilhelmina could not imagine why—and passed their bottles from man to man, drinking deep and punctuating their story with much vigorous laughter and so much elaborate detail, she suspected it was already on its way to leaving the realm of truth and crossing the threshold into legend.

When the bottle went around for a third time, she realized she had had enough.

"Excuse me!" Wilhelmina did her best to sound as level-headed and polite as she knew herself to be but when her comment caused not even a ripple in the conversation, she had no choice but to raise her voice. "Excuse me! This is intolerable. You speak like gentlemen and act like rabble. Would someone like to explain . . ." With the cloth tied over her eyes, she could see nothing, yet she knew Somerton was seated at her side. She turned and hoped she gauged the distance right so that she was not directing her comments to thin air.

"Explain yourself, sir. Now that you've bagged me, so to speak, the least you can do is explain why."

"Why?" He was closer than she thought; Somerton's voice rumbled near her ear. "You'll find out soon enough," he promised. He went back to the conversation at hand.

As if she wasn't there at all.

By the time the carriage came to a stop, Wilhelmina's anger had solidified like a rock between her stomach and her heart. The other gentlemen piled out of the carriage and Somerton hooked one arm around her waist.

"Come on," he said, his words as unceremonious as the way he latched on to her. He hauled her across the leather bench and lifted her into his arms. "It's nearly time for the Blades to arrive. Let's move, woman!"

Her feet never had the chance to touch the ground. Somerton bundled her mantle around her and heaved her over his shoulder.

Caught once again in a grip that was as unyielding as it was embarrassing, Wilhelmina screeched with frustration and tried her best to twist free, but even she recognized the plan as not only ineffective but quite possibly dangerous. The more she squirmed, the more likely it was that this drunken lout would drop her. Somerton tightened his grip, one arm around her legs, the other settled quite naturally, and quite too familiarly, on her buttocks.

Thus trussed like a Christmas goose, he carried her up what felt like a broad and endless flight of stairs, through what was certainly a large and stately doorway and from there, up yet another flight of steps. At the top, they stepped into what could have been nothing other than a room of enormous proportions. The laughter of his companions echoed all around and Somerton's footsteps rapped against first marble floor and then, plush carpet.

Without warning, he stopped and set Wilhelmina on her feet.

It took a moment for her head to stop spinning and for her stomach to settle back where it belonged and it wasn't until it did that she realized that she was surrounded.

When she turned from side to side, the conversation faded into a hushed and expectant hum.

One man cleared his throat. Another coughed. She heard any number of pairs of feet shift anxiously against the carpet.

Wilhelmina took a deep breath. She shook out her

mantle and straightened her gown. Because no one thought to do it and this time no one tried to stop her, she reached behind her and worked at the back of the blindfold. Her fingers were stiff and she fumbled over the clumsy knots.

She worked at them the way she worked at everything else, with a single-mindedness that—had they not been so foxed as they obviously were—would have given the gentlemen assembled around her a moment's pause.

The last of the knots loosened, finally, and Wilhelmina whipped the cloth from her eyes and threw it on the floor.

The first person she saw was Somerton.

"Sir!" Wilhelmina's voice was as frosty as the look she shot his way. "I have had quite enough of this tomfoolery. From all of you." She cast a gaze around the gentlemanly cavalcade and the rest of the men pulled in a collective breath of wonder. As if by design, they took a step back.

Somerton, however, kept his place. "Miss Culpepper." He dropped her a bow that was far more showy than it was steady.

If he'd been drunk when he arrived at the Church of Divine and Imperishable Justice, he was doubly drunk now.

Somerton's hat was off and his golden hair was tousled. His neckcloth was undone. A silly smile sat upon his handsome face at a cockeyed angle. Like the perfect host he no doubt thought himself, he looked delighted to see her. He also looked thoroughly pleased with himself.

It was all too much for any woman of sound mind and able body to abide.

In the second before she cocked her arm, Wilhelmina remembered her Old Testament: Judges 15:13–16.

In the second before she closed her fingers into a fist, she thought of Samson and his righteous anger against the Philistines.

In the second before she curled her thumb over her fingers, she thought that her own cause might benefit as did God's, from a strong arm and the jawbone of an ass.

She didn't have a jawbone but one look at Somerton and his friends and she knew there was no shortage of asses.

Wilhelmina reached back and with all her might, punched Somerton square on the nose.

Much to her surprise, her attack was met with a general cheer of delight and a great deal of laughter. Even Somerton joined in.

"Damn me for an idiot!" Staggered but largely undamaged, he shook his head and dabbed one finger under his nose, checking for blood. There was hardly more than a trickle. When Somerton looked her up and down, the dull glaze of drunkenness was gone from his eyes, replaced with a gleam of admiration. "You are more lively than I imagined you would be, Miss Culpepper. And so willful, I think we shall dispense with your Christian name and take to calling you Willie. And damn, Willie!" He grinned. "You have a right cross worthy of Mendoza himself." He fished a handkerchief from his pocket, wiped his hand and cleaned the blood from his face. "If I were a betting man—"

The comment was met with jeers and laughter from his friends.

"If I were a betting man," he said again, challenging his friends to dispute his assertion with one artless and completely innocent look, "I would wager that you could take on any one of us, Willie. And win inside three rounds."

Wilhelmina could not be so easily mollified. In spite of Somerton's seemingly good humor, she bristled like a hedgehog. "Well, what did you expect of me? You are insufferable! The least you deserve is a sound thumping. You snatch me away from my home and bring me here . . ." She glanced around, taking a good look at the salon for the first time. It was a grand and glorious place filled with light and crystal, damask and velvet. Not far away, tables were set with food and drink, as if for a celebration.

She pulled her gaze back to the blue and bleary eyes of the man before her. "I don't know where I am and I don't know who I am with. Only the good Lord knows what you intend to do next."

Most of the crowd had the good sense to meet the comment with the silence it deserved.

Except for one man.

One fellow standing somewhere behind Wilhelmina dared to snigger at the unspoken suggestion and she turned to aim a withering look in his direction.

She needn't have bothered.

Before the last snicker was even out of the man's mouth, Somerton had the fellow by the throat. He dragged him across the room. There were tall French windows along the far wall and seemingly impervious to the man's sputtered protests, Somerton yanked open one of them and pitched the fellow outside. He disappeared into the darkness, the last sign of his presence a muffled yell, a sharp screech and a whimper that had something to do with rosebushes.

Somerton brushed his hands together. "That's the last the Dashers will ever see of Monteford," he said, and it was apparent from the glint in his eyes and the lift of his chin that he expected no objections.

There weren't any.

Somerton strolled back to where Wilhelmina was standing and if his steps were a little unsteady, the look in his eyes no longer was. He stationed himself directly opposite her, linked his hands behind his back, and regarded her much in the way she had seen her father eye his wayward flock.

"I have told you more than once this evening, Willie, no one is going to harm a hair on your God-fearing head. You have my word on that and though you hardly know me, I can assure you that these fine fellows will vouch for me." He glanced around the room and his look was met with nods and smiles that were hardly more sober than his own. "We simply need your assistance."

"My assistance?" Wilhelmina could not help herself. It was an astonishing revelation and it deserved all the skepticism she could pack into her words. "How would I ever be able to provide assistance to you? And why should I? You have treated me badly. Now you say you want me to help? How can I possibly help you?"

Now that the time had come for him to lay out his plan in all its endless glory, Nick found himself singularly tongue-tied. He knew it wasn't the daunting size of his audience that left him dumbstruck.

It wasn't the claret, either.

It wasn't the hour of the night or the temperature in the room or the fact that his neckcloth was constricting either his breathing or his voice, for it was hanging so loose as to be nearly completely undone.

It was Willie Culpepper.

The realization burned through Nick as effectively as did his last drink.

He had expected Wilhelmina Culpepper to be the rigid and foreboding pasteboard figure he'd seen with her pretentious papa that afternoon. He had expected her to be cold. He had expected her to be unassuming and unemotional, sanctimonious and stiff.

He hadn't expected a real woman at all.

Steadying himself for a better look, Nick let his gaze wander from the tips of Willie's slippers to the top of her sensible, perfectly plain and just-this-side-of-out-of-fashion poke bonnet.

She was not a pasteboard figure. She was a real woman, and if he needed any more reminder, he need only recall the warmth of her body against his back at the church. He had expected her to be self-righteous and he wasn't wrong there. Somehow, he knew she would be stubborn and again, he had not been disappointed. But he had never thought she would be so warm. He had not expected the well-shaped nose, either, or the perfect chin, the mouth that looked ripe enough to kiss. In spite of her drab clothing, he could see that her breasts were full and high, her hips were nicely rounded, her waist was made to be circled by a man's arms. He had not expected such attributes. Certainly, he never expected her to have a wicked right cross.

Gingerly, Nick touched his nose.

It wasn't that he thought his plan any less brilliant now than he'd judged it earlier. It wasn't that he didn't want to take a well-earned one thousand from the Blades. And, damn it, it wasn't as if he were reluctant to show the world that he could pull off a caper as easily as he could be made the butt end of one.

It was simply that it was difficult to think with any clarity when Willie was looking at him so.

"You. Help us." Nick screwed up his face and fought to find the right words, as angry at himself for feeling so embarrassed by the whole thing as he was at his inability to lay it out as the logical, fiendishly clever plan it was. "You see, we have this wager and—"

"Wager?" Willie's chin came up. Her shoulders shot back. Her gray eyes, which Nick imagined were as placid as pussycats most days, looked more now like threatening thunderclouds. "You abducted me as part of a wager?" As regal as an empress, she turned and headed for the door. "Well, you can simply un-abduct me. Right now. Your carriage must still be here about. Call it, and—"

"But, Willie!" The last thing Nick wanted was to look desperate but he could hardly help himself. He pictured Willie slipping out of his grasp along with one thousand pounds.

He darted forward and stopped her, his hand on her arm.

He was saved from doing any more when the double doors snapped open.

"Excuse me, m'lord." Newbury coughed politely behind his hand. "There are some gentlemen here to see you."

Whatever pangs of conscience Nick felt disappeared in a flash of exhilaration. This was it, his moment to cut a shine.

"Well, what are you waiting for, man?" he asked. "Show them in!"

Newbury's grizzled brows snapped together with worry and he darted a look down the passageway before he turned back to Nick. "Are you certain, m'lord?"

Nick grumbled an oath beneath his breath. Had he been more sober and less anxious to give the Blades their just and well-deserved due, he might have questioned Newbury's hesitancy. Instead, he slapped one hand against his thigh.

"Of course I am certain," he said.

"But, m'lord, they've brought—"

"Damn it, Newbury! I don't care what they've

brought. It hardly matters, at any rate. They cannot top our offering. They could have Julius Caesar himself, dressed as the Archbishop of Canterbury and sporting a purple peruke and they would not have anything nearly as splendid as we have."

"Yes, m'lord." His expression as blank as a sheet of foolscap on the first day of Michaelmas term, Newbury retreated. Willie might have gone right along with him if Nick hadn't noticed her fall into step behind Newbury. "Oh, no!" As if it were the most natural thing in the world, he hooked an arm around her waist. "We've nearly bested the blighters. You cannot leave now." He glanced around, planning his strategy.

"You!" He handed Willie off to Hexam. "You keep her out of sight. And you . . ." He pointed to the Dashers standing behind Willie. "You get there near the door. You . . ." He waved to Latimer and Palliston. "You stand in front of her so they cannot easily see her from the doorway."

"Stand in front indeed," Willie protested. Nick paid her not the least amount of mind. His brain already working over how the Blades would look when they realized they'd lost the wager, he stepped back and waited for Newbury to return.

Within minutes, the passageway outside the room filled with the sounds of shuffling feet, barely contained laughter and more than a few good-natured oaths. The door clicked open.

"M'lord." Newbury stood back so that Nick's guests might enter. "It is His Grace the Duke of Ravensfield and his companions, m'lord," he said as if Nick could not see the men who stood in the passageway beyond. "They have come to call."

"Well, let them in, Newbury. And be a good man, will you? Get us a few more bottles of claret. Our guests have come a long way on a chilly night. No doubt they are thirsty and cold."

"Yes, m'lord." After only one fleeting and quite dubious glance at something in the passageway that Nick could not see from where he stood, the butler went about his duties.

"Ravensfield." Nick made a cursory bow to the only man who came through the doorway. Thomas Flander, the Duke of Ravensfield, was as much the unofficial head of the Blades as Nick was of the Dashers. He was the same age as Nick and though Ravensfield's title was more prestigious and his fortune a good deal larger, Nick had always taken some small bit of satisfaction from the fact that the ladies of their mutual acquaintance had never been quite able to decide which of them was the most handsome. There was no similar debate about which of them was the most notorious rakehell. They ran neck and neck there. Or so the gossips all said. They also said that was where the similarities ended.

While Nick was golden-haired, Ravensfield's hair was as dark as midnight. While Nick's eyes were blue, Ravensfield's were as black as coal. Nick favored buff-colored trousers, well-cut coats in claret, brown or the shade of indigo that Wenterly, his valet, insisted brought out the color of his eyes to their best advantage. Ravensfield had the habit of dressing entirely in black, except for a linen that was blindingly white and neckcloths that were so perfectly arranged they made him the envy of every other buck within miles.

They were so different in appearance that they were known about the ton as *Night* and *Day*, and standing across from each other now, Nick could well see why the labels not only had been conceived but had also taken hold.

Ravensfield looked as if he could smell success riding the night air. He smiled with all the warmth of a snake eyeing its dinner.

Nick tossed a cursory look at the clock in the corner. "You're early."

Ravensfield popped open the gold watch that hung from a chain in his fob pocket. "Right on time." He snapped the watch shut and slid it back into place. "I do believe you have one thousand pounds that belongs to us."

Nick could hardly help himself. He had to laugh. The man was as bold as brass. "What? Are you willing to dispense with the formalities?"

When Newbury appeared at the door with a tray of refreshments, Nick signaled for him. He handed one glass to Ravensfield and kept one for himself. "It's early," Nick said, holding up his glass in salute. "And though the Blades may be old and ready to retire . . ."

The Dashers applauded Nick's stroke of wit and buoyed by their loud and enthusiastic encouragement, he goaded Ravensfield further.

"Though the Blades may be old tabbies ready to sleep

before the fire, the Dashers say the night is young! Finish your drink, Ravensfield, and have another. My claret will help soften the blow you're sure to feel when you hand us that one thousand pounds."

"You crow well enough. But you know it's all fustian." Ravensfield downed his drink in one long swallow and came up smiling. "I am afraid this night, there will be disturbing echoes of that fateful weekend at Weyne's. Another loss, but at least this time, you will not do it with your trousers down." Laughing heartily he clapped Nick on the shoulder and continued on.

"No. It's neither the hour nor your esteemed company that compels me to cut short my visit. I have a charming bit of muslin waiting in my carriage. She's as skilled at what she does as she is pretty," he confided with a wink. "My share of the one thousand pounds ought to be enough to please her and that should make her very, very grateful."

"Then I hate to disappoint her. And you. You will have to pay the doxy with your own blunt, not mine. You'll get none from the Dashers this night."

"We'll see about that." Ravensfield's dark eyes flashed. He set his glass on the nearest table and Nick knew it was time to get down to business.

With a flourish, Ravensfield motioned toward the doorway. "Gentlemen! I give you the most amazing, the most astounding, the most remarkable thing you Dashers have seen or will see in a good long while!"

On cue, the Blades who had been waiting in the passageway outside paraded into the room two by two.

Nick recognized every one of them: Ravensfield's cousin, John, side by side with the Earl of Whiting; Archie Greene, the celebrated novelist, with Stephen Wolf, the astoundingly wealthy banker; Joseph Heathe, James Varclay, Thatcher Kent, Maynard Hudson. Each of them carried a bottle and each was drinking to the health of the Dashers as they entered. Bringing up the rear of the procession was Lewis Hinter-Paxton.

Nick wasn't sure if there had ever been a Royal Italian Opera House production about India, but if there had been (or if there ever would be), he imagined that the native characters in it would be dressed in much the same theatrical way as was Hinter-Paxton.

He was wearing wide white trousers that were gathered at his ankles just above his bare feet and a sort of waistcoat that exposed his arms and a good portion of his bare torso. He sported an elaborate, saffron-colored turban with a large and very real-looking emerald pinned to the front of it and a huge feather sprouting from the top.

As exotic as the outfit certainly was, it was not the most singular aspect of Hinter-Paxton.

That was certainly the fact that he was leading a baby elephant.

"No Julius Caesar!" Nick laughed and when Ravensfield looked at him in wonder, he laughed even harder. "No Archbishop of Canterbury! And not a purple peruke in sight!"

Obviously, he had expected something a little more rhapsodic. Ravensfield sniffed decorously. "I do not know how you can be so cavalier," he said, casting a glance over Nick and on to the rest of the Dashers. "It took a great deal of ingenuity to pinch the little brute from Astley's and a good deal of convincing to get it into a carriage and bring it over here. I take it you're in shock, Somerton, or you'd have the sense to recognize defeat when you see it."

"Defeat. Hmmm." Being careful to stay away from the probing and inquisitive trunk the elephant moved from side to side, Nick did a turn around the scrawny little beast. He wrinkled his nose. "It's singular, right enough, Ravensfield. I will admit that much." He let the comment register and just when the Blades were looking damned pleased with themselves and damned sure they'd won, he added, "However . . ."

"However?" His voice edged with disbelief and just the slightest touch of annoyance, Ravensfield pulled back his shoulders. "You can't possibly tell me you've seen anything like it," he said, jabbing a finger toward the animal. "At least not here in Somerton House."

"That's where you're wrong." Nick came to a stop directly across from Ravensfield. "You're forgetting the times we've all spent here together sharing a bottle or two. I can myself attest to the fact that on those nights when we've landed under the tables and up in the altitudes, there has been at least one elephant on the premises. I'd wager you've seen a few yourself."

While Ravensfield and the other Blades laughed at the quip, Nick took the opportunity to signal to Latimer and Palliston.

As if they'd practiced the maneuver and drilled it to perfection, the Dashers backed away in concert, and Hexam marched forward with Willie Culpepper on his arm.

"Zounds!" Ravensfield was enough of a man of the world to be suitably enchanted by the young lady so surprisingly revealed, enough of a gentleman to know not to say anything more suggestive lest he offend, and enough of a realist to take a startled step back when Willie's steely eyes met his.

"Zounds!" He murmured the word this time and closed in on Willie, taking much the same kind of turn around her as Nick had done around the elephant.

There were spots of dark color in Willie's cheeks. Her eyes flashed, not at Ravensfield or at the other Blades and Dashers who had made her the center of their attention, but straight at Nick.

Like lightning.

"I trust this means our business is concluded," she told him. "And you, sir . . ." She shifted her gaze to Ravensfield. "You can stop eyeing me like a bolt of cloth in a shop."

Never one to be easily deterred, Ravensfield's smile grew broader. "You've had one too many drinks this night, Somerton," the duke said. "She may be charming in her own steadfast sort of way, but the young lady is hardly extraordinary. As you yourself mentioned, we have all seen elephants here in Somerton House on nights when the spirits are flowing and the candles are burning to their stumps. But we've seen young ladies here on those nights, too, Somerton. Dozens of them. Just like this one."

"No. Not like this one."

Nick marched over to stand nearer to Ravensfield and Willie.

"Your Grace," he said, turning to Ravensfield and addressing him in formal fashion. "Gentlemen." He looked at the others. "While you may think the young lady all-too-familiar, I tell you this: she is unique. And far different from anything any of us have seen in a good, long time. Gentlemen, may I present . . ." He paused for effect, enjoying the moment nearly as much as he knew he would enjoy spending Ravensfield's money. "A virgin!"

"What!" Willie's infuriated gasp was nearly lost beneath the sounds of a hearty ovation and a good deal of laughter.

Ravensfield had chosen that unfortunate moment to take a drink. He choked it down, coughed and pounded his chest. Eyebrows quirked with curiosity, he gave Willie one final look. "She's a beauty in her own way. But the gown . . . the bonnet . . . her crusty demeanor . . ." He shivered. "I have no doubt you are right about her, Somerton. However did you find her?"

Latimer stepped forward and because his peerage was equal to Ravensfield's and his family line was even older, he presumed to put a sympathetic hand on the duke's arm. "Somerton's a genius. Admit it, Ravensfield. The man is above your touch when it comes to being clever."

Though he wasn't about to admit it, Ravensfield

knew he had no choice. He reached into his coat pocket and produced a stack of banknotes.

"Success!" Nick brandished the notes for all to see and the Dashers cheered. "And drinks," he called. "Drinks all around!"

The preliminaries over, the score evened—at least for one night—the Dashers and the Blades linked arms and exchanged greetings. Chatting and laughing, they adjourned to the nearby tables where an army of servants had earlier set out plates of figs and bowls of dates and platters of Westphalian hams and plump sausages.

Nick said his farewells to Ravensfield (who, in spite of the fact that he was not any richer, was anxious to get back to the woman who waited in his carriage) and made a move to join his guests at table. He was pulled to a stop by the unyielding pressure of a hand against his sleeve.

He turned and found himself nose to nose with Willie.

Her eyes blazing, Willie dropped her hand the moment she had Nick's attention. She propped her fists on her hips. "Are you simply going to walk away?"

It was not a question as much as it was an expression of outrage. Had Nick been as wary of women when he was drunk as he was when he was sober, he might have realized as much. Instead, he took Willie—and her comment—at face value.

"Of course I am going to walk away. That's it. That's all. I told you as much when you got here. I promised you wouldn't be touched. I guaranteed you that you would not be harassed in any way. So you see, we don't need you any longer. You were anxious to leave earlier. You can leave now."

Which didn't explain why Willie didn't budge.

The realization trudged through Nick's head as if in heavy boots. But he had to give himself credit, it didn't take him long to figure out the thing. "Do forgive me, Miss Cul . . . Cul . . . Culpepper." He spoiled the fervor of his apology with a hiccup and slipped a sovereign from his pocket. He held it out to Willie. "Here you go. For your trouble. I will have Newbury tell Burnam to bring my carriage around. You'll be home in no time."

Her expression turned from a glare to a grimace. Nick couldn't think why. He poked the gold coin in her direction again.

This time, Willie's spine went rigid. She stood up straight and tall, suddenly looking less like an innocent virgin and more like the unyielding figure Nick had seen beside her father that afternoon.

"I will not be paid off and dismissed like one of your friend Ravensfield's doxies," she said, her words clipped by her clenched teeth. "And I will not head off in a carriage in the middle of the night all by myself. You brought me here, you'll take me home. Now."

"Yes. Er . . . Well . . ." Nick glanced over his shoulder to where his friends were digging into their suppers. "That's all well and good, but we're having a feast here, you see. If you'd like to stay—"

"I would not." Folding her hands together, Willie clutched them at her waist. "And I will not be turned into the street. You can be certain of that."

The two bright spots of color Nick had seen in her cheeks earlier were gone. Her skin was the color of fireplace ashes.

At least Nick supposed it was the color of fireplace ashes. He'd actually never gotten close enough to a dirty fireplace to see what color the ashes were. That was a job for servants.

And so was this.

"Newbury!" His voice revealing far too much of the panic Willie's level gaze caused to erupt inside him, Nick caught his butler's eye. He took hold of her hand and hauled her over to where Newbury was stationed.

"Be a good fellow," he told Newbury, "and see Miss Culpepper home. Here." He added another sovereign to the stack and dropped both coins into her hand. "That ought to more than make up for your trouble. Good night, Miss Culpepper. Good-bye."

There wasn't much Willie could say in the face of such a straightforward, albeit heartless, dismissal. She raised her chin and held her jaw so tight, it felt as if it would snap. With a toss of her head and a look at Nick that would have withered any man not so wet to the gills with spirits, she followed Newbury out the door.

If Nick wasn't quite so foxed and not so eager to join his guests for an evening of drinking and cards, he might have noticed that Willie paused outside the door, her eyes suddenly bright.

As if she'd just thought of a very clever idea.

$\mathcal{N}$ick dreamed of an angel.

Not an angel of the sort he'd seen in picture books. No flowing white gown. No downy white wings. No halo of pure, white light around its golden head.

This was a fiery angel.

An avenging angel.

An angel with granite-hard eyes and hair the color of an August sunset. An angel with posture like a pikestaff and a personality to match.

Solid.

Rigid.

Unbending.

Being careful not to move too quickly, Nick groaned and dug his shoulders farther into his featherbed. His head pounded like a military band. His mouth tasted like the bottom of a birdcage. He could see light against his closed eyelids and the very thought of a world waking to morning sunshine and chirping birds made his stomach turn.

He knew beyond the shadow of a doubt that it would hurt like hell to face the day, so he took the only rational course of action.

He decided not to.

As he had done so many times before on so many mornings after so many such nights in the company of the Dashers, he lay perfectly still because *still* was the only thing that didn't make his head thump. With any luck at all, by the time the sun slipped into the afternoon sky and he stumbled out of bed, his head would be blessedly free of the hammering inside it and his stomach would settle back where it belonged.

Pity it didn't work.

"Damn!" Carefully, Nick opened one eye. When he suffered no more ill effect than a swooping in his stomach and a fierce pain behind his forehead, he summoned the fortitude and what little of his energy had not been pickled in claret to open the other.

And sat up in bed like a shot.

There was a woman in the room with him. A woman dressed all in black who was stationed at the foot of his bed looking for all the world like the fiery avenging angel in his dream.

Only far more cantankerous.

"Willie?" Even as he said the name, he prayed she would not answer. That way, he would know she was nothing more than a spirit-soaked vision.

"It's about time," she said, dashing Nick's hopes. "I

thought you would never wake. It's nearly eight. Most decent folk have been up and about their business for hours. Do you always lay in bed so long?"

The face was familiar.

The voice was unmistakable.

Nick's stomach lurched and he held up one hand as if that alone would help keep the memories at bay. "Wait a minute! Are you telling me . . . I didn't dream you? You're real? It . . . It really happened?"

"Since I cannot say what you dreamed, I cannot say one way or another if your dreams coincide with reality or collide with it. However, if you are talking about last night—"

"Yes."

"And if you're remembering your trip to the Church of Divine and Imperishable Justice—"

"So it seems."

"And if you are referring to the fact that I was unceremoniously bundled up and brought here against my will—"

"I am." Nick's spirits plummeted. It was not some twisted trick of his imagination. "Is there any more . . ." Almost afraid to look, he glanced at the pillow that lay beside his. It was not crumpled; it hadn't been used.

Nick sighed with relief.

Willie followed his gaze as clearly as his thoughts and her expression darkened along with the color in her cheeks. "You needn't worry on my account," she assured him. "You were quite foxed, you know. Even had you been inclined to debauchment, I doubt you would have been capable. No, you have quite enough to be remorseful for without adding seduction to your sins."

"Do I?" Nick scrubbed his hands over his eyes. "I remember you didn't want to come with us. I remember you took a chunk out of Hexam's hand." He scrubbed a finger under his nose and winced. "You poked me in the nose. I remember that, too. I also remember that I sent you home with Newbury."

Willie clutched her hands at her waist. "It is not Newbury's trustworthiness you need question and you must not hold him accountable. He went to fetch your driver, just as you asked. By the time he returned, I was nowhere to be found. I suppose he assumed I'd grown weary of waiting and had gone home on my own. As you can see, I did not. I found my way here instead and I spent the night right over there." With a tip of her head, she indicated a chair that stood next to the door that led to Nick's dressing room.

"But why? Don't you realize . . ."

The full import of the situation washed over Nick like a cold wave. "Good heavens, Miss Culpepper, don't you see what you've done? Do you realize you've spent the night? Here. With me! And though you assure me there was no impropriety between us and I have no reason to disbelieve you . . . The rest of the world doesn't know that. Surely, Miss Culpepper, you will be ruined!"

"Do you think so?" If Nick didn't know better, he would have thought the expression that crossed Willie's face was nearly a smile. "Are you saying, m'lord, that no righteous man will ever marry me?"

"I'm afraid so." Nick knew enough of the ways of the world to know it was true, even if Willie didn't.

"What on earth possessed you?" he asked her. "Your father—"

"Do you suppose any father as virtuous as mine would ever welcome such a daughter back into the fold?"

"You make it sound like a good thing." Nick knew it was not. Especially if the Reverend Mister Culpepper or one of his strapping sons decided this was a matter of honor and, as such, needed to be dealt with at dawn. It was bad enough he'd had a part, however unwilling, in ruining Willie's reputation. He had no desire to splatter Culpepper blood in the process.

He might actually have had the chance to point that out if Willie hadn't marched to the windows and dragged open the draperies.

Sunlight flooded the room and like a vampire in a folk tale, Nick moaned and turned away from the light, ducking his head beneath the blankets.

That was when he realized that he hadn't a stitch on.

Blinking against the combined glare of the light and Willie's steady and growing-more-impatient-by-the-minute gaze, he peeked over the edge of the blanket. "You say you've been here all night?"

"That's right." Willie threw open the window and a stream of bracing morning air poured into the room. She headed for the door. "And now, I shall be waiting downstairs." She paused with her hand on the brass doorknob and gave him a look so much like the one of the avenging angel in his dream it made Nick shiver. "You are going to take me home, aren't you?" she asked.

"Do you think that's wise? I mean, staying out all night and then arriving home with a worse-for-wear gentleman . . ." He didn't need to explain; he knew she was fully aware of the consequences.

Which didn't explain the smile that flitted across Willie's face.

Nick had no choice but to acquiesce. Though he had known her for but a short time, he knew to do anything else in the face of Willie's determination would be about as successful as convincing the Blades and the Dashers to end their rivalry. It would also be less than honorable.

"Yes. Of course I'll accompany you home. It's just that . . ."

Thinking that he might have undressed in front of Willie Culpepper should have stirred at least some remorse in him. She was a virgin, after all. And he had the one thousand pounds to prove it.

Yet the thought that she had played him false and made herself at home here against his orders and without his knowledge sparked a note of mischief. Nick grinned.

"If you were here in the room when I came up. . . . You are too wicked, Willie. How much did you see?"

Willie's spine went rigid. She threw back her shoulders. "See? You mean—"

"I mean that I apparently did not disrobe in my dressing room." Nick braced himself on one elbow, enjoying the chagrin. "Which must surely mean—"

She clicked her tongue at the same time she opened the door that led into the passageway beyond. "I assure you, sir," she said, her voice as icy as the look she shot him, "virgins are not so desperate as you might think. I turned my back when you undressed."

Nick would have liked nothing more than to believe her.

He actually might have, if she had not left the room smiling.

Although she had been accused of as much by her father, Willie was not a willful woman—except on those occasions when she knew beyond a doubt that she was right. She had never thought of herself as cunning, either, though there were more times than she cared to remember when Papa insisted she was. Having made the acquaintance of any number of Madame Brenard's girls who did not suffer the woes of either her flaming hair or her freckled skin and Madame herself who was so clever with her sewing needle, she did not hold too high an opinion of herself when it came to either her artistic skills or her appearance. She was certainly not deceitful—unless some extenuating circumstance demanded it. Nor was she uncaring, mean-spirited or likely to go about spreading a Banbury story of a cock and a bull.

Still, she could not help but grin when, in the passageway outside Somerton's bedchamber, she leaned against the door and breathed a sigh of relief.

As willful, cunning, mean-spirited and deceitful as it was, she'd done it, and successfully, too!

Thank goodness Somerton's brain was still muddled from the night's revels. Otherwise, he might have noticed that all the while she was doing her best to sound dispassionate about spending the night in his bedchamber, her hands were shaking and her breaths were coming far too fast.

It was nearly three o'clock when Somerton had finally stumbled up to bed. With only the light of the single candle he carried to show him the way, he staggered into the room, slamming into furniture and using words Willie had never heard at home and would not have known at all had it not been for the conscientious tutelage of Madame Brenard. Unaware of Willie where she stood in the deep shadows, he went about his business.

He pulled off his neckcloth and dropped it on the floor. The warm glow of his candle brushed his skin and added lines and planes to his face that made it look as if it had been sculpted by an artist with a sense of the divine and a penchant for temptation.

He undid his shirt, slipped it off, and tossed it over his shoulder.

And she noted the fine sprinkling of golden hair on his chest, the definition of the muscles in his arms, the bare skin that glowed warm and so inviting in the candlelight that her fingers itched to touch him.

He discarded his trousers.

And Willie's fantasies took flight.

Somerton's legs were long and well shaped. His backside (her cheeks flamed simply at the memory) was firm. The rest of him . . .

Then and now, the very thought caused Willie's breath to catch in her throat.

There was only one consolation in the whole business. She had not lied when he questioned her about what she'd seen. When she realized Somerton meant to undress, she had turned her back.

She considered it a kindness that she had neglected to remind him that there was a mirror in the room.

Like the scalding touch of the Indian sun, heat curled through Willie.

If she wasn't careful, she would lose sight of her purpose.

And that would not do at all.

Her mind made up, Willie headed down the passageway in search of Somerton's breakfast room and the meal she had no doubt Newbury would have laid out even though his master was in no mood for it. A cup of tea would fortify her against the ordeal that yet lay ahead.

All she needed was for Somerton to rise, get dressed and accompany her home so she could follow through with the rest of her plan.

And the rest of her life.

A life without being shackled to the loathsome Reverend Childress Smithe.

There was no joyfulness in revenge.

Or so Papa always said.

Obviously, he had never been fortunate enough to have a moment such as this.

Already seated in Somerton's carriage, Willie sat forward and watched him maneuver his way from the front door of his grand home and down the stairs, each of his steps careful and calculated, as if moving too thoughtlessly or too quickly would be too painful a prospect to even consider.

He was scrubbed as bright as a new penny, wearing doeskin trousers that showed his muscular legs to perfection above half Wellingtons. His cutaway coat of superfine was of the deepest brown, a splendid contrast to his golden hair. His neckcloth was flawless and so blindingly white, it provided a particularly stark contrast to the decidedly green cast of his face.

"Miss Culpepper." Ducking his head as he entered the carriage, Somerton offered a greeting and glanced a look over Willie as if to assure himself that she was real and not a creation of his drunken imagination. To his credit, he did not look disappointed—at least not too disappointed—to see that she was, in fact, quite genuine.

The carriage started out at a leisurely pace and though the horses were so perfectly matched and the appointments of the carriage so perfectly luxurious as to make it the smoothest, most comfortable, most perfect ride Willie had ever enjoyed, Somerton pulled a face. He closed his eyes and rested his head against the leather carriage interior.

Except for his occasional moans when they turned or his groans when they encountered other street traffic and were thus delayed in their journey, they rode in silence. Finally, the scene outside the carriage windows changed from the lavishness of the West End and its elegant homes and parks to the less vaulted and far more ordinary quarters of the masses. The streets narrowed and the light did not flow so freely into the carriage as it did in the wide avenues of the fashionable. Gingerly, Somerton sat up. He ran his tongue over his lips. "Miss Culpepper, before I return you to your home, we must talk. You must understand. I—"

"Must I?" As ready as she was to make him a part of her plot, Willie was not certain she wanted to forgive him. At least not so easily. "I think you'll agree, it is too early in the morning for rationalizations."

"If that's what you were expecting then I am sorry to disappoint you. I never rationalize. I also make it a habit never to ask for forgiveness before noon."

"No doubt because you are usually not up and about before that hour."

"True. But I have been known to make exceptions. Both to the hour of my rising and to my usual habit of not begging for forgiveness. This is an unusual circumstance, I think you'll agree."

If it was as close to an apology as he would ever come, Willie thought it only right to provide fair warning: It was not nearly close enough. "Do you mean to say that it is unusual for you and your friends to drink yourselves senseless?" she asked.

"Not that, of course, but—"

"And that it is unusual for you to involve a young lady in one of your ridiculous wagers?"

"Well, we have been known to do that occasionally,

but only when the young lady in question is someone we know and she is eager to take part in our lark and—"

"And do you often embarrass her, then? In front of a whole host of strangers? Do you often kidnap a young lady and then parade her in front of your friends while you announce to all the world that she is a monstrosity? A misfit? A freak of nature because she happens to hold true to those virtues I daresay you would consider as old-fashioned as powdered wigs and breeches?"

"Never have before," he admitted and he looked at her with far more honesty than was proper for a man who hardly knew her. His expression softened until, finally, one golden eyebrow slipped up to a particularly cocky—and quite unexpectedly charming—angle. "If it's any consolation to you at all, rest assured that I am paying for my sins."

"It is no consolation," Willie announced. She forced herself to look away and concentrate on the scene rolling by outside her window. Otherwise, she might be tempted to admit that his words caused her heart to soften.

She did not have time to consider it. At that moment, the carriage pulled to a stop and Willie's heart leaped into her throat.

"Home," she said, glancing out the window, then glancing away again, lest the very sight of the Church of Divine and Imperishable Justice cause her to lose heart. Before she could talk herself into cowering in the corner, she put her hand on the door. "I will simply—"

"Oh, no." In one fluid movement, Somerton removed

her hand. Now that it was too late to redeem himself, he was playing the gentleman.

"I promised I would accompany you home and damn it, that's exactly what I'm going to do," he said. The pressure of his hand against hers increased ever so gently. "All the way home. It is a thing you need to learn about me, you see. When I decide to do a thing, I do it the way it is supposed to be done. If you'll allow me, Miss Culpepper—" With his free hand, he reached for the door.

Before he ever had a chance to touch it, it flew open.

Like a storm cloud, a shape filled the carriage doorway and blocked the sun. Compact frame. Thick neck. Bald head. A man rolled up on the balls of his feet and poked his head into the carriage and an all-too-familiar face came into thunderous view.

Now that the moment had arrived, Willie found herself feeling as if she'd run up a flight of stairs. Before she even knew she was doing it, she had Somerton's fingers clutched in hers.

"Papa." Willie tipped her head in the kind of greeting she was used to giving her father as she bustled back and forth between the table where he ate his meals and the kitchen where she cooked them. "I trust you are well this morning."

"Well?" Her father's question rumbled right over Willie's words, grinding them to dust. His eyes as piercing as a hawk's, his face mottled with emotion, the Reverend Mister Culpepper's gaze settled on the spot where Willie's and Somerton's fingers were entwined.

"What is the meaning of this?" Culpepper's gaze shot up and he glared at Somerton who, much to the good reverend's consternation, met the look as affably as if they'd been introduced over tea. "I asked you a question, sir. What is the meaning of this? Who are you? And what in the name of Peter and Paul do you think you are doing with my daughter?"

"What we are attempting to do is descend from my carriage." The chill of his words caused Culpepper to back away. Still holding Willie's hand, Somerton climbed down, cringing only slightly when he encountered the sunshine. He assisted Willie to the pavement and it wasn't until she was settled that he let go of her hand.

They found themselves in the middle of nothing less than chaos. All around them, work-hardened fellows carried trunks and furniture and loaded it onto waiting wagons. Nearby, a coach was standing in the ready and Jacob, Aaron, Ezekiel, Hosea, Jedidiah, and Isaac were waiting nearby. One or two of them looked relieved to see Willie. One or two looked to be on the verge of smiling their greetings. One or two more looked as outraged as their father. Her brothers knew better than to insinuate themselves into their father's business, and Willie knew better than to expect them to. They did, however, stare in wonder and their staring caught the crowd's attention.

The workers stopped in the midst of their labors. The members of the church who had come to wish the family Godspeed on their journey to the wilds to convert the even wilder and unquestionably godless heathens stood with their mouths open. Quiet descended, broken only here and there along the street by the sounds of windows being opened and neighbors sticking out their heads to see what the fuss was all about.

"Ah, the scent of scandal's in the air!" Somerton did not sound especially happy at the prospect. He did, however, sound as if it were exactly what he had been expecting.

Which was fine with Willie. It was what she had been expecting as well.

Raising her chin, she cast a glance over the people who, only the night before, had stood shoulder to shoulder with her in church, singing about their obligation to feel charity and kindness for their fellow man (or woman), no matter what his (or her) sins happened to be. Already, most of them refused to meet her eyes. A few others whispered behind their hands. Her gaze far steadier than her singing voice had ever been, Amabel Miller gave Willie a long and careful look, then pointedly turned to gaze at the closed front door of the church.

As if irate papas and public scenes were nothing new to Somerton—and nothing he couldn't easily handle—he managed a pained but cordial grin aimed all around and a second grin, no more cordial and just a bit more pained, at Culpepper. "So sorry for the inconvenience," he said. "And sorry to tell you, sir, that you've got it all wrong. I do hope you will allow me to explain."

Showing far more self-control than was his custom,

Culpepper rolled back on his heels. "Very well, sir," he said. "Explain."

Somerton smiled his gratitude and much as he'd done the night before when he was speaking to the Blades and the Dashers, he eased himself into the telling of the story. He cleared his throat. He drew in a breath. He opened his mouth, ready, Willie was sure, to lay out the whole of the story as logically and as clearly as he could.

The words never came.

"Explain . . ." Somerton mumbled the word. "Well, you see, it's devilishly hard to explain but I can tell you, sir, that you have a lovely daughter." He cast a brittle smile in Willie's direction that spoke volumes. "She joined me for . . . well, something of a lark."

"A lark, eh?" Culpepper gave the word the kind of emphasis that said he wouldn't know a lark if one came calling. "Tell me this, sir, though I am loath to call you that, for I am not certain you are the gentleman you claim to be. Tell me, why did you want her?"

It was clear that what had seemed so splendid a plan the night before paled in the light of day. Somerton gave Culpepper a blank look. "Well, I didn't want her," he said. "Not really. That is, I did not want Willie . . . er, that is, Miss Culpepper, specifically." He shook his head, clearing his thoughts. "What I really mean is, what I really wanted, you see, was a virgin and—"

"What!" The reverend's voice boomed through the narrow street like cannon shot, overpowering the outraged gasps of the people standing all around.

Willie coughed behind her hand, fighting to hide the smile that might betray her satisfaction. Things were progressing exactly as she'd hoped. Not pleasant, perhaps. And certainly not in an orderly fashion. But once the hue and cry of the scandal quieted and the gossips had their fill, she knew she would be forgotten as easily as last year's fashions. By that time, her father and her brothers would be back in India and the Reverend Childress Smithe would, no doubt, already have his sights set on another unfortunate miss to turn into his even more unfortunate missus.

It all might have gone reasonably quickly and remarkably well if not for the fact that Somerton had a conscience.

Who would have suspected?

Somerton stepped forward and raised his voice. "Reverend Culpepper, you simply must listen. There's no reason for you to be angry. Not at Willie. If you insist on pointing the finger of responsibility at someone, then point it squarely at me. And if you . . . any of you . . ." He glanced around. "If you insist on the black book for anyone in regards to this muddle, then it surely must be me. Name's Pryce, by the way. Nicholas Pryce. I am the Viscount Somerton."

The look of astonishment on her father's face convinced Willie that he was not expecting anyone with so glib a tongue or so charming a manner.

He was certainly not expecting a viscount.

Too late, she noticed the sparkle that suddenly lit her father's eyes.

"Viscount, eh?" Culpepper grinned. He reached around Willie and tilted the carriage door shut. As if the pattern of lions and squares and the spread of Latin words meant anything to him, he pursed his lips, studying the coat of arms painted on the door, then swung his gaze, sizing up the matched pair that pulled the carriage and the livery on the coachman. When he was done, he glanced at Willie and the look in his eyes spoke volumes. He was as surprised as the rest of his assembled congregation that a viscount had taken note of so ordinary a woman. But he was not so surprised as to let the opportunity pass him by.

Panic shot through Willie and she scrambled to save a situation that was quickly getting out of hand. "Viscount or not," she told her father, "this gentleman is half mad by all accounts. He took me from the very steps of—"

"Willie!" Somerton shot her a sidelong look of warning. "He's warming to the idea of me," he said. "Keep your tongue and you'll be safely back in your family's arms before—"

"All night." Willie stomped her foot, the more to add emphasis to the statement. "He kept me with him all night!"

It was a valiant attempt, but it seemed that Willie's words could not be heard over the jingle of coins that filled her father's head.

"You being a viscount, sir, and a gentleman and all . . ." The expression on Culpepper's face was as close to a smile as it was ever likely to get. "You must truly understand, sir, how important a man's daughter is to him." He cleared his throat and lowered his voice so that the people standing around them could not hear. "What I mean, of course, is in a monetary sort of sense."

"Monetary?" Somerton was clearly surprised. His shoulders shot back and his chin came up in much the same way Willie had seen the night before when he'd tossed the unfortunate Monteford out the window. He disguised his reaction behind a smile bright enough to charm the birds out of the trees.

"Are you telling me, sir, that we might easily settle this matter?"

Culpepper nodded. "That's right. And with no muss and fuss. I understand, after all, that you do not want to keep the girl. What man would, I ask you? Her being as red-haired as a ginger cat and as fiery-tempered as any three Irishmen. But now that you've had her and are done with her, we can be civilized about it. Eh?"

"Are you telling me, sir, that you don't want to poke me in the nose or call me out at dawn?"

"Nah!" Culpepper made to clap him on the shoulder, then thought better of taking such liberties with a viscount. "Can't say I ever expected anything else from this baggage." He tossed a look at Willie. "She's a willful gel, she is. Stubborn and far more sure of herself than any woman should be. Too many o-pin-ions." He shuddered. "And not enough sense in her head to keep her on the straight and narrow. I blame myself." He shook his head sadly. "I should have taken a switch to her far more often. It would'a done her good."

"Indeed." Somerton's hands curled into fists.

"Things will be different once we're away from here." The reverend nodded sagely. "Away from the temptations of the city. Away from the temptations of sin and of . . ." He weighed the wisdom of speaking further and decided a situation this potentially lucrative would not present itself again. "And of the temptations of viscounts, if you'll pardon me for saying it, sir. I'll keep her in line. And once we're settled at our mission in India and the Reverend Mister Smithe joins us, he will take over and do the honors, so to speak. I daresay he wouldn't be averse to taking the strap to her once in a while just to remind her of her place and her obligations."

"Willie, get in the carriage. Now." Somerton opened the carriage door. "I will not see your honor traded for a handful of guineas, or your person violated—"

"Violated?" Culpepper clutched Somerton's sleeve. "If we're to talk violated, sir, then we must talk about how I've been violated. A father's trust. A father's love—"

"A father who would ignore his daughter's dishonor if he received payment in return?"

"It's what's fitting, sir. It's what's right."

Somerton didn't so much hand Willie into the coach as he bundled her into it. While she did her best to get her bearings, he turned to Culpepper and lowered his voice.

"It is heartless and it is ignorant. You, sir, are heartless and ignorant. And if your daughter was not here watching, I would beat that greedy smile off your face and use your arse to wipe the street."

He swung into the carriage. "Barnum!" Somerton called and the horses took off.

"You can't do this!" Culpepper trotted along beside the carriage. "You can't just up and leave me with no daughter and no compensation. It ain't fitting!"

The horses picked up speed. The Reverend Mister Culpepper did not.

The last they saw of him, he was standing in the middle of the street, shaking his fist and screaming after them, "If that's the way it is to be then the sin is on your head. As of this day, the little Jezebel is all yours!"

. . . .

*A*ll his.

It took a few minutes for Nick's anger to abate and a few more after that before the words made their way past the furious pounding in his brain.

All his.

Quite suddenly, his head thumped harder than ever.

As the carriage plodded on toward home, he pulled in a breath and sank back against the plush seat, massaging his temples with the tips of his fingers.

It didn't help, and mumbling a curse, Nick shifted in his seat and stared across the carriage to where Willie sat as silent and as indecipherable as the Sphinx, her lips compressed into a thin line and her jaw so tight, it looked as if it might snap.

Sooner or later, he knew the weighty meaning of her father's pronouncement was bound to sink in but as the carriage neared Somerton House, sooner changed little by little to later and Willie still did not react. Nick decided that she must certainly be in shock. He had seen the signs enough times to know. He'd seen Hexam in such a state the day the poor man's mistress announced she was in a certain delicate condition. He'd seen Latimer suffer such a trauma when he learned that the sweet bit of muslin he'd had his eye on over at the Surrey was, beneath the paint and all those layers of costume, very much a young man.

Hell, he'd been in shock himself less than twenty-four hours earlier when he pressed Willie close against the church door and what had started out as an expedient way to keep her from escaping had turned into a moment of stunning and quite unexpected delight.

The thought crept up on him unawares and Nick tried his best to dash it from his mind. It was the claret, he told himself, just as he had the night before. It was the excitement of a lark the likes of which even the Dashers had never been harebrained enough to attempt. It was the lateness of the evening. The smell of spring in the air.

It was the heady excitement of planning the abduction and the exhilaration of actually carrying it out. The allure of the dark and the danger of doing something no gentleman had a right to do. It was the romance of the wild adventure and the pure satisfaction of besting the Blades. It was the thrill that ran along his spine when he pictured himself spending Ravensfield's money.

It certainly could not have anything to do with Willie.

Just to remind himself, Nick took another long look at her.

As rigid as the angel of his dream, Willie sat staring ahead of herself, her breaths coming in sharp succession, her eyes sparking a color that reminded him of lightning. It wouldn't last. Nick knew that as surely as he knew his own name. The shock was bound to give way sometime or other.

He only hoped that when it did, she did not turn into a watering pot.

Nick braced himself against the inevitability.

"Frightful old blighter." Though they were far from the church and Willie's odious father, just thinking about the man made Nick's arm muscles tense. "Can't understand how a man as disagreeable as that can have a daughter as pleasant as you."

Willie didn't say a thing, and Nick's strained smile faded.

He tried again, forcing a camaraderie he didn't feel into his voice. "You're better off, you know. India is no place for a girl like you. You'll see. This whole disowning thing . . . it is a blessing in disguise. One of those silver linings every cloud is said to have."

His cheerful observation was met with stony silence.

"What I mean is . . ." Nick hauled off his top hat and raked his fingers through his hair. A suggestion of genuine concern had somehow crept into his voice and if Willie was as surprised by it as he was, she at least had the good sense not to embarrass him by pointing it out.

"You do have somewhere you can go, don't you? Friends?" Nick winced at the memory of the leering, self-satisfied looks on the faces of the people outside the church. "No. I suppose not. Well, I know a great many people. Good families. Good homes. There has to be someone who can help." A thought struck and Nick sat up.

"The Earl of Malmsey needs a governess for his horde of offspring, or so I've heard. There are seven little ones to ride herd on and by all accounts, they are frightful, and of course, the earl himself is something of a lecher, but . . ." Carefully, he rubbed the spot on his nose that felt much as if it had met with a stone wall. "If the old boy gets too familiar, I daresay you could simply wallop him."

Willie didn't respond but he saw something flare in her eyes that looked nearly like interest. Sure he had her attention now, Nick warmed to the subject.

"If not Malmsey, then someone else perhaps. Last I lunched with the Countess of Ashbury, she did nothing but complain about how hard it is to find a competent lady's maid. A suggestion only, of course," he added, as if anticipating a protest that never came.

Eager for more of a reaction, Nick had the most idiotic urge to take Willie's hand in his. He leaned forward, his elbows on his knees, and it was only the memory of what had happened the last time he'd taken such a liberty that kept him from making the same mistake again. He wondered if he might feel all the same things he'd felt then: the quick flutter of surprise that made Willie tremble when his fingers closed over hers, the warmth of her hand, the answering warmth that had grown inside him at the very touch and blossomed when she chanced him a look.

The memories raced through him and Nick balled his hands into fists to keep them where they belonged.

"I never intended to disrupt your life," he said, capturing her gaze and holding it. "Not like this. And I do take full responsibility." He gave her time to disagree and when she did not, he raced on. "The Dashers may have been in agreement on the thing, but it was my idea from the start. It was the madness of the moment. Seemed damnably funny at the time. It isn't nearly as amusing now, is it?"

Willie might have answered if the carriage had not pulled to a stop in front of Somerton House. She was out the door and onto the pavement before Nick had a chance to move. Pulling in a breath to steady himself, he followed.

And stopped in the doorway of the carriage, paralyzed by the sight of everything going on outside his home.

It was a duplicate of the kind of chaos that had reigned supreme back at the Church of Divine and Imperishable Justice. There were carts and coaches everywhere and people scurrying about carrying trunks and boxes. The broad stairway that led up to the house was filled with both people and parcels.

"Newbury?" When his butler passed hauling a bundle that looked to be filled with clothing, Nick climbed down from the carriage and stopped him, one hand on his sleeve. "Newbury, what is the meaning of this? What's happening?" He glanced around, confirming his suspicions. "This is my staff. These are my servants. What the devil is going on here?"

Newbury was dressed in a kind of traveling outfit, rough trousers and a sort of jaunty cape that made him look as if he were starting out on a fishing expedition to the Highlands. Though he stopped and set down his bundle, he firmly refused to meet his master's eyes.

"We're leaving, m'lord," Newbury said.

"Leaving?" Nick's voice came out a full octave above its usual pitch. He cleared his throat and held tight to his composure, glancing all around again, as if this time, the scene might be different and everything back to normal.

It wasn't.

Nick dodged two footmen shouldering a trunk between them. "What do you mean, leaving? Don't be ridiculous. Of course you're not leaving. Get your things back into the house where they belong."

"I'm afraid we can't do that, m'lord."

"*We?* What do you mean *we?* And where are you all going?"

"All of us, m'lord." Newbury chose to answer the first question and ignore the second. "We're all . . ." He looked up at the sky, then down at the tips of his boots. "We're all leaving."

Nick scoured his hands over his face. "I'm still dreaming," he said, hoping to convince himself. But when he looked again, Willie was standing exactly where he'd left her, looking as confused as he felt. Newbury was no more than two feet away, still dressed in his ridiculous traveling costume. Nick's words came out uncommonly calm, surprising even him. "I can see that you're leaving," he said, packing as much noblesse oblige as he could manage into the carefully measured words and hoping it was enough to disguise the cold dread he felt coursing through him. "What I don't understand is where you're all going. And why."

This time, Newbury chose to answer the last question first. "The why of it is easy enough, m'lord, if you'll pardon my saying it. And I may as well be the one to tell you, m'lord, as I've been with your family all these years and you should sooner hear it from me than from a stranger." He glanced at Willie out of the corner of his eye and his cheeks darkened.

"It's her, m'lord." Newbury stood as straight as a pound of candles. "It's the young lady."

"Willie?" Nick looked from Newbury to Willie. "What's wrong with Willie?" He sidestepped away from her. "I say, you haven't gotten some tropical disease or something, have you, Miss Culpepper? For surely, my servants are afraid you might contaminate them."

He had to give her credit. She knew a jest when she heard one, even a poor one, and she sent him an acerbic look in response.

Newbury, apparently, didn't have Willie's sense of humor. "There's nothing wrong with the young lady, m'lord. At least not as far as I can tell." Newbury looked her up and down and his neck reddened. "She seems virtuous and honorable, if you'll excuse me saying it, m'lord. And that, you see, is the crux of the problem."

"It is?" Nick could not seem to make his way through the tangle of Newbury's logic and he looked to Willie for help. It was some small comfort that she looked to be no more enlightened than he.

"You see, m'lord, we talked about it. All of us. All of this morning after you departed. It is one thing when you bring young ladies to Somerton House who are . . ."

Nick didn't think it was possible for Newbury to get any redder. He did. This time, even the tips of his ears colored.

"Young ladies who are not quite ladies, if you catch my meaning, m'lord. It is one thing when you bring such as that home and it is your business, surely, and none of my own. As such, it is above my comment and my reproach. But when young ladies of good family and good reputation are involved in your revels, m'lord . . ." The repercussions were obviously too grievous for Newbury to vocalize.

But while Newbury may have been at a loss for words, Willie certainly was not. "Involved?" The single word echoed against the stately façade of Somerton House, each syllable ripe with outrage. Willie stepped forward to face Newbury. "How dare you accuse your master of impropriety," she said, and when the rest of the staff stopped what they were doing and did their best to pretend they weren't listening at the same time they strained to hear, she narrowed her eyes and shot them a look that was no less infuriated than her voice. "You've got it all wrong. All of you. It was not his idea that I spend the night, but mine and the fact that nothing happened—"

"Be that as it may . . ." The very fact that Newbury

would presume to interrupt was a sign of his distress. "We had a bit of a meeting this morning, m'lord. All of us." He gestured toward the crowd, most of whom— now that their mutiny was public knowledge and their lord was looking at them—turned away or stared down at the ground. "It took us a while to hash the thing out but we finally decided. We will not . . . We cannot . . . be a party to such depravity."

While Willie managed a sputtered protest, Nick could manage nothing at all. There was a knot in his throat the size of Gloucester. It matched the one in his stomach. He stared at Newbury in dumb amazement, fighting to take in everything the man was telling him and feeling not unlike he'd felt the night before when Willie's fist came out of nowhere and connected with his nose.

The fact that it was completely unlike Newbury to disregard his master's feelings should have told Nick just how far past hope the situation had progressed. As if pronouncing a death sentence, Newbury pulled back his stooped and scrawny shoulders. "Surely you under-stand, m'lord," he said. "We have our reputations to con-sider. Even if you do not."

One part of Nick wanted to argue with the man. An-other wanted to throw up his hands in disgust. A third wanted to throttle him. He decided on a strategy some-where in between. "But where will you go?" he asked. "I mean, there's a damned lot of you. Upstairs maids and downstairs maids and tweenies by the score. Where will Cook go?" His mouth watered at the memory of Cook's superb meals.

"And you, Newbury? You're not Moses. You can't lead the masses out of here and into the bally desert and wait for manna to fall out of the skies to feed you. There are other considerations. You'll need work and no one is going to hire—"

"Good morning, Somerton!"

Nick's words stopped as if they'd been sliced with a knife. He didn't need to turn around to know who'd come up on him unawares. He recognized the voice. After all, he'd heard it only the night before, when the leader of the Blades admitted defeat at the hands of the Dashers.

And suddenly, everything made sense.

"Ravensfield!" Hiding his distress, Nick turned and smiled at the duke with a sangfroid that was famous in ton circles and a smile cold enough to freeze the devil himself out of hell. "I might have known you'd be at the bottom of this."

The corners of the duke's mouth twitched with the effort of controlling a smile. "I don't know what you're talking about," he said. He sauntered over to where Willie was standing and lifted her hand. He kissed her fingers.

"I don't know what you see in the man," Ravensfield said to Willie. "But then, Somerton's appeal to women has always been something of a mystery to me. He's not a bad fellow, though he does tend to be a bit hasty at times. I think you'll agree with me there. And if the stories I've heard are to be believed, he has something of a temper. Besides that, let's see . . ." He pursed his lips, thinking. "He takes too many things far too seriously," Ravensfield declared and added with a laugh, "Except for love, of course!"

"And is that how you expect me to react to the mass desertion of my entire staff? By not taking it too seriously?" Nick snatched Willie's hand out of the duke's grasp. "Explain yourself, Ravensfield."

The words were simple, but there was no mistaking the edge of anger that honed them. Ravensfield gave in with enough of a smile to make it seem as if it were his own idea. "I called around to see you this morning. Seems that last night, I was in so much of a hurry to get back to my most delightful companion that I left my hat behind. I could have sent a servant around, of course, but as luck would have it, I was passing this way on other business. Imagine my surprise when your good Newbury informed me that you were not in. That you had taken the young lady home. At ten o'clock in the morning!"

Ravensfield's knowing gaze appraised Willie from head to toe and though he was clearly amazed that such a plain-as-Salisbury miss could attract the attention of a man as discriminating as Somerton, there was something in his frank assessment that said he approved nonetheless.

It wasn't until Ravensfield's gaze rested on Willie's hand that Nick realized he was still holding it. He dropped it as if it were on fire. "It isn't what you think," he said.

"Me?" Ravensfield's expression was the picture of innocence. "I don't think a thing. And if I did, it is no more my business than my . . . business . . . is any business of yours. But your servants . . ." He shook his head. "They were in a terrible quandary when I arrived. And quite upset by all accounts. I couldn't help but hear what was going on. There was some talk of how you'd done it this time, besmirched the family name well and good, and one little scullery maid was in tears. Seems she was worried what might happen when her sainted, white-haired granny discovered that the Viscount Somerton's supposedly respectable home was really a house of ill repute." Ravensfield shrugged his broad shoulders.

"What else could I do?" he asked. "I tried to help as much as I was able." He paused long enough to make sure Nick got his message. "They had worked themselves into quite a state. You know how the serving classes can get when they are provoked. Finally I realized there was no soothing them. I did what any friend would do, what you yourself would have done had I been in such a predicament. I stepped in and set things straight."

"You stepped in and stole them out from under me!"

As if Nick had meant the accusation as a compliment, Ravensfield beamed a smile. "I've just finished construction on Broadworth Hall, my new country home in Berkshire. Seven thousand acres. Fifty-nine rooms not counting the servants quarters. I have to admit, I was beginning to wonder where I'd find a trained staff to step in and get the place up and running.

Not that they are nearly enough." Ravensfield let go a long-suffering sigh.

"But for now, they will have to do. And I have always admired your Newbury." He laughed. "*My* Newbury," he corrected himself. "He is a man of impeccable manners, even if his taste in traveling clothes is rather less than might be hoped for. So . . ."

Savoring the moment, Ravensfield drew in a deep breath. "We are off to Berkshire where the air is clean, the skies are blue. Don't blame them for leaving, by the way, and don't be angry. I've more than doubled their yearly wages. They couldn't possibly refuse my offer. Sorry, Somerton." He clapped Nick on the back and smiling like a brewer's horse, he signaled to the convoy of servants to get started at the same time he headed back to his carriage.

"Oh and by the way . . ." Halfway there, Ravensfield stopped and turned. "You've done it again," he said with a wink and a sly smile. "More fodder for the gossip mills. Word's gone around as word always does. They're talking about this little incident from one end of London to the other and from what I've heard, there are more tongues wagging this time than the last. Last time, there was no mistaking what you had in mind when you pounced through that window, naked as the cuckoo in Christmas. This time . . ." He touched the brim of his hat and bowed in Willie's direction.

"This time, you've got them guessing. Drives them mad, you know. The rumormongers hate it when they don't know all the details. It looks like they will do what they always do. They will simply have to invent them. Good day, Somerton." He nodded. "And to you, miss." His parting words hanging in the air like oil on a stream, Ravensfield hopped into his curricle, grabbed the reins and started off, and the long line of carts filled with Nick's former servants followed behind.

Paralyzed with disbelief and numb with anger, Nick watched them go and it wasn't until the last cart had turned the corner that he shook himself out of his daze. He headed for the house, covering the distance quickly, his steps hammering the pavement at the same time his gaze darted from house to house along the street.

They might pretend to fine manners and flawless up-bringing, but his neighbors were no more circumspect about their interest in the goings-on in front of Somerton House than were the people who lived around Culpepper's church. There wasn't one house on the elegant street where the draperies weren't open, and not any window in any of those houses that didn't have a nose pressed to the glass and a pair of overcurious eyes behind it, watching the peculiar farce taking place outside Somerton House.

The dazzling smile Nick aimed at his nosy neighbors was enough to inform them he'd seen them, and taken note. One by one, the faces disappeared from the windows and the draperies fell back into place.

As a matter of habit, Nick paused outside the imposing front door of his home, so used to having someone step forward to open it for him that he nearly forgot there was no one there to perform the service. Mumbling a curse, he hauled open the door and slammed it shut behind him with enough force to make the crystal chandelier in the entryway chink. He stalked up the stairs and into the library and headed straight for the sideboard. There was a bottle of brandy there and he peeled off his gloves and tossed them aside. He reached for the bottle, splashed three fingers of brandy into a glass, downed it, and poured another before he plopped into the nearest chair.

"Have you eaten anything today?"

Startled by the voice, Nick looked up and found Willie toeing the line between the passageway outside and the library. "I'd forgotten about you."

"There's a fine thing to say." They were far beyond formalities and she didn't wait to be invited in. She crossed the room, the sound of her steps like a whisper against the carpet. She perched herself on the chair opposite his. "I am sure I am not nearly as talented as your cook but I can prepare something if you like. It's the least I can do."

"The least you can do?" Nick laughed. "Surely you're confused, Miss Culpepper. As all of London is sure to know by now, I am the guilty party here." Even if Willie could not, he could well imagine that the air over the West End was already blue with the rumors, the story gaining more fanciful and scandalous details with each recounting. He could hear it now: a pretty and virtuous girl whisked from the doors of a church against her will; a house full of wild and drunken men; a journey home the next morning, just the reckless and notorious viscount and a miss who was by this time, no doubt, a mistress.

The very thought gave Nick the all-overs.

"There's nothing at all for you to feel contrite about," he assured her.

"Isn't there?" Willie glanced away. It was a strangely hesitant reaction from a woman who was direct enough to speak her mind and sure enough of herself to let a right cross punctuate her words, and it was that more than anything else that convinced Nick he needed to take control and set things right.

It was damned inconvenient to be made to feel so guilty so early in the day.

Damned awkward to be reminded that he had principles.

Damned annoying that his conscience should remind him that there was a solution to the problem.

Suddenly finding himself at a place he had hoped to never venture, in a situation he had hoped not to have to face for a very long time, Nick knew exactly what to do. He downed his drink in one gulp and pulled himself to his feet.

"Willie . . . er . . . Miss Culpepper . . ." He didn't much like the way his voice wavered over the words but now that he'd begun, he couldn't stop.

"Miss Culpepper, I should be most honored if you would accept my offer of marriage."

◈ 6 ◈

....

It was difficult to take a proposal of marriage seriously when the man making it looked as if he were standing before a firing squad.

His body braced as if for the punch of bullets to his chest, his breath tight, Somerton waited for Willie's answer. From the look of complete and absolute panic on his face, there was no doubt that he thought he knew exactly what that answer would be.

Earlier, Willie had admitted that she enjoyed watching Somerton's discomfort, both physical and mental. But though she might be small-minded, she was not cruel. Outside the Church of Divine and Imperishable Justice, Somerton had stood at her side and defended her honor and because of it—and her own cunning plot to rid herself of Childress Smithe—he found himself in a bumble bath.

The least she owed him for his trouble and his willingness to put it right was a measure of honesty.

"I . . ." Willie scolded herself for sounding no more steady than Somerton looked. She drew in a breath, collecting her thoughts and because she refused to let him see that her hands were shaking, she busied herself untying the ribbon on her bonnet. She slipped the bonnet off and set it on the nearest table. "I couldn't possibly," she told him. "You see—"

"Damn! Of course you couldn't." Somerton slapped one hand against his thigh and his mouth thinned in disgust, not at her but at himself. "That isn't the way it's supposed to be done. I realize that, of course. I wasn't thinking."

Before she could tell him he had it all wrong, he grabbed her hand and held it between both of his own. "A man should be more sentimental when he's broaching such a delicate subject, even in circumstances like these." Somehow, he managed to disguise what he must certainly be feeling behind a charm so natural that had Willie been more naïve, she might actually have believed him.

"I know this is sudden." Somerton recognized the irony of the statement and added, "Hell, this entire situation is sudden. But . . ." He tightened his hold on her hand. "It would be an honor, of course. I said that before, didn't I? You would make me the happiest man in the world if you would agree to be my wife."

"Don't be absurd!" In spite of the serious nature of the situation, Willie could not keep from laughing. "You hardly know me."

"I know enough about you to know you would make

a serviceable companion." It seemed Somerton was not persuading her nearly as well as he was convincing himself. Hell-bent for leather, he barreled on. "In the short time I have known you, I have learned that you are determined and dutiful. I suspect you are conscientious and I know from your background and your upbringing that you most certainly must be honest, faithful, and loyal, as well."

All this fervent persuasion was beginning to make Willie feel light-headed.

She twitched aside the thought and got back to the matter at hand. "Are you looking for a wife, sir? Or a dog?"

"I'm sure you would keep the house running like clockwork," he added, not missing a beat. "You'd keep the servants in line—if, indeed, we ever had servants again—and you'd keep the books in order and the silver counted and my social calendar shipshape and in Bristol fashion. I could use that. Someone to remind me of my social obligations!"

"Ah, not a dog, then. You're looking for a secretary! Or is it a housekeeper?"

The absurdity of the situation completely escaped him. He continued to stare into her eyes, his expression nearly as earnest as she knew it to be false.

It looked as if humor would not dissuade him. Something more serious was in order. Willie wiped the smile from her face.

"And what of romance, then?" she asked. "You haven't said a thing about it. How can you offer me marriage unless you can also offer me love?"

Somerton stood as still as if her words had turned him to stone. "Very well." His words came out like stones, too. Willie swore she could see them falling from his lips. Clearing his throat, he grimaced and dropped down on one knee.

"Miss Culpepper, the sun that shines outside this very window shines no more brightly than on your face. The moon that dances across the night sky does not rise unless at your command. You are the light of my life, the rhythm of my heart. I pledge you my . . ." He clenched his teeth. "My love."

She had the most ridiculous urge to call his bluff and agree to the proposal.

Willie dismissed the thought along with the tingle that sped up her spine when she looked into Somerton's eyes. Tingling was not in her own best interests, she reminded herself. Nor was it in his.

"And what of Ravensfield, then?" The question popped out of her before she could stop it. "What of the things he said?"

"Ravensfield?" For a second, Somerton allowed his skepticism to poke its head out from under the stifling wrappings of his romantic notions. He hauled himself to his feet. "What did Ravensfield say?"

"He said you took far too many things far too seriously. Don't you remember? He also said that love wasn't one of them. He said you were never serious about love. And though I think there are things you and Ravensfield do not agree upon, something tells me this is not one of them."

Somerton tossed the objection aside. "Never before. It's true. I never before have taken the notion of love seriously. But if you were to be my wife—"

"If I were to be your wife . . ." Willie pulled her hand from his and stepped back, away from the maddening gleam in Somerton's eyes and the little voice inside her own head that asked what it would be like to spend the rest of her life with him. It would be impossible, she reminded the voice. Impossible, infuriating, inconceivable. Even though there was a part of her that thought it might also be intriguing to wake up each morning with him beside her and to go to bed each night wrapped in his arms. Even though that same little voice and the pictures that flashed through her head reminded her of the way his naked body had been gilded by candlelight and of the way just looking at him made her feel.

The thought caught her off guard, but Willie was too practical not to recognize it for the airy nothing it was. "We would not have a happy day between us," she told him and reminded herself. "You would be only too eager to be away from me and would retreat to your club and gamble away your troubles. You would satisfy yourself with a variety of doxies who would sympathize with the true but very sad fact that you are shackled to a ginger-headed, bran-faced bluestocking."

Somerton looked genuinely hurt. "Do you think so little of me, then?"

"No," Willie told him and it wasn't until she said it that she realized it was true. "I think too much of you. I do not know you, sir, and last night, it was no mistake that I cuffed you on the nose. I had decided, you see, that you were little more than a drunken lout. Arrogant. Maddening. And far too sure of yourself for your own good. I have no doubt that all those things are still true. But this morning . . ." She turned away from him, certain she would not be able to continue if she kept looking into his eyes.

"This morning you proved yourself a true friend and the least I can be is honest in return." She went as far as the mantelpiece, then turned again to face him. "Think of what you are asking! I am no society miss and I would never meet with the approval of your friends or your family. I don't know how to behave at a ball because I have never attended one. I don't know how to ride as do so many ladies, because I have never had reason to learn or the leisure to practice. I don't know which colors are fashionable this spring or what fabrics might make the most fetching gowns. I'm abominable at making small talk and would embarrass you the first time you trotted me out to tea. As you heard my father say, I have too many convictions and too little inclination to keep them to myself. I would make you a poor wife and a poorer companion and we would be heartily miserable for the rest of our natural days. You do not deserve so severe a punishment for what was, after all, really a very poor escapade."

"Poor? Do you think so?" It was clear she was assailing Somerton's opinion of his cleverness and just as clear no one ever had before. He cocked his head. "I'd say the look on Ravensfield's face when he realized he'd lost a thousand was well worth the effort."

"And is it also well worth spending the rest of your life with me?"

She had him there, there was no denying it. Still, Somerton refused to give way.

"What of your reputation, then?" he asked. "Ravensfield said people are talking."

"Let them!" It was as close as Willie had ever come to thumbing her nose at the conventions her father held so dear and the heady feeling of it made her laugh. "I can only think that whatever they say—true or not—will only enhance your reputation. As to mine . . . I brought this on myself. By staying the night. And what you don't know . . ." She hesitated, wondering first how his opinion of her might change when he knew the whole of the truth and second, why she cared.

"I knew what would happen when I did. Or at least I hoped. Don't you see? This is exactly the outcome I expected. I wanted my father to disown me. So that I might avoid a marriage in India."

"The Reverend Mister Smithe?"

"One and the same." A chill touched Willie's shoulders. "He's a repulsive fellow. Eyes like a dead cod's. Hair that is dark and oily and nearly touches his shoulders. His parson's clothing hangs from a body that is too thin and too tall and altogether too horrible for words."

Somerton looked surprised that he had not put two and two together earlier and come up with the proper answer. His eyes sparked and his hands curled into fists. "Ah, the fellow who would not be averse to taking the strap to you once in a while." He drew in a breath, mastering his anger and when he looked at Willie again, one corner of his mouth crinkled into a smile.

"I say, Willie, you are clever!" He went over to the sideboard, poured another glass of brandy and handed it to her. He bowed in her direction, then lifted his own glass in a toast. "Here's to you, miss! You more than come up to scratch. You have the ingenuity of a Captain Sharp and the courage of a battalion!"

"And because of me, you have no staff." When he motioned to her to drink up, Willie took a sip. Because her father never permitted them in the house, she was not used to spirits, and the brandy burned her throat and settled in her stomach like fire. It was not an unpleasant sensation. "What will you do?"

He waved away the question with one hand. "It is of little consequence. I'll manage. The real question, of course, is what will you do? Did you have any plans? I mean, you hoped your father would toss you out. But if he did, did you think where you would go or what you would do?"

"There's always the Earl of Malmsey," she suggested, even though from what he'd said, she thought it would be a most undesirable position. "Or that duchess you spoke of. The one who needs a lady's maid. Or . . ." Another thought occurred to her and Willie set down her glass and faced him. "You need someone."

Was it her imagination, or did Somerton hesitate just a bit too long?

"Yes, I do," he said, pulling his gaze from her and

frowning into his glass. "I need a butler and a I need a housekeeper. I need maids by the score and a cook—a good cook. If you know someone—" He looked up at her and saw that she was serious. "You're not saying—"

"And why not?" Perhaps it was the brandy. The more Willie talked about it, the more reasonable it seemed. "I owe you something, surely. If it wasn't for me, your servants would not have exited *en masse*."

"But . . ." Somerton held out his arms and looked from one end of the expansive room to the other. "Somerton House is large and though you pack the punch of a regiment of seasoned troopers, there is only one of you."

"There is only one of you as well," Willie countered. "How much work can it be? I can cook. I've done it for years for my father and brothers. I can clean. I've done that, as well. I can read better than most, write a cleaner hand, keep more careful books."

"And it is quite simply out of the question."

That's all there was to it. Somerton's tone of voice as much as told her so. It was just as well. It was surely a cockle-brained idea from the start. Which did not explain why for one short-lived moment, it had sounded so good to Willie. Almost as good as it would have been to see Somerton each day.

It was that realization more than anything else that helped Willie make up her mind. She had never been a flighty girl, nor was she a woman inclined to romantic notions. She had never had the time or the inclination nor had she ever met a man who inspired such castles in the sky.

And now that she had, she recognized how impossible the whole thing was.

With a fleeting smile, she retrieved her bonnet and headed for the door. "You are right, of course," she told him. "It would never work."

"Not in a million years."

"Of course." She glanced over her shoulder to where he was standing. It must have been a trick of the light that filtered through the windows at his back. She thought when she did, he pulled himself to a stop, as if he'd been about to come after her.

She scolded herself for being far too fanciful. "I appreciate all you've done for me. More than I can say. I'll just let myself out, why don't I." She reached for the doorknob and only stopped when she heard his voice.

"I say, Willie . . ."

She turned to find that he'd come a few steps closer.

"Are you any good at toast and jam?"

Willie was, in fact, quite good at toast and jam. She was also good at preparing a more substantial breakfast on those days—few and far between as they were— when Somerton wasn't feeling the nasty aftereffects of the night before. She was good at hauling water, good at beating carpets, good at scrubbing floors and pots and the stone stoop out front. She was a dab hand at dealing with the flurry of invitations that came down upon

Somerton each day like snowflakes out of a January sky. She was good at keeping his schedule running as smoothly as possible considering how often he was inclined to sidestep his social commitments in favor of an evening of revelry with the Dashers.

She was not, however, good at all of them. And not all at once. And certainly not all by herself.

Her face covered with grime, her clothes spotted with fireplace ash and her hair hanging loose and in her eyes, Willie groaned.

Somerton House was as big as a highflyer's dreams and as hard to manage as any six churches.

Even after a week, there were entire rooms she'd never entered, passageways she'd never had a chance to walk down, windows she'd never had the opportunity to look out of because she was always so busy taking care of the necessities.

She was deathly tired and more and more lately, she rued the day she had rejected Somerton's marriage bargain and vowed that she could handle things on her own until a new staff was hired. Especially when it looked as if that might not happen anytime soon.

Though in fashionable circles her kidnapping had done nothing but put a shine on Somerton's standing as a rakehell of the first order and thus, a man to be admired for his daring and his brass, news of the escapade was not so well received with the working classes. The scandal was still too new and while it was, it qualified Somerton as far too wicked a master. Willie had dutifully advertised for staff. To date, she had no candidates.

She turned the problem over in her head at the same time she reached for a stiff-bristled brush and tried her best to get rid of the ashes that had somehow managed to powder the carpet from one end to the next.

In the last week, she had seen little of Somerton. He slept late and came in at the hour when most decent people were nearly ready to wake. He said little and ate much. He came and went as carefree as a summer's day and while he did, Willie cleaned and cooked and waited up late until her eyes were heavy and her head bobbed, just to hear the sound of his carriage and know that he had returned home safely.

She may as well have accepted his proposal of marriage.

As disgusted with the thought as she was with herself for having it, Willie tossed down the brush. It landed with a dull thud in the pile of ashes she had already gathered and they rose like smoke into the air, scattering to the four corners of the room.

"Damn!" She mumbled the word and when the clouds did not part, thunder did not rumble and lightning did not strike, she repeated it, louder and with far more feeling. But while the outburst might have made her feel better, it did little to help with the mess.

What she needed, Willie decided, was a miracle.

That, and a bucket of water.

Because she didn't expect the one at all and because she knew the other would never arrive on its own, she headed to the kitchen. She'd just gotten there and filled a bucket when there was a knock on the door.

She wiped her hands against her apron and scooped

a curl of hair out of her eyes. She opened the door and sucked in a breath of surprise.

Something told Willie that her miracle had just arrived.

It was habit alone that made Nick pause at his front door. Habit, and a lifetime of being waited on hand and foot by an army of discreet, perfectly mannered and impeccably trained servants that made him step back, as if he needed no other gesture than that to make a liveried footman materialize from the nighttime mist to open the door.

"Ridiculous," he mumbled.

"What's that you say?" The fog that filled the midnight air was thick enough to hide even a man as substantial as Arthur Hexam. Little by little, he came into view as he climbed the stairs to the door of Somerton House. His pudgy cheeks were the color of summer cherries, his breaths strained from the effort of mounting the twelve steps up from the pavement.

"You're not talking to yourself again, are you, Nick?" Smiling, Hexam retrieved a handkerchief from his pocket and wiped it across his forehead. "You've been doing that a good deal lately, you know. Talking to yourself. Ever since—"

"Ever since my household has been in an uproar and my life has been in chaos." Nick didn't need Hexam to remind him that he'd been mumbling like a bedlamite this past week. He didn't need Hexam to point out that it was this past week that Willie had been in the house.

"She's trying her best," Nick said below his breath,

and even he wasn't sure if he was trying to assure
Hexam. Or reassure himself.

"You mean Willie?" Roger Palliston joined them at
the front door. "Latimer is instructing his grooms to
wait upon our return," he said, glancing back through
the mist to where they'd left the duke's crack new drag.
"You are talking about Willie, aren't you?"

Nick sighed. He'd hoped the mention of Latimer's
well-appointed carriage would be enough to change the
subject. He should have known his friends would not let
it go so easily. They were never ones to drop what could
be an interesting topic. Most especially when the topic
was a woman.

"Yes, we're talking about Willie," Nick said, unac-
countably annoyed by the realization. "Though for the
life of me, I don't know why. She's made a shambles of
my home."

"Perhaps." If Nick didn't know better, he'd say that
Hexam's expression was dreamy. "But she's got eyes that
can light a fire in a man's soul."

"Do you think so?" Nick asked. Now that he thought
about it, he realized Hexam was right: Willie's eyes were
particularly attractive, and looking into them did cause
a little flame of awareness to lick at Nick's imagination.

He shook away the preposterous thought. "She's
made a muddle of my wardrobe."

"Come man, what's a wardrobe?" Palliston laughed
and clapped Nick on the back. "A wardrobe is nothing.
Not when you're talking about a woman with hair as
pretty as a Scottish sunset."

Pretty?

Now that Palliston mentioned it, Nick realized Willie's hair was remarkably pretty.

He cast that thought to perdition along with Hexam's observation. "She's nearly made me feel guilty enough about the mountain of invitations that arrive here daily that I've actually been tempted to accept a few of them."

"That's bad." One corner of his mouth pulled into what was nearly enough of a smile to make Nick even more irritated, Palliston shook his head sadly. "That's very bad."

"And that's not the worst of it," Nick conceded. "She sings. In the morning. Great, thunderous hymns filled with the promise of fire and brimstone."

"That's terrible." Hexam hung his head.

"She doesn't know the importance of keeping absolute quiet in the house before half-three in the afternoon. She doesn't understand the value of knowing how to turn callers away at the door. And at table, she doesn't even know the difference between claret and port."

"Now that is a problem." As gracefully as a dancer, Latimer ascended from the fog and landed lightly on his feet. Considering the amount of both port and claret they all had consumed that evening, it was a wonder he—or any of them—could walk at all.

"So . . ." As if preparing to encounter one of the more enchanting women of their acquaintance, Latimer straightened his neckcloth and smoothed his bottle-green waistcoat. He strode toward the door. "What are you going to do about her?" he asked Nick.

"Do? About Willie?" It was the same question Nick had asked himself a dozen times over the past week. What he needed to do about Willie had been foremost on his mind. Right after the fact that when he thought about what he needed to do about Willie, he also thought about how guilty he'd feel when he dismissed her.

"What I'm going to do," he told his friends, "is get inside and make myself comfortable. I'm going to open a bottle of brandy and with your help, I'm going to drink the entire thing."

"Now there's a man with a plan!" Hexam laughed and stepped aside so Nick could get to the door.

Before he had the chance to open it, they heard the noise of a great hubbub from within.

Someone grumbled a curse. It was not Willie's voice.

Someone else mumbled a word of warning. The warning did not come from Willie.

There was a shuffling of feet as if a great many people were being assembled at great speed.

Nick looked at his friends in wonder. "It isn't my birthday."

"We wouldn't have remembered if it was," Palliston assured him, and he knew it was true.

"And there can't be any relatives visiting."

"If there were any great-aunties on the other side of that door . . ." Latimer eyed the house with trepidation, ". . . we would be on our way as fast as hell could scorch a feather."

The mystery of the thing was solved when the front door of Somerton House flew open.

A vaguely familiar looking lad of no more than ten stepped forward, tilting the door closed behind him. He was dressed in the most astonishing livery: golden satin knee breeches, linen shirt, a brocade vest in a deep, rich shade of blue. He even wore a powdered wig.

The boy was as thin as a rasher of wind and though the two circles of scrubbed pink skin on his cheeks showed that some effort had gone into the washing of his face, the cleanliness of the rest of him was questionable. His fingernails were caked with grime, his shirt was just this side of filthy. His nose wasn't much cleaner.

He looked up uncertainly at the four gentlemen staring at him in astonishment. Then, as if he'd finally remembered what he was supposed to be doing there, he made a quick, jerking bow.

"There you 'ave it," the boy said, so proud of himself that he grinned and revealed several missing teeth and several more that were just a shade brighter than his breeches. "Welcome to Somerton 'ouse, sirs. We be most pleased to 'ave you 'ere."

Had it been earlier and had he not spent the evening at a gaming hell in Jermyn Street where he'd passed the time losing heartily and drinking even more vigorously, Nick may have been tempted to toss the young pup out on the street where he belonged. As it was, he barely contained a smile.

He backed away a step or two and might have gone bumping down the stairs if not for Hexam, who put a hand on his shoulder to warn him. Steadied and on sure footing, at least as far as his balance was concerned, Nick looked the boy up and down. "Pleased? Are you, sirrah?" He pulled himself up to his full height and glared down at the child. "Then perhaps you might explain who the devil you are. And what the devil you are doing in my home."

The boy's jaw dropped. His scrawny shoulders trembled. "I didn't know, sir . . . I mean, I am . . . What I mean is 'ow to say, sir, is I'm—"

"He's Jem." The door opened just enough to let a bright stream of light onto the front stoop along with Willie. She put a reassuring hand on the boy's shoulder. "His name is Jem, m'lord, and as to what the devil he's doing here, that is simple enough. Jem is your new footman."

❧ 7 ❧

....

In the week she had been in residence as house-keeper, butler, cook and maid-of-all-work, Willie had learned a great deal about Somerton. She knew that if it was cooked properly and seasoned liberally, he liked leg of mutton for dinner, and that the sight of kippers too early in the day made him blanch. She knew he preferred silence to noise—especially on those mornings when he was looking a little the worse for wear—and though she tried her best to stay out of his way and keep the clamor of her work to a minimum, she also knew that in a place as vast and as quiet as Somerton House, she would have gone stark, raving mad if she worked in silence.

She knew that Somerton was not an especially friendly man and though once or twice she caught herself regretting his lack of sociability and wishing for more from him than a distracted *good morning* or a hurried *good night,* she also knew better than to expect too much from the master-and-servant relationship they had established.

And if occasionally she found him casting a glance at her when he thought she wasn't looking?

Then and now, Willie set the thought aside as nothing more than a figment of a too-active imagination.

Yes, there were things she knew about Somerton.

But she never realized he had so great an amount of self-control.

And she was never so grateful for it as now.

His expression devoid of emotion, his posture as steady as any man's could be considering that he had been out with his friends all night and that meant he was undoubtedly foxed, Somerton looked from Willie to Jem and back again to Willie.

"My footman, you say?" One of his golden eyebrows slid up in an expression that teetered between amusement and bewilderment. "And when did I engage a footman?"

"You did not engage him at all. I did." Willie returned his look with one that was far steadier than she was feeling. For most of the day, she had been much too busy to think what might happen when the moment arrived and Somerton returned home. Now that the moment was here, her stomach felt a bit as if it had been tied into one of the elaborate knots Somerton used to arrange his neckcloths. "You will recall that we discussed it. Engaging a staff. You will also recall that you told me to take care of the details. Jem is one of the details."

"Is he now?" Somerton turned to his friends. "She's

taken care of the details," he told them before he turned his attention back to Willie. "Would you care to elaborate?"

"Certainly." Taking one breath for courage and another to calm the sudden pounding of her heart, Willie stepped back. Since that moment earlier in the day when there was a knock on the kitchen door and she'd decided her prayers had been answered, she'd been assuring herself—and the people she'd found standing out on the back stoop—that things were going to be as right as a line. It was time to prove it. To them and to herself.

With a look that served as a gentle reminder of all she'd drilled into him in the past hours, she told Jem that it was time for him to take over.

Watching the boy steady himself with a deep breath—much as she'd just done—Willie couldn't help but smile. What the lad lacked in training, he certainly made up for in panache. Just as she'd instructed him to do, he marched to the door with his head high and his shoulders as stiff as a soldier's. He opened the door and with a flourish of his hand that looked a little less like the grand obeisance it was supposed to be and a little more like a rude gesture he was—no doubt—more used to making, he stepped back to allow his master and guests into the house.

Somerton tipped his head, instructing Willie to go first and it was just as well, for when he stepped into the doorway, glanced into the imposing entryway and caught sight of people he neither knew nor expected to see lined up on either side of the magnificent, winding stairway that led up to the first floor, he stopped as if frozen.

Never one to let something as simple as another person's stupefaction impede her when there was work to be done, Willie motioned, first to the men who waited in a straggling line to the left of the stairway, then to the women who stood in a slightly more orderly fashion on the right. "M'lord, allow me to introduce your new staff," she said.

"My new—" Somerton might never have moved at all if not for a poke from behind from Hexam. Jolted into action, he stepped over the threshold and into the entryway and once his friends were in behind him, Willie reminded Jem to stop staring and close the door.

"M'lord . . ." Willie motioned toward the man who waited closest to the door. He was a bull of a fellow, compact and muscular, with a crooked nose, a bruised jaw and one eye swollen shut. "This is Mister O'Reilly. Your new valet."

"O'Reilly?" Somerton looked the man up and down, which really took no time at all considering that he came no higher than Somerton's shoulders. "Not Charlie the Rooster O'Reilly? The prizefighter?"

"Sure and you have a memory there, sir! Imagine the likes of you remembering the likes of me and my bit of a career." The valet's smile showed that his front teeth were missing. He touched a tentative finger to his left eye and winced. "Retired, as it were, sir. As of last night."

"And this . . ." Before Somerton could comment,

Willie moved to the next man in line. "This is Mr. Finch. He will be your butler."

Though he would be the first to admit that he had been inside the home of more than one aristocratic gentleman in the course of his career, Finch might also confess that he had never actually been formally introduced to anyone of standing. Because he didn't know what else to do, he grabbed Somerton's hand and pumped it. "Five Fingers Finch, they call me," the butler said. "But don't you pay that no mind, guv. All that talk of cat burglary and larceny. All in the past, guv. All in the past."

There was no point in staying too long with Mr. Finch. The look on Somerton's face told Willie as much. Anxious to distract him, she looked down the line of waiting men. "The others are footmen, coachmen and such," she said. "You will meet them all in good time. But there is one other I would like you to meet now. This . . ." She stepped back and did her best to sound chipper as she introduced a tall, rail-thin man with a pallid face and sunken eyes. "This is Mr. Marquand. Your cook."

"Marquand? Simon Marquand?"

Willie cursed Somerton's memory. She'd hoped the absence of Mr. Marquand's Christian name would circumvent explanations that were better given later. Or never at all.

Though he lost none of his legendary aplomb, she couldn't help but notice that Somerton's skin went a bit pale. "Simon Marquand the—"

Rather than deal with questions that might be as unfortunate as they were embarrassing, Willie breezed over to where the ladies waited.

She stopped before the first of them and smiled at the woman who, all along, had been anxious about what Willie saw as a most commonsense plan. She was not above reminding Willie that she was surely jeopardizing her own place in the viscount's home for want of helping the rest of them. All day, Willie had defended her decision and she stood by it even now. Still, she knew that of all of them, this was the most crucial introduction she would make to Somerton.

"M'lord . . ." She offered Somerton a cordial smile, hoping it would pave the way. "This is your new housekeeper. Madame Brenard."

"I say!" Before anyone else could move, Latimer stepped forward, his eyebrows nearly as high as his voice. He peered at Madame, who all along had been too nervous to do anything but look at the floor.

As soon as she looked up and saw the handsome young duke, Madame's face lit with recognition and her eyes beamed as bright as her painted cheeks. "Evenin', Your Grace, been a while and no mistake." Remembering herself, Madame slipped into a French accent that was as heavy as Willie knew it to be spurious.

"That is, *bonsoir, Monsieur. Enchanté!*" She dropped him a curtsy and held out her hand and ever the gentleman, Latimer smiled and kissed her fingers. Madame grinned and apparently feeling on more solid ground, gave the duke a knowing wink. "Just 'ere to 'elp out, so to speak," she told him in a stage whisper. She tipped her head farther down the long line of waiting servants. "Me and the girls."

"Girls?" The muddled smile Hexam had been wearing since he walked into the house widened into a look of absolute delight. "Look at that, will you!" Grabbing on to Palliston's sleeve and tugging him along, he hurried down the line of waiting servants and stopped in front of four women who giggled in unison.

"It's Flossie!" he said. "Flossie, Bess, Marie, and Clover!" He looked from the yellow-haired girl with a gap-toothed smile to the black-haired beauty whose substantial bosom could not be concealed, no matter how expertly Willie had attempted to tie the white apron over Bess's low-cut gown. From there he cast a glance over petite, frisky Marie with her dancing eyes and ready laugh to Clover, a quiet girl with wide hips and a mane of curly hair the color of strong coffee.

"Good God, man . . ." When he turned away from the girls and toward Somerton, Hexam's expression was beatific. "Flossie, Bess, Marie, and Clover! All together! Right here under your roof. It's like a dream come true!"

"Indeed." The expression on Somerton's face did not match the anticipation of Hexam's expression, the amusement of Latimer's, or the laughter of Palliston's. His hands clutched behind his back, his voice as calm as if they were discussing nothing more significant than the day's weather, he strolled over to where Willie was standing.

"We need to talk," Somerton said, his words as clipped as his jaw was tight. "Now."

*   *   *

As many times as Nick thought about that night, he was never quite sure how he got to the library. He didn't remember marching up the steps. He didn't remember grabbing on to Willie's hand and hauling her up behind him, either.

He did remember—or at least he suspected—that he must have held very tight to his temper, because he knew for a fact that upon finding a second-story man, a prizefighter and a madam suddenly on his staff and in his home, his first inclination was to give Miss Culpepper the verbal drubbing of her life.

He didn't, though he couldn't imagine why, just as he couldn't imagine why once the library door was closed behind them and he turned to face Willie, he found himself with his breaths coming hard and fast, his heart pounding double time and her hand still clutched in his.

As if it were as hot as coals, he dropped her hand and moved back a step, away from the unseen but all too real aura that seemed to hover around Willie like the heat off a candle flame.

"What the devil—" Nick caught himself just as a stream of invective was about to leave his lips. It wasn't that Willie didn't deserve every last word he was tempted to hurl at her, it was just that watching her watch him—her arms tight against her sides, her chin high and steady though her lower lip trembled the slightest bit, her simple and prim hairstyle looking even more simple and prim framing a face that, in this light, looked to belong to a goddess—he suddenly realized that he did not have the heart.

"Would you like to explain what's going on here?" Nick asked.

"Explain?" Willie laughed nervously. "I am sorry, m'lord," she said instantly, and some of the starch went out of her shoulders. "It's just that I'm a bit surprised. I did not think you would give me the chance to explain before you threw open the door and kicked me down the front steps and into the street."

"Really?" Nick whirled around and walked over to the magnificent mahogany desk that took up a good portion of the far wall of the room. It had once belonged to his father and his grandfather before that. He wondered what either of them would say if they knew that now that they were at their rest, the family home was filled with the likes of Rooster O'Reilly.

Nick laid his palms flat against the desktop. "I never realized I was such a turk, or that you thought I could be as heartless as that."

"Heartless, no. Practical, yes. Especially when it comes to your home. And I was afraid when you met the new staff—"

"Who are wholly unsuited."

"Who are wholly unsuited. Yes, I do quite agree with you there. Which doesn't, of course, mean they cannot be trained or that they shouldn't be given a chance." She pulled in a breath. "I was afraid when you met them you might—"

"Toss them out right as you hit the bottom step?"

As much as she was trying to put up a brave front, Nick couldn't help but notice that Willie swallowed hard. "There are a good many of them," she said. "And I think you'll agree, m'lord, that I am the only one who deserves tossing. From a practical standpoint, there is only one of me. It would be far easier for me to find my way on my own than for all of them, all at once, to be searching for work. If anyone is to go—"

"It should be you. Yes. Yes. I couldn't agree more." It was the truth and Nick knew it. Which didn't explain why the knowledge sat in his gut like the remains of a bad joint of mutton. Anxious for something to do to dispel the nervous energy that built inside him like thunder in a summer cloud, he reached for the nearest stack of papers. They were notices from his tailor, letters from his haberdasher, invoices from his greengrocer, and he shuffled through them unseeing, waiting until he thought the appropriate time had passed to give Willie the chance to develop what at least might look like a bit of remorse.

When he glanced up, she hadn't moved an inch and she didn't look the least remorseful. Then again, if she had, something told him he would have been disappointed.

Nick let go a sharp breath. "You're still here."

Willie had the good sense not to say a thing.

Too agitated to keep still, he tossed the papers back down and rounded the desk to stand before her. "You are no green girl, Miss Culpepper, and I do not like to treat you like one, but as your employer, I do have a certain amount of responsibility toward you. I have to ask. Do you know who those people are? Do you know what they are?"

"What they are?" Willie was not a tall woman, and she had to raise her chin to look at Nick. "I know they are folk who were turned out of their lodgings today. They could not meet the rent, you see, and they were put out on the street, every one of them, along with all their worldly possessions, by a landlord who was asking more than he knew they could ever pay. I know there are some who are looked upon as thieves and trust me, m'lord, if they are allowed to stay and I am allowed to oversee their work, I will not tolerate thievery. I know there are some who are rough around the edges and I do not expect that they shall ever polish into diamonds, but—"

"But?"

"But they can at least try."

"But surely, Miss Culpepper, a woman of your background would not—"

"Know people such as those?" It was Willie's turn to break the tension between them. She turned and walked as far as the windows, then came back again, her head tipped in thought. "I met Madame three years ago," she said. "It was raining. Quite vigorously. She stepped into the Church of Divine and Imperishable Justice to escape the deluge."

"And?"

"And my father sent her away. Unceremoniously. Unemotionally. Unsympathetically. He said a church was no place for sinners such as Madame. It wasn't the first time I'd seen him treat someone in need so poorly. At the time, we were collecting clothing for our mission in

India and I saw that Madame's gown was worn. I followed her and apologized. I took her another gown."
She watched Somerton's eyes as she relayed the information and seemingly satisfied by whatever she saw
there, she went on. "We have been friends since and
through her, I have met the others."

"Then surely you know—"

"That Madame is an abbess and that Flossie, Bess,
Marie, and Clover are Cyprians? Yes, I know that well
enough but then, I daresay you probably know that as
well." Her gaze still locked with his, Willie paused for no
more than a heartbeat. It was time enough for Nick to
know she had not missed the look of recognition that
washed across his face when he saw Madame, nor had
she failed to notice the eagerness his friends displayed
when they realized that Flossie, Bess, Marie, and
Clover—who had the reputation as four of the cleverest,
most inventive and most eager-to-please demireps in
London—had literally been dropped in their laps.

"From the conversation, I take it you and your
friends are very well acquainted with Madame and her
girls."

It was true and it was not anything he needed to be
embarrassed about. Which didn't explain why Nick suddenly felt as if he were standing naked and exposed
under the scrutiny of Willie's straightforward gaze.

"And Marquand?" he asked, anxious to change the
subject and annoyed at himself because of it. "Correct
me if I am wrong, Miss Culpepper—and I have no
doubt you will—but I remember the stories that went

around town a year or so ago just as readily as anyone. My new cook, Simon Marquand, is a poisoner!"

"An *alleged* poisoner." She clicked her tongue, apparently surprised that he did not know the difference. "And even if it were true—and no one ever proved it was—he did not poison an employer, so you would have nothing to fear. If I remember correctly—and I am sure I do—it was a ghastly fellow named Cryle who *allegedly* died at Mr. Marquand's hand, a man who was suspected of having lured Marquand's daughter into a life of depravity."

"And poisoning isn't depraved?"

"That is not the point."

"Then what is, Miss Culpepper? What is the point?"

"The point is that you need a staff. I cannot continue to be the only one working here, partly because it is unfair to me and mostly because it is unfair to you. You have a vast household and a vast household needs a good many people to keep it running smoothly. I do not need to remind you that respectable people have been put off by the thought of service here in Somerton House. Someday, I expect that will change. The story of the scandal that surrounds the both of us is sure to lose its luster as soon as the next bit of juicy tittle-tattle comes along. But until it does, someone needs to work here. With Mr. O'Reilly taking care of your personal needs and Mr. Finch handling the staff and Madame taking care of the household responsibilities, I will be free to get your books and your finances in order." She glanced at the stack of tradesmen's bills Nick had tossed onto the desk. "As you can see, there is some need for a tight hand and a closed purse."

"And you will be what, then? My secretary?"

"Secretary. Steward. I care not what you call me."

"And when the silver disappears?"

"I swear it won't. I'll count it myself each night before I go to bed."

"And that little urchin at the front door?"

"Jem is Clover's son and worked at Madame's before today. He may have looked familiar to you because of it." She did not pause to allow him time to confirm or deny the fact. "We didn't have time to clean him up completely but once he's had a bath—"

"Once he's had a bath and all the dirt is washed away, there won't be much left of him but bones and a runny nose."

"He is a rather scrawny thing, I'll give you that much. But he's bright. And eager to please. He would make a serviceable footboy once he's cleaned up, or a crack tiger."

"And the doxies?"

"Chambermaids. And why not? They have proved that they are used to hard work, there's no doubt of that."

"You are surely mad, Miss Culpepper!" Somerton had had enough. He turned and stalked across the library and when he got to the door, he threw it open and marched into the passageway without another look at Willie or another word.

Watching him go, Willie's shoulders sagged and her

spirits plummeted. She had promised Madame and the rest of them that she had the situation well in hand, and that when things looked their bleakest, the Viscount Somerton would surely not let them down.

And now he was on his way belowstairs to prove her wrong.

The very thought gave Willie impetus to hurry after him.

She raced from the room but by the time she got to the bottom of the stairway, Somerton was already there. Madame was chatting amiably enough with the woman who was to work in the scullery. Rooster O'Reilly, Mr. Finch and Simon Marquand were standing in a knot with the other men Willie had engaged as staff, glancing somewhat enviously at the door to the morning room. It was open when Willie accompanied Somerton upstairs, It was now firmly closed.

Flossie, Bess, Marie, and Clover were nowhere to be seen.

Neither were Hexam, Latimer, or Palliston.

Fortunately for Willie, Somerton paused to look over the scene, too, and when he did, she had time enough to scramble to catch him up. She was right behind him when, eyes flashing blue fire, he stalked to the morning room and threw open the door.

Over his shoulder, Willie saw Latimer and Bess standing near the window, his head on her bosom. Palliston and Flossie were locked in an embrace over near the mantelpiece. Hexam had both Clover and Marie with him on the sofa, the result of which looked to be a tangle of legs and arms and an Arthur Hexam who was smiling broadly in anticipation of what might come next.

"What the devil!" Somerton's voice boomed through the room. Hexam rolled off the sofa and ended up on the seat of his pants on the floor. Latimer stood at attention. Palliston laughed and looped an arm around Flossie's shoulders.

"Hexam! Latimer! Palliston!" Somerton bellowed. "Get the hell away from my chambermaids!"

"Dun territory?" Somerton's voice cracked over the words. "What do you mean, dun territory?"

Willie closed the ledger book that sat on the desk in front of her and linking her fingers, rested her hands atop it and looked across the desk at the viscount.

She would have been a fool to think she would get little or no reaction to her announcement. After all, it wasn't every day a man learned he had somehow managed to live well beyond his considerable means. She had expected anger, or even disbelief, and to counter his response, she had carefully laid out her case in neat rows of neat numbers written on the stack of papers piled neatly at her left elbow. She was more than prepared to defend each and every one of the sums it had taken her the better part of a week to compile, especially the ones that added up (or more precisely, subtracted down) to negatives.

She had not thought that instead of fury or skepticism, Somerton might meet her statement with absolute astonishment.

As if he hadn't quite heard her correctly, he cocked his head to one side and stared at her in silence. It was early in the day and his blue eyes were still slightly blurry from a night at the gaming hells, the clubs and the schools of Venus, the same gaming hells, clubs and schools of Venus where he had no doubt spent the better part of his adult life squandering his family fortune, reducing his personal wealth and amassing so great a debt, that even Willie—always a wizard with numbers and logical enough to understand what they meant— could hardly believe the sums herself.

His hands against the desktop, Somerton leaned forward.

"Dun territory," she repeated, trying to break through Somerton's astonishment with reasoning and careful explanation. "I don't know a better way to explain, m'lord, than to put it in plain words. I've gone over the figures again and again and there's no mistaking any of them. You've hit the low water mark, I'm afraid." Still, she had no reaction from him and she decided to be more direct.

"You are out at the heel," she told him, carefully pronouncing each word. "In the suds. Cleaned up."

"The hell you say."

It was a good thing that Bess had moved a chair directly in front of the desk the last time she cleaned the library. Unseeing, Somerton dropped into it. "You can't be serious, Willie. There must be—"

"Some mistake? No." Willie shook her head. "I'm sorry to say there is not. Between the tradesmen's dunning notices . . ." She lifted a hefty stack of papers, "and the debts you have voweled . . ." She held up a sheet he should have recognized, one on which he kept a running—and she suspected, incomplete—tally of the IOUs he'd signed to various creditors. "You lose a great deal gambling," she said, a fact that should have been no surprise to him.

"Of course I lose a great deal gambling." His voice teetered on the edge of awareness that was sure to bring a rush of anger along with it. "That's what gentlemen do. We spend money. On gambling. And clothes. On drinking. And—"

No doubt, he was going to say *bits of muslin* but instead of pointing it out, Somerton swallowed his words and Willie was just as glad. As difficult as it was to inform her employer that he was under the hatches, it would have been even more difficult to sit across from him and hear him admit what she already knew, that a good deal of his fortune had been spent on women like Bess and Flossie, Marie and Clover.

As good-hearted as they were and as good-natured as they had been about taking on responsibilities they had never thought to assume, Willie couldn't help but feel a stab of emotion every time she thought about the girls. It had taken her a long time and a great deal of soul searching to discover—and then to admit—what that emotion was.

When she thought about Somerton with the likes of Bess and Flossie, Marie and Clover, she knew envy.

The very idea caused a spark to sizzle its way through

her and startled both by it and by her reaction to it, Willie sat up straight and tall. She refused to meet Somerton's eyes, afraid that if she did, he might see some evidence of the completely inappropriate thoughts that rattled through her brain.

Apparently, he mistook her reluctance to look at him as a sign that she was backing down from her assertion about his finances.

"I always lose a great deal," Somerton said, trying for the jolly, devil-take-it attitude she had heard ring through his voice when he was in the company of the Dashers. "I can lose a great deal because I have a great deal to lose."

"*Had* a great deal to lose." Willie stood. The rest of what she had to say was better delivered on foot. "Unless you have some kindly relative who would be willing to—"

"Afraid they've always depended on me for that sort of thing."

"Or some equally unfortunate gentleman who might owe you—"

"There have been a few such debts." Somerton shrugged. "I've forgiven them."

"Then you are—"

"Not plump?" He caught Willie's gaze.

"Thin." As tempted as she was to turn away, she forced herself to meet his eyes. "Very thin, indeed. I do not think we can keep the household running past—"

"That bad?" Somerton got up and spun around, pacing to the far side of the room and back again, his hands clutched behind his back.

"There is a solution to the problem."

Willie's statement stopped him in his tracks. His back was to her and he turned. "You're not proposing we send Mr. Finch in to pinch someone's jewels, are you?"

Willie wished she were.

At the same time she wondered why the thing she was about to suggest was more troubling, even, than a little larceny.

"Actually . . ." Stalling for time while she searched for the best way to offer the suggestion, she rounded the desk and went to stand nearer to him. "You do have something quite valuable," she said, and because the subject was much too serious to allow him to make light of it, she continued before he could venture a guess as to what that something might be.

"Your title," Willie reminded him. "You are the Viscount Somerton, after all, and I do believe your family has deep roots and a fine lineage."

"Are you saying—"

"I am saying that there is one and only one thing that can redeem your present financial state of affairs, m'lord. A rich wife. It is time for you to marry."

❧ 8 ❧

....

"*Y*ou are not listening to me."

"You're wrong." Nick glanced over his shoulder to where Willie was trailing behind him like a gray cloud threatening a summer picnic. He crossed the entryway, looking around one last time to make sure that everything was as shipshape as it was likely to get considering the current state of his household staff. Satisfied that the brass was polished (except for Jem's sticky finger marks), the paintings were free of cobwebs (except for the ones that couldn't be reached) and the furniture was dusted (except for a spot on the table near the morning room doorway that he wiped away with his shirt cuff), he paced to the far end of the entryway, then turned to head back the other way. When he did, he nearly slammed right into Willie.

He stopped just short of doing either of them any damage and realized it was lucky that he did; it was clear she was not about to give an inch. "I am listening," he told her on the end of an exasperated sigh. "I cannot fail to listen. You won't let me."

"Then why won't you stop just for a moment and simply look?" She fluttered a paper on which he could see a long list written in her neat hand. "If you are indeed listening, m'lord—"

"Listening and planning to act on what I'm hearing are two different things," he reminded her. "If that is a list of women who you think might be possible marriage candidates—"

"It is."

"Then I am simply not interested."

She glowered at him, her ginger-colored brows low over eyes that were as steely as any he had ever seen. He refused to give her the satisfaction of rising to the bait. "Willie, I told you . . ." A carriage pulled to a stop outside the front door and Nick glanced at the window. His guest had arrived. "You'll see," he said, stepping aside so that Mr. Finch could be ready to answer the door at the first knock. "You may think you have the solution to my problem—"

"I certainly do not have the solution. But one of these ladies . . ." She read the name at the top of her list. "Devonna Markham, perhaps. She has at least six hundred pounds a year from her grandfather and another eight or nine hundred—depending on who is telling the story—from an elderly aunt, another Miss Markham, who named our Miss Markham the only heir to her estate. Then there is Emma Greenlaw." She glanced at the second name on the paper, then up at Nick, as dispassionate as if they were discussing consolidated annuities rather than flesh and blood women—and the flesh and blood man who, if he was not careful, would find himself strapped to one of them.

"Miss Greenlaw's father is in trade," Willie explained, "and to some, that might make her less than satisfactory, but by all accounts, the Greenlaws are respectable and as plumb in the pockets as any. Then there is Lady Catherine Sutcliffe who is a widow, and of course, Sylvia Moore-Paget and—"

"Charming. All of them."

And just hearing their names read like the roll of the Doomsday chronicle struck terror in Nick's heart.

He cast aside the thought and consoled himself with the sure knowledge that there was light, yet, at the end of the tunnel and hope, still, that he would not be backed into a corner with pen in hand, ready to sign a prenuptial settlement.

"I have no doubt that they are splendid girls with splendid families and splendid family fortunes. But don't you see—" There was a knock on the door and Nick's face lit with a smile at the same time his spirits lifted far higher than they had been since the day a week earlier when Willie had so clearly spelled out the sorry state of his finances.

Rather than be seen waiting at the door and look far too eager, he ducked into the morning room and Willie followed.

Nick peered around the half-closed door and watched as Mr. Finch ushered his visitor into the entryway. "You'll see, Willie." He backed away from the door so that Mr. Finch might announce his visitor and when he thought a sufficient amount of time had passed to send the clear message that he was not overanxious, overly concerned or overwrought at the news of his financial ruin which, no doubt, had already gone through town like wildfire, he told Mr. Finch to show the man in.

Waiting, Nick gave Willie a smile that told her he was supremely confident and so sure of his plan, she need think about hers no longer. He was not about to be ensnared by some modest miss with a smile on her pretty face and naught in her heart but the desire to shackle a husband to herself and control his fortune, his thoughts, and his very life.

"Yours may be one solution to my problem but it is not a satisfactory one," he told Willie in a whisper. "And it is not the only one. Wait here. You'll see."

Willie did not have to wait long. A second later, Rawdon Farleigh stepped into the room.

A lifetime of dealing with his betters in a capacity that, by nature, needed to leave room for both discretion and a little healthy competition had made Mr. Farleigh into exactly the kind of man Nick expected. Just as those of Nick's acquaintance who had dealt with the man (ever so secretly, of course) had described, Farleigh was small and slight, with a pointed chin and eyes that were yellow, like a rat's. He was well dressed—even if he was a bit dandified, well mannered—even if he was a bit unctuous, and cognizant enough of the ways of society—and his place on the fringes of it—that he knew exactly what to say, how to say it and when to keep his mouth shut.

When he was introduced to Willie, he kept his mouth shut. After all, it was not often that a viscount introduced a young lady in his household as his secretary and steward, and if Farleigh thought better of the designation and that, perhaps, it was a grand and glorious title for a different sort of profession altogether, he was too mindful of what might be at risk to give an opinion.

Which was a very good thing, Nick decided. He would have hated to throw Farleigh out before they ever had a chance to get down to business.

Farleigh wasted no time. Chafing his hands together as if against a chill, he scanned the paintings that hung around the room.

"Excellent." Farleigh headed straight for a portrait of Nick's great-aunt Hermione and Nick's mood brightened even more. He had never liked Great-Aunt Hermione and he liked her portrait even less. She was a gray-faced, hatchet-jawed, rock-ribbed old lady and it would do his frame of mind—not to mention his purse—a world of good to be rid of her.

"Wonderful, isn't she?" Nick could hardly believe the words that poured out of his mouth. Great-Aunt Hermione, wonderful? He controlled the shiver that spilled down his back and got on with it. Better to lie to Farleigh than to spend the rest of his days with Great-Aunt Hermione staring over his shoulder.

"It is a Gainsborough," Nick said. He directed the comment at Farleigh at the same time he glanced

Willie's way as if to underscore what he had told her earlier. There was more than one way to save a family's fortunes. Even if it meant selling off the long-dead
ancestors, one by bloody one. "Been in the family for
years."

"I have no doubt of that." Farleigh brushed a finger
against the frame and came away covered with dust. His
top lip curled and without ceremony, he pulled out a
silk handkerchief and cleaned his hands. When he was
done, he retrieved his quizzing glass, held it up to his eye
and took a good, long look at Great-Aunt Hermione.

He nodded and mumbled to himself. He clicked his
tongue. He stepped back and looked at the painting
from the right, then from the left. He stepped back even
farther and squinted at Hermione. Step by careful step,
he got closer to her—closer, Nick suspected, than any
man had ever gotten in life. He ran a finger along Great-
Aunt Hermione's massive bosom.

Another thing Nick suspected had never happened to
the old lady in her lifetime.

While Farleigh was still staring deep into Hermione's
eyes, Nick decided it was time to start the negotiations.
He made sure to look at Willie as he did, so she could
see that, in spite of her dire warnings, he had his financial situation well in hand. And he didn't have to chain
himself to an iron-ball of a wife to do it.

"I've been told at least two hundred pounds." It
wasn't what he'd been told at all but Nick thought it
would be bad form to let Farleigh think there was a bargain to be had.

"Two hundred?" Farleigh's sandy brows rose. He pursed his lips. He lowered his quizzing glass and looked at Nick with an expression that teetered between pity and indignation. "Are you suggesting, my lord, that I give you two hundred pounds in exchange for this painting? Or that you pay me two hundred pounds to take it off your hands?"

"What!" Nick could hardly believe his ears. "You don't mean—"

"That it's a forgery? Most certainly." Farleigh nodded vigorously. "Well done, no doubt of that. But a Gainsborough?" He tisk-tisked ever so politely. "Hardly, my lord. It is nothing but an imitation, and nearly worthless."

"But it can't—" Nick stopped himself just short of a full-blown protest. But only because he refused to give Willie the satisfaction of seeing his plan dashed and hers on the verge of being resurrected. Not one to surrender so easily, he went across the room and pointed to a landscape.

"Van Ruisdael," Nick said.

Farleigh gave the painting no more than a quick look. "Not."

Nick tried the painting on the wall next to the landscape. "Reynolds."

"Definitely a counterfeit. And not a very good one."

"The Romney?"

This painting, at least, Farleigh considered. Unfortunately, his final opinion was no different.

The same might be said of the paintings in the library,

the suit of armor that stood in a little-used upstairs passageway, and was, according to family legend, said to have once belonged to Henry VIII, the collection of medieval manuscripts which, Nick's father had always assured him, were as priceless as they were unreadable.

By the time they got done with a tour of what he had always thought were the family treasures and back down to the morning room, Nick was numb from head to toe. Still, he was not about to give up. He had his mother's jewelry brought out to a table near the window where it could be examined in the light and he hovered behind Farleigh, watching as the little man bent over his work.

"Paste." Farleigh pronounced. "Colored glass. Hunks of metal."

"And worthless?"

"Worthless." Farleigh pronounced the single word like a death sentence.

By now, Nick was hardly surprised. He was no fool. Some Pryce who had gone before him must have been just as short of the blunt as Nick now found himself. That same Pryce must have had the same idea Nick had to save the family name. Unfortunately, that Pryce got to everything of value first and apparently needing to hide the fact (probably from his wife), had replaced it all with reproductions.

Worthless reproductions.

"I am sorry we are not able to do business, my lord." Farleigh's mouth was pinched, but at least he had the good grace not to point out that he'd spent his day on a wild goose chase. He bowed his way out. "Good day."

Nick waited until the door clicked closed behind Farleigh. "Good?" The word echoed in the morning room and sounded hollow in Nick's ears. "How can anything be good? How can I possibly—"

A small, rustling sound behind him brought him turning around.

He found Willie exactly where she had been throughout the ordeal, at his shoulder, looking remarkably calm in spite of the bad news Farleigh had delivered.

Without a word, she drew her list of marriageable ladies from her pocket, unfolded it, and handed it to Nick.

"This isn't a good idea." Nick tugged at his neckcloth and though he did not ordinarily fall prey to the kind of pettifogging philosophy doled out in rhyming couplet doggerel and had little patience for those who read too much imagery into commonplace events, even he could not miss the symbolism.

Rooster O'Reilly's knots were tight around his neck.

Just like the stranglehold some marriage-minded miss was sure to tie around his life.

"Are you sure—"

"Yes." Behind him, he heard the rustle of Willie's skirts and a second later, caught her reflection in the mirror that hung at the top of the winding stairway that led up from the entryway.

Though Somerton House was resplendent—decorated with brightly colored hothouse flowers and sparkling with the light of innumerable candles—Willie looked as plain and as practical as ever. Her hair perfectly arranged, her black dress spotless in spite of the fact that she had spent the better part of the day scurrying about making last minute preparations for the evening's dinner party, she glanced quickly over at Nick and nodded her approval.

"Miss Markham will no doubt find you most acceptable."

In spite of the edginess that clutched at his insides, Nick laughed. "Acceptable?" He turned from the mirror and though he knew it was unseemly to be so informal with a member of his staff and utterly improper to tease a properly raised, properly mannered woman such as Willie, he simply couldn't help himself. "I hate to tell you this, Willie . . ." He offered one of his signature smiles, the kind that had been known to melt female hearts—proper and otherwise—from one end of London to the next. "But I am used to women finding me more than simply acceptable."

"No doubt."

Was it relief that scurried through his insides when he realized his devastating smile had no effect on the starch in Willie's shoulders or the level look she aimed his way?

Nick liked to think so.

Which made him wonder why it felt more like disappointment.

He cast aside the thought with a twitch of his shoulders inside his formal black cutaway coat, reminding himself in no uncertain terms that there was no cause for dashed hope. It was exactly the kind of reaction he had expected from Willie. She was, after all, the most straightforward woman he'd ever met. The most uncomplicated. The most plainspoken. With Willie, there was no artfulness as with so many women of his acquaintance, no maidenly blushes and shy glances deliberately delivered and just as deliberately designed to ensnare a man as surely and as painfully as a bear trap.

In fact, he suspected she was the exact opposite of Devonna Markham, the wealthy, yet-to-catch-a-husband chit at the top of Willie's list of likely marriage candidates, the woman who—along with a mob of London's tulips of fashion—would be arriving at Somerton House in less than an hour's time for the first dinner party hosted by the Viscount Somerton in as long as anyone could remember.

Once Willie had convinced him of the worth of her plan and the invitations had gone out, it did not take long for the ton to put two and two together: If the Viscount Somerton was eschewing the company of the Dashers in favor of more refined pleasures, it could mean only one thing. He was looking for a bride.

The reaction was predictable.

Suddenly, he was receiving more social invitations than ever, most of them from eager mamas looking to snag a title for their daughters along with the unfortunate Lord who went with it. Not long ago, he would have declined. Politely, of course, and secretly, with great relief. Now that his social life was in Willie's hands—and now that she had convinced him that he must marry or certainly outrun the constable—he found his days filled with soirées and balls, rides in the park and musicales. She had even accepted an invitation to Almack's on his behalf.

The very thought made Nick groan.

"It's not that I thought to never marry."

The sound of his own voice surprised him and he snapped out of his reverie to find Willie watching him carefully. "I knew it would have to happen," he admitted. He turned and gave his neckcloth another tug, then smoothed his gold brocade waistcoat into place. "I am the only son, after all, and it is my duty to make sure the line survives. I've never deluded myself about that. I knew it would happen eventually. I'd only hoped—"

He caught himself before he said too much. It was one thing admitting his reluctance to Willie. It was another to voice what he had never confessed to anyone before—that he had always harbored a hope that he might marry for love rather than because of family obligations or the expectations of society or, most especially, for money.

It was an impracticable thought at best and probably as old-fashioned as frill collars and buckled shoes, yet he'd seen too many instances of the hurt that could be done when love did not accompany a couple to the altar, the most monumental and painful from his own parents.

He was not looking to duplicate their mistakes and there was a time he would have sworn he would never let it happen.

But as much as he'd hoped to circumvent the misery that plagued his parents' lives at the same time he sidestepped the vicar, he had always been cognizant of the fact that he had an obligation, to his country, to his ancestors, to the generations of Pryces who would come after him. He must keep the family name above reproach.

"I'd only hoped *eventually* would not arrive so soon," he told Willie.

"Just as I'd hoped the marriage my father always talked about arranging for me would never happen."

As grateful that she understood as he was that she had effectively changed the subject, Nick laughed. "Are you suggesting that I might get myself out of this predicament by getting kidnapped?"

"It has been known to work before."

The gleam of amusement in Willie's eyes outshone the candles flickering around them and for a moment, Nick could do little but smile in response. When he realized it, he only felt worse. There was little point in smiling about anything when the noose was tightening around his neck.

"I would face Lord Harry himself and not struggle against a kidnapping straight to the hottest fires of hell if it would get me out of this." He glanced toward the stairway and the entryway below where already, Mr. Finch was standing near the front door waiting for the first guests to arrive. The butler was doing a nervous sort of little dance, hopping from one foot to the other, his anticipation of the night's event a perfect reflection of the atmosphere that pervaded the entire staff.

And their master.

"Perhaps she won't come," Nick said.

"Miss Markham?" Willie shook her head. "I hear she is over the moon at the prospect of meeting you, m'lord. Word has it that you are the most eligible bachelor of the ton."

"Just as word has it, no doubt, that I've lost my mind." Too edgy himself to watch how edgy Mr. Finch looked, Nick spun around and paced over to where Willie was standing. "Are you sure Miss Markham is a good choice?"

"She was presented at court last Season and apparently made quite an impression. She did not, however, find a husband and has arrived back in town, or so I hear, with fresh enthusiasm and her mind quite made up to not leave again until there is a ring on her finger."

"All that money and no husband?" Nick could hardly believe it. He knew half a dozen men at least who would not let so fat a fish squirm so easily off the hook. "What's wrong with her?" he asked, considering for the first time what he had not considered before. "Does she have a squint? A limp? Some sort of defect of personality that makes the men keep their distance?"

"Word has it, m'lord . . ." As if gauging his reaction, Willie looked at him levelly. "It is said that Devonna Markham refuses to marry until she finds the man of her dreams. Unfortunately, no matter how much I inquired of her friends, relations, and servants who I rather boldly pumped for information, I could not fully uncover what those dreams might be. If her attendance here is any indication, I would guess that she's holding out for someone rather above the station of the baronet who offered his heart and his hand last Season."

The news was not encouraging.

"Don't worry." Willie reassured him with a smile. "Your friends will be here. Mr. Hexam and the duke of Latimer and the rest of them. They will, no doubt, offer great moral support. And I will be—"

"You'll be at dinner?" It was the most absurd thought and completely impossible, yet the very idea gave Nick a shot of much needed courage.

"Not at dinner." At least Willie had the courtesy not to point out how ridiculous the very notion was. "But I will be in the kitchen the entire night and if there's anything you need or any question you have, you need only have Mr. Finch come and tell me."

That, at least, made him feel better. The idea of a husband-hungry Devonna Markham did not. "What in the world am I supposed to say to the woman?" Nick asked.

Though it seemed the most logical question, Willie's only response was a laugh as clear as church bells on a frosty morning. The sound was so unexpected and the smile that accompanied it so bright, it took Nick's breath away.

It was a blessing that Willie didn't notice. "I cannot believe that you are ever at a loss for words!" she said, still smiling. "Especially when it comes to conversing with women. I need not remind you that your reputation precedes you, m'lord. And your reputation—or so

I've been told—is that of the most charming man in all of London."

"Charming?" As much as Nick would have liked to believe it, he wasn't the sort to lie to himself. "I may be charming with a certain sort of woman—"

As if to underscore what he was too much of a gentleman to admit to a woman who was too much of a lady to hear it, Bess and Clover rounded the corner, their cheeks pink with excitement, their voices tight with the anticipation of the event that promised to be the most elegant thing they had seen in their lives. Three weeks of Willie's tutoring had done wonders for the girls. Though Nick suspected they would always be too spirited to blend into the woodwork as good servants were supposed to do, both Bess and Clover (as well as Marie and Flossie) had made great strides.

After the first few times they brazenly offered themselves and Nick made it clear that he was not disposed to treat them as he had when they were part of Madame's nunnery, they had become cognizant of their place in his household and conscientious, too. They completed their tasks as well as might be expected and except for the times they allowed their hips to sway or the necklines of their gowns to droop just enough to expose a delicious and wholly inappropriate bit of flesh, they looked presentable in the gowns Willie had procured and Madame Brenard had tailored. Though there were times he heard words from their mouths that would make the most hardened sailor blush, they were, for the most part, quiet, and mostly, they only spoke when spoken to—unless, of course, they forgot that was the way things were supposed to be done.

As they neared, Bess and Clover dropped neat curtsies in Nick's direction, just as Willie had taught them. Giggling, they hurried away.

"You cannot speak to Miss Markham as you might to women like Bess and Clover."

It was as if Willie were reading his mind.

"I know that," Nick told her. "And that's the devil of it. With women like Bess and Clover, a man can be himself. He doesn't need to equivocate and make polite excuses and act as if he doesn't have a backbone. He doesn't need to follow some ancient dowager's idea of what's proper or improper to say or do. He can relax. Speak his mind. Give—and get—opinions, even from a bit of muslin such as that." He looked toward where the girls had disappeared toward the back stairs.

"And even if the opinions a woman like that hands out are only an echo of a man's and said only to make him happy, at least it is some sign that the girl has a brain. But the Miss Markhams of the world . . ." Nick shivered.

"It cannot be as bad as all that!" Though Nick could not see the humor in the situation, Willie laughed again. "Surely you must have grown up around women such as Miss Markham."

"Exactly." Nick hoped the acid in his voice spoke volumes and when the expression on Willie's face made it clear that it did not, he pulled in a long breath. "They are raised that way, you see. No thoughts. No beliefs. No aspirations at all except to find a husband who can give them a title or money or preferably, both."

"And are you telling me women like Bess and Clover have the sort of intellect you find appealing?" The tone of her voice told him that while she might well believe that Cyprians had all the intelligence in the world, she simply didn't believe that was why Nick sought them out.

"They may not be the great minds of our time but at least they are not afraid to show some life. Some passion."

"I daresay."

He harrumphed at the comment and apparently feeling some remorse—or perhaps it was because she took pity on him—she did not press the issue. "I've been instructing the staff," she said, though what that had to do with the fate that awaited Nick, he did not know. "Ever since we planned this dinner party, I've spent time with them, day after day. We talk about the appropriate way to serve and the way they are to behave and how they are to stand and walk and respond if someone should speak to them. At each lesson, I have found that one of the best ways to reinforce what they've learned is to try a bit of make believe."

He looked at her uncertainly.

"It seems to be working," Willie assured him. "For instance, this afternoon, I sat at table and had Mr. Finch come in and act as if he were serving tonight's dinner."

"Playacting, do you mean?"

"Exactly."

"It's ridiculous!"

"Perhaps. But a little playacting has helped assure us that Mr. Finch will not be serving the turbot with his fingers tonight as he was tempted to do." Her point well made and just as well taken, Willie walked as far as the stairs, then turned. She pulled back her shoulders and lifted her head, suddenly looking for all the world as regal as a duchess and as supercilious as most of the women Nick had had the misfortune to meet since he had ventured into the deep waters of the marriage pool.

"I am Miss Markham," Willie said. "And I've just arrived. Jem has opened the door. Mr. Finch has shown me in and taken my wrap. We have just been introduced and—"

"And do you suppose she's as pretty as you?"

Even Nick wasn't sure where the remark came from. He knew only that it was true. With the lights reflecting in Willie's eyes and a bit of high color emphasizing the sprinkling of freckles across her nose and cheeks, she suddenly didn't look as prim as he remembered and he just as suddenly remembered that though she'd been at Somerton House for weeks now, he hardly bothered to look at her at all. Willie was Willie and as such, she was the one who kept the household running as smoothly as a well-oiled clock, and the servants on task and Nick's life—at least as much as she was able—in some semblance of order.

He had, he admitted, taken her for granted, and that meant he had never noticed how clear her skin was or how her eyes shone with exactly the kind of intelligence he'd just told her he found so admirable. He hadn't noticed her figure much, either—at least no more than any man would notice a woman who was neither too old or too young or too close a relation to pay any attention to at all. But now that he looked, he realized that Madame Brenard must have been as hard at work on Willie's gown as she had been at fashioning suitable clothing for the other women in the household.

Though the dress would never grace a fashion plate, its simple lines, high waist and delightfully scooped neckline brought out the best of Willie's figure and its dark color made her hair, in contrast, look as bright as flame. With a sensation that felt a bit as if a hand had been inserted into his gut to twist it tight, Nick realized what he'd thought that first day he'd set eyes on Willie. She had all the right curves in all the right places. And now he saw that all her right places looked to be as delectable as any of the right places he'd ever been placed rightly enough to see.

"La, sir!"

The sound of Willie's voice snapped Nick out of his thoughts and he found himself grateful for the fact.

"I see you do quite live up to your reputation, m'lord," she said, sounding as practiced as every marriage-minded girl he'd ever met. "You are not above flattering a woman both to make her feel welcome in your home and to turn her head."

"Except I wasn't. Flattering, that is. Simply telling the truth." One hand behind his back, Nick reached for

Willie's right hand and at the same time he bowed over it, he brushed her fingers with his lips.

For what seemed too long a time and not nearly long enough, Willie stood as still as he knew Miss Markham would not. Miss Markham, he would wager, would take the opportunity to preen like a peahen and glance at the other women in the room just to make sure they noticed that the Viscount Somerton was paying her special court.

Willie's hand was small and well shaped, her fingers short and tapered. Her skin was not nearly as soft as that of the impures he was used to being so close to, yet there was something about the work-roughened touch that sent a singular sizzle through Nick.

Perhaps Willie felt it too. When he tightened his hold, she pulled her hand back to her side. "Miss Markham will be wearing gloves, of course," she said, looking up into Nick's eyes. She was Willie again and not some pampered wet goose with more social-climbing skills than brains. A restive smile came and went over her face.

"She'll giggle nicely, if I am not mistaken, and then she is bound to look around for her mother to be sure she's done the right thing. She will get Mama's approval and once she has it, she will wait for you to say—"

"That your eyes are as soft as April clouds and your smile bright enough to make the sun hide in shame."

"You are too bad, m'lord."

Was it Nick's imagination, or did Willie look relieved to think they were back to playing their game?

As if she held an imaginary fan, she tapped his arm. "You will make me so giddy, I will not be able to eat a bite at dinner, m'lord."

"We'll cancel dinner."

"But sir . . ." As if they were in the crowded salon of Somerton House, she glanced around. "You have other guests and—"

"We'll toss the guests into the street." The more Nick thought about it, the better the idea sounded. One careful step at a time, he closed the gap between them, until he was close enough to look down into Willie's eyes. "We'll have Mr. Finch bring us a bottle of wine and we'll bar the doors and close the curtains and—"

"Gads, m'lord!" As if she knew enough about Devonna Markham to know that she'd spent her life being instructed in exactly how to deal with men who were too forward for their own good but too well-connected to be put aside, she backed away a step and gave him a practiced, coquette's smile. "We are hardly acquainted and yet you tease so! Certainly what you mean to speak of is how fine the weather has been these last few days." She gave him a pointed look. "Or perhaps you might mention the excitement of Princess Charlotte's upcoming marriage to Prince Leopold of Saxe-Coburg-Saalfeld. Like the rest of the ton, I cannot help but think you must be keen with anticipation."

"Keen with anticipation, yes. But not about Princess Charlotte." Nick again stepped nearer. "It's not too late to extinguish the candles and pretend we are not at home."

"You are standing too close, m'lord."

It was not some callow miss who looked up at him with an expression he could not fully read, not some cast-in-stone Miss Markham who ran her tongue over her lips as if they were suddenly dry. And she was suddenly nervous. It was Willie, and the realization should have been enough to bring Nick to his senses. For reasons he could barely understand and never explain, it only served to make him more determined.

"I am thinking that I'm not nearly as close as I'd like to be." Nick voice dipped along with the look he skimmed over Willie's freckle-dotted shoulders. He brushed it along her collarbone and across the hollow at the base of her throat. He skimmed it over where the swell of her breasts peeked ever so demurely over the neckline of her gown. There was a warm, soft shadow between her breasts and he imagined how smooth her skin must be there. And how it might taste.

"Miss Markham will be frightfully unnerved should you speak to her so shamelessly." Willie's voice carried an edge of nervous laughter.

"But you are not." Nick raised his gaze to her eyes.

"Of course not." She forced a smile that lasted no longer than the bump of Nick's heart against his ribs. "We are playacting, after all, and there is no sincerity in the things you say."

"And if there was?"

The question hung in the air between them like the scent of the yellow roses in a vase set upon a nearby table. Heady. Tantalizing. Compelling.

Before Willie could answer—and before Nick could

decide what he wanted her answer to be—they heard the sounds of a carriage out front.

Something very like relief washed over Willie's expression and she backed away and glanced toward the front window. "It is sure to be your cousin, Lynnette," she said, her voice breathy. She moved quickly toward the stairway. "She is back from Bath, you know, and I asked her to arrive early so that she might be here to greet your guests. It was kind of her to agree to act as your hostess tonight."

"Kind. Yes." Away from the magnetic pull of Willie's smile, Nick felt more his old self again and instantly determined that he had never been all that satisfied with that person. Reluctant to break whatever fragile bond he had established with Willie and just as sure that if he did not let it go he would lose both her trust and her friendship, he caught the gaze that had been so sure and steady before and now refused to meet his eyes.

"I'm sorry. I think, perhaps, that I've made you uncomfortable. It was not my intention."

"Of course not." She gave him a gracious nod. "We are all on edge and I, perhaps, overreacted. After all, it is not every night that something so momentous happens at Somerton House."

"No, it isn't."

She was talking about the dinner party.

Nick was not.

The front door opened and Lynnette—all dark hair and ringlets and girlish laughter—sailed into the entryway like a ship headed into port.

"I must greet your dear cousin," Willie said and before Nick could make a move to offer her his arm and accompany her, she hurried down the steps.

Nick was not a man who believed in luck. But watching Willie go, he breathed a sigh of relief. Without the fortunate and well-timed arrival of Lynnette, he was sure he knew exactly what would have happened.

He had nearly kissed Willie Culpepper.

And the devil of it was, he couldn't quite decide if that was a bad thing.

Or a very good thing indeed.

....

"**I** say! Did you see the look on the old man's face?" Arthur Hexam could barely control himself. His plump body settled comfortably on the settee in Nick's library, his head thrown back against the pillows and a glass of claret in one hand, he laughed so hard, he nearly choked on the bite of biscuit he was chewing. He popped the rest of the biscuit into his mouth so that he might pound his chest with one hand and even when he caught his breath, he kept on laughing. "I thought ol' Jack Markham would have apoplexy right there at your table!"

"That would have capped off the evening nicely." Nick doubted if Latimer, Palliston, or Hexam noticed the sarcasm in his voice; they were all laughing so hard. He tossed back the last of the claret in his own glass but even when he swallowed and felt the slow, familiar burn of the spirits in his throat, he couldn't quite bring himself to join in the merriment.

There wasn't anything funny about the way the evening had gone.

The thought sat upon his shoulders like a January chill and though his first inclination was to reach for more claret to melt it, Nick set down his glass. No amount of spirits was going to make him feel better about the fact that he'd been tempted to overstep the bounds of propriety—not to mention sanity—and kiss Willie.

Just as no amount of claret would dull the fact that he still wanted to kiss her.

More than he wanted his next breath.

He caught himself just as he was about to sigh and glanced around. Fortunately, his friends were too busy recounting the events that had unfolded at the dinner table to notice that he was brooding. It was, perhaps, the only consolation in what had turned into the social disaster of this—or any other—Season. That, and the fact that things had gone so badly at the dinner party, it had nearly made him forget what happened with Willie.

Except for the incident of Jem being distracted by a stray dog and leaving his post at precisely the moment Devonna Markham and her parents alighted from their carriage and a second, more disturbing, occurrence when the Duchess of Amberly noticed that her diamond bracelet was missing only moments after Mr. Finch had served her an orangeat, the evening had started out well enough.

The bracelet was soon found on the floor near where the duchess had been standing (but only after Nick saw

Willie out in the passageway having a quiet but firm talk with Mr. Finch), and conversation was as lively as it can be in a group of both men and women. His duties as host kept Nick busy and he was grateful for that much. The more he had to do, the less he had time to deal with the memories that tickled his imagination—memories of Willie's voice and Willie's laughter and the way Willie's eyes sparkled in the light of the chandelier. Though it served much the same purpose, he was less grateful for the obvious and quite terrifying realization that Devonna Markham took an instant and rather intense liking to him.

Even that might not have been enough to ruin the evening.

But then it was time for dinner.

There were too many guests for Mr. Finch to serve by himself and though some of the other men of the staff did their best to help, there was a time between the second course and the third when the dishes weren't whisked from the table nearly quickly enough. Extra help was in order.

Unfortunately, it arrived in the form of Flossie.

Jack Markham, Devonna's father, was deep into the telling of a story when Flossie entered the room. He was a big man, he was loud, and he was impossible to miss.

"Godamercy!" Flossie blurted out the moment she saw the man. "If it ain't Jackie Markham. Well, don't you look a sight different, sir. What, with your clothes on and all!"

Just as it had then, mortification raced through Nick

and he scraped a hand through his hair. "Damn, but Jack's face was red," he said.

"Jack's face?" Latimer finished the claret in his glass and got up to pour himself another. "As red as his face was, you should have seen his good wife's. She went as pale as porridge."

"And Miss Markham herself . . ." Before Hexam could get it, Palliston snatched up the last biscuit on the plate set on a nearby table. "She was muddled, right enough. At least for the first few moments. And then the truth dawned—"

"And she was as spitting outraged as her dear mother!" Smiling, Hexam ran a finger around the perimeter of the plate, picking up the last biscuit crumbs and licking them off his finger. "What a predicament, eh? They couldn't up and leave because even though Jack pretended he'd never seen Flossie and didn't know what she was talking about, that would have been as much as admitting his guilt. That gimlet-faced wife of his couldn't wait until the meal was over so they could make their excuses and fly out of here."

Halfway toward taking up the seat he'd vacated, Latimer stopped and held up one hand to silence their laughter. "We are surely being insensitive," he reminded them and the somber expression on his face embarrassed them all into silence. "There are more important things to consider here than our amusement, gentlemen. We must surely convey our deepest regrets . . ." Latimer's mouth twitched into a smile. "To poor Somerton here . . ." His smile turned into a grin. "Who surely through this incident has lost a lady who was most taken by him and would have made him a most worthy . . ." His grin grew to a chuckle. "A most worthy . . ." He laughed too hard to say another word.

And it was just as well. Because he knew they would have it no other way, Nick joined in the fun with as much enthusiasm as he was able to muster. Which was little enthusiasm, indeed. "No regrets necessary," he told them. "Miss Markham was . . ."

"Trying much too hard?" Hexam suggested.

"She shouldn't have to be. Not with an income like she has. No." Nick thought about it for a moment. "Those are not the words I would use. What I meant to say, of course, is that Miss Markham is—"

"As ordinary as apples," Latimer suggested.

"And chatty enough to set a man's teeth on edge." Palliston shivered.

"And quite obviously . . ." Hexam set down his glass so that he might clutch both his hands to his heart. "Desperately head over heels in love with Somerton!"

"Laugh if you will," Nick told his friends. "I find no amusement in the thing. Not only was Miss Markham too tall for my liking, she was also, as Palliston was so wise to point out, far too garrulous. Which is not necessarily a bad thing in a woman except on those occasions when she has nothing of any interest to say. Which, in case you didn't notice, certainly applies to Devonna Markham. It is no wonder the girl hasn't found a husband. She must scare them off by the dozens with her endless prattling. Besides . . ." He did not usually send his friends home this early in the night, but it had been a far too eventful dinner party and he was drained. Nick stood, effectively announcing that it was time to end the evening. "Miss Markham is simply not my type."

It was an honest enough admission. Which didn't explain why his friends met it with smiles.

"Somerton is getting pensive." Latimer clapped Nick on the shoulder and headed for the door. "There was a time when the only *type* that concerned him was the female type."

"Perhaps he *is* ready to get buckled." Following Latimer, Palliston shook his head sadly. "Otherwise he would not be so concerned with matching to the right personality."

"Which makes a man wonder, of course . . ." As if there might be more biscuits hiding beneath it, Hexam lifted the plate. Disappointed in his search, he shrugged and set it back down. "Tell us, Somerton . . . which type of woman is your type?"

It was the last thing Nick wanted to think about. Especially when the memories of his encounter with Willie were still so fresh and vivid enough to make his body tighten in response. He was saved from answering altogether when there was a knock at the door.

Latimer was standing the closest and he opened the door to reveal Willie standing in the passageway outside.

"Excuse me, m'lord."

One look at Willie and Nick realized he wasn't the only one having a long night. Earlier, her hair had been pulled back into a neat chignon. Now, it looked as if two cats had been fighting atop her head. A flaming red curl hung in her eyes. Another few dangled from the knot of hair at the back of her head. Earlier, her clothing was pressed, brushed and clean. Now, there was a streak of some sort of dark gravy across the front of the white apron Willie wore over her gown. Her face was pale and she refused to meet Nick's eyes. "I'm sorry to bother you, of course, but—"

"No bother at all!" While Latimer held the door open wider so that she might enter, Hexam was not nearly so patient a man. He reached for Willie's arm and tugged her into the room.

"The biscuits," Hexam said, apparently thinking the subject far too important to wait a moment longer. "Somerton says there's a new cook. You must ask him about the biscuits."

Willie was apparently expecting a different sort of reception. She glanced at Nick as if to gauge his reaction, and seeing that he was not inclined to interrupt his friends, she addressed Hexam. "They are called kaju badam. The recipe is from India. I thought it would be something a little different and that the guests might enjoy them, but of course . . ." She didn't need to add that after the fiasco in the dining room, Nick's guests had followed the Markhams' suit and had left as soon as possible after dinner, long before they could enjoy the kaju badam or any of the other sweets that had been laid out for their pleasure. "I made the biscuits."

"Madame, you are a goddess!" Palliston bowed in Willie's direction. "They are quite delicious and—"

"If you have more . . ." Hexam stepped between Palliston and Willie.

"There are many more in the kitchen." Automatically, she made a move toward the door. "I could get—"

"Oh, no! I will get them myself." Before Hexam could move, Palliston headed down the passageway, and not to be outdone, Hexam followed.

"I suppose I, too, will say good night." As was only fitting, Latimer's leave-taking was directed at Nick. Which didn't explain why he looked at Willie when he spoke.

Now that Nick thought of it, ever since she walked into the room, Willie had been the center of attention. It was bad form, especially considering that she was in his employ. It was worse form, he decided with something that felt a bit like a jolt out of the blue, because if anyone was going to pay attention to Willie, it should have been him.

Latimer nodded briefly in Nick's direction, bowed toward Willie and was gone.

For far longer than was polite, Willie toed the edge of the brightly patterned rug. Ever since word had gone around Somerton House about what Flossie had said— and word had gone around as fast as smoke rising up a chimney on a cold day—she had practiced what she would say to Somerton when she finally came face-to-face with him.

And now that she was face-to-face with him, she found that every one of the pretty apologies she'd rehearsed refused to come.

It was his fault, of course, and Willie consoled herself with the fact.

If her head wasn't still spinning from the encounter with Somerton earlier in the evening, she might not have found it so difficult to talk to him.

He was the one who had been gracious and charming. The one whose secret looks and fleeting glances had sparked an emotion so powerful, she hardly knew how to contain it. He'd spoken, and his words had sent a shiver like icy fire down her spine and into the private places of her body and her soul.

She knew better than to let her head be turned. After all, Somerton was doing nothing but playacting.

And even though she knew it, Willie couldn't help herself. She had taken his words and his looks and the touch of his hand to heart.

The realization was still too fresh and too painful to deal with and rather than even try, she decided to say exactly what she came to say so that she could be on her way.

"Brandy." The word sounded as dry as Willie's mouth felt and she cleared her throat and tried again. "I wonder, m'lord, if I might have a glass of brandy."

"Really, Willie!" Somerton crossed the room toward the bottles that were set on a sideboard near the window, his manner no more intimate now than it had ever been except for the stolen—playacted—moments at the top of the stairway.

He poured a glass of brandy and held it out to her. "You hardly look the type to console yourself with spirits."

"It is not for me, m'lord." Automatically, Willie took a few steps closer but she did not accept the brandy. To do so would be to take it under false pretenses. "It is for Flossie. She's terribly upset and I thought it might help. She's down in the kitchen. Crying. She has been since—"

"Since she single-handedly tarnished Jack Markham's name in front of his friends, his social betters and most of the people he's trying to court in the hopes of making a suitable marriage for his daughter?"

"Balderdash!" Ill at ease or not, Willie simply could not listen to such nonsense and keep her peace. "If Jack Markham's reputation is tainted, it is certainly beyond Flossie to do it single-handedly. Surely Mr. Markham himself had some part in their association, and more of a responsibility for the thing, I would venture, than poor Flossie ever did. She was the one who was so desperate to put food on her table, she would do anything. With anyone. Markham, on the other hand, took advantage of that desperation just to satisfy his own physical appetites and some mistaken fantasy that women are put on this earth solely for the pleasure of the men who choose to use them any way they like."

"That is enough, Willie." Though Somerton's voice was quiet and his statement calm, there was no mistaking the warning that came along with the words.

Willie would have been wise to listen. She actually might have if she didn't find herself so incensed. "I daresay half the men in that room knew Flossie, just as Markham did. And half of the women sitting there pretending to be shocked by the whole thing know exactly where their husbands go when they leave the house each night. And yet someone dares to speak the truth the rest of them will not utter and bring the thing out in the light and—"

"I said, that's enough!" Somerton's voice echoed against the walls and the vibration of it shuddered through Willie and stunned her into silence.

Perhaps because he realized it, he was instantly apologetic. "I didn't mean—"

"Of course you did." Averse to letting him think that her hesitation had anything at all to do with doubting that her argument was less than logical and perfectly accurate, she shook herself out of the momentary silence. "I don't suppose it's right for a servant to speak so boldly to her master. Even when she is speaking the truth."

To her surprise, Somerton laughed. "Good God, Willie, even when you're apologizing, you make it sound as if you're dressing me down."

"I'm sorry, I—"

"No need." He held up one hand and with the other, set down the glass of brandy. He leaned back against the sideboard, his arms crossed over his chest, his legs crossed at the ankles, and though it certainly must have been an even more taxing night for him than it had been for the rest of them, he looked none the worse for wear. His black evening clothes and blinding white linen made a dazzling combination, and every hair on his golden head shone like summer sunshine. He cocked his head and gave her a careful look. "Is that how you think of our relationship?" he asked. "Master and servant?"

It wasn't how she'd been thinking of their relationship all night long.

And there was no way on God's green earth Willie was about to admit it.

Too restless to stand in one place, she walked to the window and nudged the draperies aside.

There was no point in confessing that while she'd directed the taking of wraps and the ushering of guests into the salon, while she'd overseen the cooking of dinner and the serving of it, while she'd handled the sudden and quite unexpected rush of Somerton's guests to leave and the predicament Five Fingers Finch had nearly put them in by resorting to his old ways and the inconsolable sobs of Flossie who—after her impetuous outburst—was sure she would be shown the door at any moment, she had been thinking of everything that had happened with Somerton before his guests arrived.

Even now, her insides were tied in knots and her brain was muddled.

Did she think of herself as a servant and Somerton as nothing more than the master of the house?

She didn't dare answer for if she did, she would have been tempted to confess the truth: that she had never had any intention of thinking anything but.

Until that moment when she thought he might kiss her.

Until she realized that it was what she wanted.

And that she wanted it still.

Willie shook herself out of her reverie and found herself staring at her own reflection in the window. Too plainspoken not to answer if he should press her for the truth, she was also too honest to face the woman who looked back at her from the glass. She dropped the drapery and turned, determined to change the subject.

"Miss Markham was a top quality choice," she said. "And it is my fault things did not work out between you. I should have known there was the possibility for such an incident. I should have been more careful about instructing the girls. I'm sorry."

"I'm not!" Somerton threw back his head and laughed. "Devonna Markham is pinch-faced!"

It was impossible not to respond to the smile that brightened Somerton's expression. Before she even knew she was doing it, Willie found herself fighting to control a smile. "Certainly, m'lord, you are not so shallow as to look no farther than a woman's face."

"She was long-winded."

"A talent that might keep a husband entertained on those nights when he and his wife are home together."

"She isn't very bright."

Willie could not deny it. Like everyone else at Somerton House that evening, she had heard Devonna Markham's high-pitched laughter as well as the cockledbrained comments the girl made. She declared the weather "fine," until she saw that the statement did not bring the instant smile she'd hoped from Lord Somerton and changed her opinion to, "Perhaps not so fine after all." She announced that the newest novel by one

Mrs. Mordefi, whose singular talent to send chills down the spines of her readers, was also "fine." Until she saw that Lord Somerton did not instantly agree and said, instead, that the book was lacking.

"She may be a gooseberry, but there is no denying that Miss Markham is wealthy enough to get you out of the stew you find yourself in."

"Something I sincerely wish no woman would ever have to do." The smile faded from Somerton's face and he pushed himself off from the sideboard.

"Still, she would have made you a good match. And now I'd venture to say that you will never get near the girl again."

"For which I suppose I must offer Flossie my sincerest thanks." Somerton held the glass of brandy out to Willie. "Take this to her. Please. And tell her to stop crying. Good gad!" A shiver danced across his broad shoulders. "There is nothing I hate more than a woman who blubbers!"

"I will gladly take her the brandy with your compliments." Willie crossed the room until she was standing within a few feet of Somerton. "She's worried she'll be sacked. As is Mr. Finch."

"Finch." Somerton's mouth thinned. "There's another story and no mistake. Did he really think—"

"It was an honest mistake." It was another lie but at least Somerton had the good grace not to point it out. "He promises to never do it again. And I . . ." Willie reached for the brandy. "I promise to watch him like a hawk!"

Their fingers met over the crystal and though Willie

was tempted to pull her hand away, she knew full well it would be the worst course of action. Poor Lord Somerton was having a bad enough evening. He did not need brandy splashed on him and spilled on his fine rug to top off the night.

They stood that way for a heartbeat or two and might have gone standing even longer if Mr. Finch did not appear outside the doorway.

"You've a gentleman to see you, my lord." The fact that Finch didn't have the nerve to look into Somerton's eyes told Willie that he knew full well what he'd done earlier was wrong. The fact that on sight of him, Somerton stood tall, squared his shoulders and raised his chin was enough to tell both Willie and Finch that the viscount would not tolerate another such slip up.

"A gentleman, you say?" Only when he was sure that Willie had firm hold of the glass did Somerton let go. "Who is it, Finch, and why—"

"We aren't standing on formalities, are we?" With a smile as bright as his coal-black greatcoat was shadowy, the Duke of Ravensfield swept into the room. "That will be all, Finch," the duke said, turning to the butler and even though the dismissal had not come from his master, it was all the encouragement Mr. Finch needed. Before Lord Somerton could find the words to give him the drubbing he so soundly deserved, he disappeared down the passageway.

Willie made to leave, too, but before she got to the door, Ravensfield stepped in front of it, effortlessly blocking her way.

"Miss Culpepper." He aimed a smile at her that was intimate enough to melt a lesser woman's heart. "No need for you to leave. As a matter of fact, I think you'll want to hear what I have to say. There are things I need to discuss with his lordship and I think you will find them interesting." He gave her a penetrating look. "I hear from reliable sources that you are the one who engineered tonight's festivities."

Willie looked to Somerton for guidance and when he did not object, she took a seat, as mystified as he was by the duke's appearance.

Ravensfield wasn't the least bit timid about making himself at home. As if he'd been there a hundred times before and had poured himself a hundred drinks—which, now that Willie thought about it, he probably had—he strode over to the sideboard, filled a glass and tossed it down. He filled it again before he turned.

"I have come to express my regrets. At not being able to attend tonight's festivities." The duke smiled, an expression that did little to soften his features. "Like the rest of the ton, I was surprised to hear you were having a dinner party, Somerton. And as pleased as can be. It's good to see you taking an interest in your social obligations."

Somerton's smile was not nearly as effortless as the duke's, though it was a good deal more cheery. "Duties of which I am fully aware. I need neither your encouragement nor your lecturing to remind me."

Ravensfield waved away the suggestion that his comments were offered with anything less than sincerity. "I was disappointed that I could not accept your kind invitation but I had other . . ." He glanced in Willie's direction and seeming to think better of what he might have said, he cleared his throat. "Other commitments," he said. "I wish I did not. It would have been most interesting to be here."

"I have no doubt you would have found it amusing."

"Cheer up!" No longer able to contain his laughter, Ravensfield walked over and thumped Somerton on the back. "It's Jack Markham's own fault, after all, and not yours. And if you did offend the terribly rich Miss Markham?" Ravensfield's black eyebrows slid up with curiosity and he glanced over his shoulder at Willie as if he thought he might find the answers to his questions with her. "That is why you had the dinner party, isn't it? To ensnare the financially plump Miss Markham?"

"You know as well as I do that it would be most unseemly for us to discuss that," Somerton spoke before Willie could. Which was, she thought, a good thing. Had she been answering the duke, she would not have been nearly as diplomatic.

"The young lady in question isn't here," Somerton said. "And Willie . . . that is, Miss Culpepper can hardly defend her honor, not being acquainted with Miss Markham."

Ravensfield could not be so easily put off. He laughed. "What you mean to say, of course, is that yes, you've ruined your chances with the good Miss Markham. Or should I say more accurately, that Flossie ruined your chances for you?"

"Word travels fast around town."

"Like the wind." Ravensfield drank down the claret in his glass. "I hope this one stumbling block on your road to matrimony has not caused you to lose heart. Then again . . ." He gave Somerton a careful look. "Perhaps it has?"

"And perhaps I should be a clod-pate not to wonder why it matters so much to you."

"Aha! There you have it!" Like a conjurer producing something both mysterious and unexpected, the duke pulled a single sheet of paper from his pocket, unfolded it and read it over quietly, nodding in assent. When he was done, he turned not to Somerton but to Willie.

"Somerton is a rakehell of the first order. But then, I daresay you know that. Women have been after him for years. In droves. Yet he's never so much as expressed even the slightest bit of interest in tying the knot. Not that I can blame him!" As gracefully as a panther, Ravensfield crossed the room and sat in the chair opposite Willie's.

"It would take a woman of great character to put up with the likes of him." He leaned a bit nearer and lowered his voice, as if sharing a confidence. "Word has it that you are the first one who's been able to talk him into getting even this close to the parson's mousetrap."

"Me?" Willie smoothed a wrinkle from her apron and though she could not bring herself to lie to Somerton, she found it as easy as an old shoe—surprisingly—to look Ravensfield in the eye at the same time she wove a bit of whole cloth. "Lord Somerton's marital state is certainly no concern of mine."

"No, I do not imagine it is." A knowing smile touching his lips, Ravensfield sat back and considered her response. A moment later, he shook himself out of whatever thoughts occupied him and waved the piece of paper in the air. "Your marital status may not concern Miss Culpepper, but it now officially concerns me, Somerton!"

Though Willie had no idea what the duke was talking about, it was apparently becoming clearer by the moment to Somerton. She saw the momentary flash of surprise that sparked in his eyes. He concealed it easily as he strolled across the room.

"Don't tell me you were enough of a gull to be drawn into a wager so fickle as that! Are you telling me—"

"Odds are running six to one that you will meet someone and marry her. This Season." Ravensfield tapped the paper with one finger. "Of course, the odds may yet change. It is early in the game."

How Somerton managed to conceal his outrage, Willie wasn't sure. When she realized what the duke was saying—and that they were talking about Somerton's future as casually as they might have talked about which fast trotter might win which race—her fingers curled into her palms. Her heartbeat quickened, nearly to the impossible rate it had achieved earlier when she looked into Somerton's eyes.

"You're taking bets?" All the outrage she was feeling was manifest in Willie's voice. "About Lord Somerton's search for a wife?"

"More specifically, about whether or not he will find a wife." Ravensfield neatly folded the paper and put it back in his pocket. "There are those who are as sure as the Creed that it will happen. After all, Somerton is not unattractive, or at least that's what the women of his acquaintance have been known to say. And he does have that rather succulent title! It's enough to make any woman's mouth water. Now that the word is out that he is in search of a mate, yes, there are those about town who are betting. And they are betting heavily that he will find a wife. And soon."

It was appalling to think there were those who would wager on so serious a matter, yet listening to the whole of the plan laid out before him, Somerton did not react. He poured another drink but rather than sip it, he rolled the glass in his hands, watching the blood-red liquid swirl inside it.

"And let me venture a guess." He glanced at Ravensfield. "Seeing that the odds are stacked that I will wed, you've wagered the other way. That I will never find a wife."

"Oh, I shouldn't say *never*. Really, Somerton, you do not think highly enough of yourself." Ravensfield rose to his feet. "I think that someday you will find a wife. But I do not think it will be soon, especially considering the current state of things here at Somerton House. Not that your staff does not hold a certain charm," he added, almost as an aside. "But the ton can be quite damnably pretentious when it comes to such as poor Flossie and her friends."

"And yet you yourself are not so narrow-minded."

"Me?" Ravensfield poked one finger at the black satin waistcoat that showed when his greatcoat flapped open. "You know I don't care a fig who serves in your home or what sort of services they provide. I have, however, had a chance to look over most of this year's crop of marriage-minded girls. Not a toast among them, I'd venture to say, and not one who looks as if she would make you an appropriate *parti*. I know you well enough, you see. I know you would never spend the rest of your life with a woman who would bore you to death and be as cold as icicles in your bed—pardon my being so blunt, Miss Culpepper—just to make sure I lose a wager. So you see . . ." Ravensfield straightened his greatcoat, flapping it around him like bat wings.

"It is the ultimate challenge between the Blades and the Dashers. Marry and you save the family name and secure the family fortune at the cost of your happiness. Fail to marry, and you'll make me a great deal of money. You'll pardon my saying it . . ." He headed for the door. "But you are damned if you do, Somerton. And just as damned if you don't. I'm wagering on the latter. Let's face it, my friend, in spite of your title, you have little to recommend yourself. You have little redeeming social value."

"That isn't true and you know it!" The words were out of Willie's mouth before she could stop them and when she came to her senses, she found she was already on her feet. "That is . . ." She swallowed down her morti-

fication and reminded herself of what Somerton had reminded her of only a short while before. He was the
master, and she, the servant. As such, she owed him her
loyalty. Not her passion.

She dared a glance at Somerton and saw that though
he was not at all surprised by her outburst, he did not
feel he needed her support. Nor did he appreciate it.

"What I meant to say, of course . . ." Willie drew in a
steadying breath and hoped that the heat she felt in her
cheeks was not as noticeable as she feared. "Lord Somerton has many fine qualities. I do believe there are any
number of young ladies who would be proud to know
that he is taking them into consideration."

"I truly hope not!" Ravensfield tipped his head in
farewell. "You've got until the end of June, Somerton.
This June. And either way you look at it, you lose and
I . . ." He had removed his tall top hat when he walked
into the house and now, he clapped it back on his head
and set it at a rakish angle. "I win!"

For a few minutes after he was gone, Willie was too
stunned by all that had happened to do anything but
stare at the place where Ravensfield had stood. She
was pulled from her thoughts by a curious sound behind her and she turned to find Somerton rubbing his
hands together.

"We'll get him this time!" He crossed the room to his
desk and pulled open the top drawer. Whatever he was
looking for, he didn't find it, and he tried the next
drawer and the next. Finally, he grumbled his displeasure. "Where the devil is it, Willie?" he asked.

"It?" His eyes were bright, his mood suddenly as animated as it had been despondent when she entered the room. Not certain what was happening or how she should respond, Willie approached him carefully. "You're looking for—"

"The list, of course." Somerton tapped a finger impatiently against the desktop. "The list you showed me the other day. The one that recorded each of the women you thought might be good matches."

"It is right here." Willie retrieved the list from her pocket. She had already crossed off Devonna Markham's name.

"How many?" Somerton asked.

She glanced over the names. "Ten, m'lord. But I'm surprised—" She thought better and swallowed her words.

Somerton laughed. "Out with it, Willie. By all accounts, you're bound to tell me sooner or later anyway. You're surprised about what?"

"That you would care. You have been most reluctant."

"Yes. Yes, I have been." Somerton rounded the desk and, plucking the list from Willie's hands, he headed out of the room, studying it. "But that was before I knew Ravensfield had his finger in the thing. You don't think I'm going to let him win this wager, do you?"

He didn't wait for her to answer and it was just as well. Watching him go, Willie whispered, "No, m'lord. I don't think you will let Ravensfield win."

And even though that would mean a successful match for Somerton and that a successful match for Somerton was what Willie had been urging all along, she wondered why the very thought of his sudden enthusiasm for finding a wife made her feel so hollow.

And why she cared so very much.

❧ 10 ❧
....

"**S**o, 'e's gone for the evenin', is 'e?"
Willie had not heard anyone come up behind
her and at the sound of Madame's voice at her shoulder,
she drew in a sharp breath of surprise and moved back
from the library window.

It was on the tip of her tongue to tell Madame that
she had no notion what she was talking about, that she
was standing there simply to see if the window had been
washed that afternoon as it was supposed to have been
and not because she was watching Lord Somerton get
into his carriage. One look in Madame's eyes, and Willie
decided against it. It was one thing lying to herself. It
was another to try and pull the wool over eyes that had
seen as much as Madame's.

Willie moved away from the window and headed for
the desk on the other side of the room. Somerton had
been in the library earlier and the neat piles Willie had
arranged that morning were now scattered. She looked

through the papers one by one, sorting them again. If her thoughts would not cooperate, she told herself, at least her work could be organized.

"He's headed for a ball at Almack's," Willie said, glancing toward the window and promising herself it would be the last time. "I hear he made good on a voucher of admission he was given earlier in the Season. Before—"

"Before we arrived. Yes." Madame's lips thinned. She turned from the window, too, but though it was obvious that neither of them was watching Lord Somerton any longer, it was just as obvious that Madame would not so easily let go of the subject. " 'Im bein' there ought to shake up a few of them toplofty Society types."

"Indeed." Because she knew it was true, Willie had to smile. Just as quickly, she put the thought from her mind. Better to concentrate on the task at hand than to let her imagination run riot. Especially when it ran in the very direction in which Somerton's carriage was headed.

Her mind made up, she read over the newest of the invitations that had been arriving at the house in record numbers. The first requested Lord Somerton's presence at a country house party in two weeks' time and Willie made a note for herself to check and see which, if any, likely marriageable lady might be attending as well. She set the invitation on the proper pile and glanced up at Madame. "According to what Mr. Hexam told me when he visited His Lordship last Tuesday evening, the ton as a whole is thrilled to see Lord Somerton in circulation, so to speak. In spite of what happened at the dinner party—or perhaps because of it—his sudden participation in Society gatherings has added a certain spice to a decidedly bland Season."

"And no wonder. Because for the first time, 'e's seriously searchin' for a wife." Madame looked none too pleased at the prospect, which surprised Willie. After all, Madame understood just as surely as Willie did that finding a wife was a fit and proper task for someone of Somerton's age, station and financial straits. " 'E's 'ad a change of 'eart and no mistake. Just think, when you first put forth your plan to find 'im a wife, 'e wanted no part of it. 'E was downright reluctant. That's what 'e was."

"That was before the Duke of Ravensfield entered the picture."

Like it or not, it was the truth and as Willie had told herself time and again, it was time to face it. The transformation of Somerton was, after all, close to miraculous. She shook her head in wonder. "There is nothing like a wager to warm a man's blood."

It wasn't meant as a jest. Which made Willie glance up in surprise when Madame laughed.

"Sorry, lamb." Madame held one hand to her ample bosom as if that might help keep her laughter in check. It didn't, and it wasn't until the laughter had settled into a throaty chuckle and she had wiped a hand across her eyes that she tried to speak again. "Wagers are one thing, certainly. But I'm thinkin' there are other things that can 'eat a man's blood even more. If only a woman knows 'ow to go about usin' them."

It was so close to what Willie had been thinking about since the night of the dinner party and her encounter with Somerton on the stairway that she had no choice but to protest. "Madame, you can't possibly think—"

"Don't 'ave to think a thing, as it 'appens. I 'ave eyes to see and ears to 'ear and even if I did not, I 'ave a 'eart and oftentimes, the 'eart does more seein' and 'earin' than it does anythin' else."

"That may be so . . ." Willie reached for the pile of papers in front of her and tapped them against the desk top, wishing at the same time that she could so easily order her emotions and the thoughts that had been speeding through her brain since that fateful night. Not to mention the sensations that coursed through her body every time she so much as thought of the way Somerton had looked at her.

"Certainly, you are being much too imaginative," she told Madame, her voice nearly choking over the words. "You cannot possibly think—"

"That you are dreamin' about the man? And wonderin' what it might feel like to be with 'im as a man and a woman are when they are lookin' to pleasure each other?" Madame's gaze was far too perceptive, her words too close to the ones that had plagued Willie for far too long.

"Am I that transparent?" Willie dropped into the seat behind the desk. "I wouldn't for the world have him—"

"Oh, 'e 'asn't any idea!" Madame shook her head, though the fact that Somerton did not know what a gooseberry Willie was seemed more a thing to rejoice about than one to be sorry over. "Like most men, 'Is Lordship does not know 'ow many blue beans make five. 'E pays too much mind to the things that 'ardly matter and doesn't notice the things that do. Like the way you watch 'im when 'e 'appens into a room. Or the fact that more nights than not, you wait for 'im to return from wherever 'e's gone. 'E 'asn't paid none of it no mind but you can be certain sure it 'asn't escaped my notice. I've seen the way when you speak to 'im, you won't meet 'is eyes. I've noticed that when you are obliged to talk to the man about some 'ousehold matter or another, you try to be as quick about it as 'ell would scorch a feather. Little things, surely, but you would think a man would be aware. At least any man with 'alf a brain."

"Then we must be thankful that His Lordship does not have 'alf a brain." Because she dared not think about it or how foolish she'd been to allow her emotions to be so visible, Willie rose to her feet, determined to put both the conversation and the thoughts it sent jangling through her aside. Horrified by all that had been said and all that it meant, she looked to Madame for assurance. "You haven't told a soul, have you?"

Madame grinned. "On my honor," she said. " 'Aven't. Wouldn't. Wouldn't 'urt you for the world, lamb. Only I'm afeared you will take care of that yourself. If you do nothing and let your feelings go unspoken."

It was Willie's turn to laugh. She wasn't sure why. There was certainly nothing at all amusing in the things

Madame suggested. "You cannot be serious." Because she feared Madame was, Willie refused to even consider the notion. "Nothing is exactly what needs to be said. And these feelings . . ." She hauled in a breath and let it out again slowly. "These feelings are misplaced. And misbegotten. They must certainly go unspoken."

"And yet a woman can say a great deal without ever speakin' a word." Madame raised her neatly arched eyebrows. "If you catch my meanin'."

"I do not," Willie said, because of course, she did. "You cannot think that I would ever——"

The very thought set Willie's heart hammering inside her ribs and her blood buzzing in her veins. "I wouldn't know how," she said, as surprised as Madame obviously was that she had dared to speak the words.

Madame waved away her worries with one hand. "The 'ow of it is easy enough! And a thing any woman knows. Any woman who wasn't raised as you was, with a madman for a father and no mother to 'elp you along when it comes to such."

"But, Madame, I couldn't——"

"Of course you can!" Madame smiled and waved Willie closer. "Come on, now. Come over 'ere, and tell me what is it Somerton's done."

"Done? He hasn't done anything. You don't think——"

The horrified expression on Willie's face was apparently all the reassurance Madame needed. "Oh, I know right enough that 'e hasn't taken any liberties. Somerton may be a rakehell but he is not lackin' honor. But there must be somethin' that makes you think so of him.

Somethin' besides those eyes like sapphires and those shoulders that are as wide as the main door of St. Paul's. And that smile . . ." A tremor skittered over Madame's own shoulders. "Don't tell me you 'aven't noticed all that. So tell me, what was it? A glance? A word? Or just lookin' at that angel's face and knowin' what a wanton devil's 'eart 'e 'as?"

The memory of everything that had happened at the top of the stairway coursed through Willie like warm honey. She caught herself just as she was about to sigh and decided it was foolish to deny what was apparently so evident. "He spoke," she said and when she looked at Madame and realized she was waiting for more, she tried again to make sense of what she had not been able to explain even to herself. "He spoke foolishly. I admit that much. We were practicing, you see. Rehearsing what he might say to Miss Markham and—"

"And he told you what pretty eyes you have and how your smile lights a room. Yes." As if she'd heard the same sort of thing a hundred times over from a hundred different men, Madame nodded knowingly. "And that's what's got you all a twitter about the man?"

Willie cringed. Listening to Madame speak the words put them into perspective and standing back to look, she realized how much of a ninnyhammer she sounded. "I told you it was foolish," she said, her shoulders slumping beneath the realization. "He hadn't a thought for what he was saying and I . . ." She leaned back against the desk. "I am afraid I have taken it all quite to heart."

"And who can blame you? There's more than one

woman in town who considers 'erself quite sophisticated and still cannot resist Somerton's charms."

It was another thing Willie did not wish to think
about. If Somerton's appeal was potent enough to capti-
vate even the most sophisticated of women, what
chance did she stand?

"Those charms are far beyond my reach," she admitted. "As is even thinking of such things. I simply must
put the whole thing out of my head." Her mind made
up—even though the sting in her heart proved she was
not totally convinced—she stood straight and tall. "I
will simply do what I have done all my life. I will mind
my own business. I will complete my work and deal
with Lord Somerton as I might with any employer. Effi-
ciently. Professionally."

"You might try a smile now and again."

Madame's suggestion hung in the air, simple yet
provocative.

Too provocative to even consider.

"I smile," Willie insisted. "Often. I smile at Jem and at
Mr. Finch when I am instructing him about how to—
and how not to—behave with guests. I smile at the girls,
surely, for they respond far better to encouragement
than they do to scolding. I smile at—"

"At Somerton?"

The very thought made Willie feel light-headed and
the starch in her shoulders dissolved, much as did her
resolve. "If I am to smile, that means I must look him in
the eyes. And if I look him in the eyes, surely he'll know
what I'm feeling."

"What you're feelin' doesn't matter. Not to any man. Not nearly as much as what 'e's feeling. And 'e can't be feelin' a thing. Not if you never give 'im any encouragement."

The very thought terrified Willie. "I do not wish to encourage him," she insisted. "Encouragement leads to—"

"Exactly!" Madame beamed her a smile. "Oh, come now, lamb," she cooed when it looked as if Willie might lose heart. "You know as well as I do what you're dealin' with. The man is lookin' for a wealthy wife. And 'e will find one soon enough. Even if 'e did not 'ave a title to dangle in front of 'im like a carrot ahead of an 'orse, 'e's got that face and that smile and that voice that sends shivers up a woman's spine when it's spoken low and shivers in other places as well when the words are right and the lights are down. You'll lose 'im."

"I never had him to lose."

"Well then, you'll lose the chance to ever know what it might be like to be with a man such as that. Once there's a woman in the 'ouse, she'll watch 'im like a hawk. And knowin' Somerton . . ." She shook her head at the wonder of it all. " 'E'll not be like so many of the others. He will honor 'is vows and no doubt. Even if 'e does find 'is bride's purse more appealing than 'er person. Sad to say but if you do nothing now, you'll miss your opportunity."

"Opportunity?" The word scraped from Willie's suddenly dry mouth. "Opportunity to—"

Madame's squeal of laughter was the only confirmation Willie needed that Madame was referring to exactly what Willie thought she was referring to. And what she was referring to was not anything Willie wanted to refer to. Much less to think about.

"You need a bit of advice. To 'elp put your fears to rest." Madame bustled closer. "Let me see you give such a smile that will make 'Is Lordship sit up and take notice."

"I cannot. I—"

"You're not smiling."

"Very well." Willie gave in but only because she knew Madame would not let go of the subject until she was well satisfied. She tried for a smile and Madame cringed.

"You don't want to look as if you're going to bite the man's 'ead off," Madame told her. "Smile. Natural-like. Like you're as 'appy as can be to set your eyes on 'im."

"Like this?" Willie tried again.

"Better," Madame assured her. "Only you'll want to remember that 'e ain't one of your brothers. Add some 'eat to it, my girl. Like 'e's the only man in the world."

"It's foolish!"

"As foolish as practicin' what 'e was goin' to say to that Markham woman?"

"More foolish than that. At least there was a purpose for rehearsing what he was going to say to Devonna Markham. He was, after all, thinking of marrying the girl."

"Well, 'e won't be thinkin' of marryin' you!" For some reason Willie could not understand, Madame was pleased by the thought. "After you're done with the man, 'e won't be able to think of a thing but pullin' you into 'is arms and—"

"Madame, really. You are too wicked!" Willie would never have the daring to do what Madame suggested. Even if she did have the desire. Yet there was a certain pleasure to be had from thinking she might have such power over any man. Especially when that man was Somerton.

"That's it!" Madame clapped her hands together, as pleased as could be by the smile that had somehow crept over Willie's expression when she did not realize it. "But just because you're smilin' doesn't mean you can stand there as if you've a broomstick up your back. Relax." She demonstrated, leaning forward just a little, the pose welcoming—and suggestive enough to allow anyone who might be looking a brief and tantalizing glimpse of her breasts.

Willie felt the blood drain from her face. "Smiling is one thing, surely. I cannot—"

"Don't be a cabbage 'ead. Of course you can." Madame took hold of Willie's arm and tugged her forward just a bit. "There. You see. You bend as well as any other woman."

"But if I did . . ." Compared to the gowns Willie had seen at the dinner party, her own plain dress was drab and austere. It was however, as was the fashion, cut low over her breasts and when she bent forward as Madame suggested, she glanced down and was shocked by all she saw. "A real lady would never—"

"Don't fool yourself. 'Ow do you think all the *real ladies* find real men to warm their beds?"

"It's shocking."

"It's an art."

"But he would think me bold."

"Men love bold women."

"And wicked."

"Though half of them would never admit it, they love wicked women as well."

"And what would I do if—" The very thought was too much to even consider, and Willie swallowed the words with a gulp.

"If 'e notices, you mean?" The ready smile Madame had been wearing faded bit by bit, replaced by a look so bittersweet and so filled with wisdom, there was no doubt Madame knew what she was talking about. " 'E'll be a married man soon enough. It may very well be all you'll ever have of 'im."

The words settled inside Willie like a weight. "You're right. And I admit that it is tempting. More than tempting, if you must know the truth. To spend even one night with Lord Somerton . . ." Her words dissolved on the end of a sigh and her foolish fantasy along with them. "I want more than that," she told Madame and reminded herself. "I don't want him to see me as just a bit of muslin he can use for his pleasure and abandon just as easily. I would rather he felt something for me. Something of the affection I have for him. And if he does not . . . well, then I would rather have no part in his life at all."

"You're talkin' about love?" Madame shook her head sadly. "Oh my girl, I am sorry. I 'ad no idea you've got it so bad!"

*   *   *

It was far too early for Somerton to return, which was why Willie decided her ears were playing tricks on her when she thought she heard the front door open and close. She glanced up and tipped her head, but as there was no other sound, she told herself she was being imaginative and went back to her book.

According to Mr. Hexam, who had been kind enough to fill her in on the details of the seventh heaven that awaited those few fortunate souls lucky enough to be invited to Almack's, the balls and suppers there often went on nearly until dawn. It would be hours before Somerton was home, and though she knew she could best spend those hours in her own room and in her own bed, Willie was not yet ready for sleep. She was used to staying up to listen for the sound of Somerton's carriage and besides, on the nights she waited for him, she had acquired something of a secret indulgence.

When Somerton was gone, she often spent time in his library reading his books.

It was a small, eminently satisfying reward for all her hard work. At least when the book was engaging. It also helped to keep her mind off where Somerton had gone, what he might be doing and if this time, the marriage prospect she had sent him off to meet just might be the woman who would win his heart.

Her current choice of reading matter was one of Mrs. Mordefi's early works and, very much engaged even as she was frightened by the story of a vengeful ghost and a ruined abbey, Willie tucked her bare feet up under her and adjusted her lightweight shawl over her nightgown, tilting the book toward the single candle that glowed next to her chair.

It would have been far easier to concentrate on the words on the page in front of her if she could forget everything Madame had said earlier in the evening. All those things about Somerton's face and Somerton's smile and Somerton's voice, the one that Madame assured her—and Willie knew for a fact—could easily send a shiver up a woman's spine.

And though she did not and never would know it for a fact, she could well imagine that the other things Madame had said were true, as well.

If the words were right, if the lights were low, she was sure Somerton's voice could send shivers to other places in a woman's body.

The very thought caught Willie off guard and she sucked in a little breath of surprise. But though in front of Madame she might have had to pretend that such thoughts did not send her head soaring at the same time they made her body feel as if it had been set down a little too close to the fireplace flames, she could not pretend so well to herself. She closed the book, tipped her head back and sighed.

"It's no wonder the family coffers are empty and I am sent out, hat in hand and carrying the old and honorable family title with a To Let sign hanging from it. My God, woman, you are burning down all my candles!"

The sound of Somerton's voice right behind her made Willie shriek and jump to her feet.

"I'm sorry, m'lord." The answer was as instinctive as

the curtsy she dropped him. It wasn't until she was already on her feet that she realized her toes were showing
and that she was dressed in nothing but a nightgown. Its
sleeves went down nearly to the tips of her fingers. Its
neck went up nearly to her chin. It was wide enough to
hold at least two of Willie and she was sure Somerton
had seen far more uncovered flesh on the women he had
danced the evening away with at Almack's.

Which didn't stop her from feeling as if she were
standing naked in front of him.

She tugged her shawl closer around her shoulders
and tried to stand so that the hem of her nightgown hid
her feet. "I didn't mean to . . . That is, you can take the
cost of the candle out of my wages, surely, it's just that
I—"

"Willie!"

By the time Willie settled herself enough to look up
into Somerton eyes, she saw that he was laughing. "I am
the one who is sorry," he said. "It was wicked of me to
tease. But I saw you here so deep in thought and I simply couldn't help myself. You must excuse my poor jest."
In keeping with his clothing—the old-fashioned knee
breeches and dress coat with long tails that was *de
rigueur* for Almack's—he dropped her a deep and showy
bow.

Damn!

The word rumbled through Nick's head along with
the realization that he was staring at the carpet and
wondering how he'd gotten himself into a situation he
wasn't quite sure how he was going to get out of.

If he had any idea of how Willie was dressed—or more precisely, undressed—he never would have dared walk into the room and start a conversation with her.

Then again, if he hadn't walked into the room, he would have missed out on a most delightful treat.

He raised himself from the bow slowly, allowing his gaze to slide up Willie as he did. Though she did her best to hide them, her bare toes peeked out from the hem of her nightgown and something about the sight made Nick smile. He looked up farther still, past the billowing yards of fabric, stopping only as long as was polite—not nearly long enough—to study the way the muted light of the candle threw soft shadows against her breasts and outlined her nipples.

As if she could tell, Willie tugged her shawl tighter around her and his mouth suddenly dry, his gut twisting with a sensation that was part pleasure, part pain, Nick forced himself to look farther still. The neckline of the nightgown was far too high to reveal anything at all interesting, yet there was something alluring about it nonetheless. The mystery? He had never been taken with modest maids before.

There was no mystery to the fact that his fingers itched to touch the hair that was down around Willie's shoulders. It spilled over her like a sunset, hugging her breasts, stroking her neck.

Much as he wanted to do.

The realization did not come at him unawares. Ever since the night of the dinner party, he had looked at Willie differently. If it was a good thing or bad, he couldn't say. He knew only that it was madness and that it sang through his veins like fire.

Not precisely correct, he reminded himself.

He also knew he could not act upon his urges.

Keeping the thought firmly in mind, Nick scrambled for words that might sound even remotely like an excuse for his behavior. "I must admit I am feeling frolicsome," he said, smiling again when his glance glided back down to her toes. "I am so damnably happy to be home!"

"But it's too early." Willie's gaze went to the tall case clock that stood in the corner. "It is not yet midnight and surely, the festivities at Almack's—"

"The festivities at Almack's were patently dull!" As if it might get rid of the remnants of the evening—and, if he were smart and particularly lucky, the uncontrollable impulse he had to pull Willie into his arms—he scraped his hands over his face. "Passing the time of day with empty-headed misses and the tabbies who keep an eye on them! Pretending for all the world as if you're enjoying yourself when all you can think is that you can't wait to be gone from the place! The dancing was pleasant enough, I suppose, but the food was atrocious and the women . . . well, they don't have much to recommend them, I'm afraid, except fathers with money."

"Even Miss Greenlaw?"

"Miss Green—" For a moment, Nick wasn't sure who she was talking about. "Emma Greenlaw? You mean the young lady you insisted I meet?"

"I can hardly insist, m'lord." Willie raised her chin in the kind of subtle act of defiance that showed a spirit he would have paid a hundred quid to see from any one of the green girls at Almack's. "I can only suggest. After all, you are the one who must make the final decision as to who you should and shouldn't meet."

"You're right, of course." Nick went over to the sideboard and poured two glasses of brandy. He came back across the room and handed one to Willie.

"Emma Greenlaw belongs on the *shouldn't meet* list," he said, lifting the glass in a toast and clinking it softly against hers. He knew it must have been a trick of the light. Willie looked as relieved at hearing the news as he did at reporting it. "She's the wrong sort of girl altogether."

"Wrong?" The way her eyebrows slanted told him it was incomprehensible. Thinking the matter through, she took a sip of her brandy and when she was done, she ran her tongue over her lips, and Nick caught himself thinking he wouldn't mind running his tongue over her lips, too.

"I looked into the young lady's background quite thoroughly," she assured him, her comment breaking into the thoughts that had no business in his head. "She has a good name and an excellent income. Whatever could be wrong with her?"

"Nothing, I suppose. That is, if you like the rugged, outdoorsy type of girl." He pulled a face, looking to make light of the situation as much to distract himself as to make Willie smile.

"She's a big girl. Taller even than I. Wide shoulders." He demonstrated, holding his hands far apart. "Jaw like a hatchet. Talks about horses. And hunting. And riding to the hounds. Wouldn't be surprised if she was wearing Hessians under that maidenly white dress of hers. No doubt they were coated with manure."

The description was preposterous, and he was rewarded for it when Willie laughed. "I thought, m'lord, that you were more anxious than ever to find a wife."

So had he.

Nick shook the thought away in time to hear Willie say, "Are you sure boots coated with manure are enough of a reason to reject the lady in question?"

"Positive!" It was the truth and Nick did not mind admitting it. "That and the fact that when she dances, she uses those boots to trod upon the feet of unsuspecting gentlemen."

If Willie had been there getting her feet stomped, she wouldn't have smiled.

"Does that mean you waltzed?" she asked and just as quickly, her smile faded and her mouth fell open. She set her glass down on the nearest table.

"I'm sorry, m'lord," she said. "It is surely none of my business to ask."

"Why isn't it?" Anxious to bring back that smile that revealed the dimple in her left cheek, Nick stepped nearer and plunked his glass down next to Willie's. "What's wrong with asking about the waltz?"

Color rose in her cheeks and she glanced away. "I needn't tell you. There are some who say it's a wanton dance."

"And the Prince Regent himself who declares it most pleasing."

"Is it?" She looked at him, her eyes gleaming with a curiosity that was impossible to resist.

Somerton bowed. "Would you care to try it and see?"

"We have no dance floor," she said, looking around as if to remind him they were in the library. "And there are no other dancers. No music."

"Then we'll just have to make our own."

Before she could remind him that it was absurd—and long before he was willing to allow himself to listen—Somerton did what he'd been wanting to do since the moment he walked into the room and saw Willie in her nightdress. In one fluid motion, he moved forward and scooped her into his arms.

. . . .

$\mathscr{F}$or a moment, Willie could not breathe and it was all she could do to keep her knees from collapsing like a poorly made pudding.

Just as quickly, she reminded herself that they were dancing—nothing more—and as etiquette demanded, she gave her hand to Somerton. His fingers closed over hers, warm and firm, and she stood as still as a stone, waiting for him to prop his hand at the place where her waist met her hip. Short of running from the room and looking all the more foolish and as guilty as her way-ward emotions made her feel, she could do nothing at all when he reached for her but take a deep breath, let it out slowly, and enjoy the heat that flowed from his hand and through the thin fabric of her nightdress.

"This is how we begin," he said, and if she wasn't so busy grabbing for any shred of composure she could, she might have taken the time to notice that he sounded just as breathless as she felt. "The gentleman greets his partner, leads her to the dance floor and then we stand just like this, just for a moment."

A moment was not nearly long enough.

"Then the music begins," Somerton said, "The rest, as they say, is as easy as falling off a log."

"Only if one knows how to fall off a log," she told him and because she did not dare to look up into his eyes, she kept her gaze on his lips. She watched them quirk into something that was almost a smile.

"Are you telling me, Miss Culpepper, that you have never fallen off a log?"

Something told her that ever so subtly, the subject had changed. Unable to resist, she glanced up and was met with an expression that hovered somewhere between *I expected as much* and *what a shame.*

She had no doubt they were no longer talking about dancing.

"I have never fallen off a log," Willie admitted and in spite of the fact that it terrified her to think what it might mean and where it might lead, she could not help it; suddenly, she found herself offering him the kind of smile Madame had said no man could resist.

Madame was right.

As if it were a physical thing that traveled through the air and struck with a force that was both unexpected and impossible to defend against, she saw Somerton flinch beneath the potency of her smile.

He did not, however, shy away. Rather, she felt the pressure of his hand increase against hers and the small, nearly imperceptible movement he made to draw her closer. It was that—along with the thread of satisfaction that wound through her when she realized that her smile could have such power over him—that made her bold.

"I have never danced, either, m'lord," she said, her voice as light as her spirits suddenly felt. "My father thought it immoral."

"Your father is a fool."

"He said it wasn't right. For a man . . . and a woman . . ." She glanced down to the place where his body was only inches from hers and when she glanced up again, she realized she had leaned closer—much as Madame had instructed her to and she had insisted she would never be so impudent to do. "He said such familiarity would surely lead to wantonness."

"I suppose it might."

At the hint of the suggestion that shimmered in his voice, Willie raised her eyes again to Somerton's. She found him looking amused. And attentive. She also saw some other emotion there, one she could not name even though she could feel it to her very core.

Not for the first time since he'd come into the room, she wished she was not dressed in her nightgown. But this time, she realized it was not because she was embarrassed. If she were wearing one of her everyday gowns, she decided, she might lean closer still just as Madame had shown her. That way, she could give Somerton a glimpse of her breasts.

The very thought sent heat shooting through Willie's cheeks but rather than be dismayed by it—as she knew she surely should be—she found a certain pleasure in the sensation. Emboldened, she leaned forward until her breasts were only a hair's breadth from brushing his chest. "We are supposed to be dancing, m'lord," she told him, her voice as muted as the light of the single candle that flickered beside them. "And we are not."

"No. We are not."

The words stuck in Nick's throat and the breath in his lungs could not make its way past them. He stood like a man struck by lightning, every inch of his flesh tingling even as he was pierced to the heart.

He looked down into the face that was Willie's.

But it was more coolly self-possessed than any he had ever seen.

And into the eyes that were Willie's.

And belonged to a woman who was confident in her ability to entice a man.

The smile was Willie's, right enough. He remembered it from the night of the dinner party. It was the smile that sometimes crept over her expression unawares, the one that could light a room and haunt a man's dreams at the same time it tickled his imagination. It was poised. Self-assured. Amorous.

Amorous?

The word burned through Nick's brain and started an even hotter fire in his blood. In spite of the fact that he told himself it was not wise, he glanced down to the small space that separated their bodies and when he glanced again at the face and the eyes and the smile that were all Willie's—and weren't—he wondered what she'd think if she knew how eager he was to close the gap that separated them so that nothing kept them apart. Not their inhibitions. Or their pride. Not even their clothing.

"What of the music?"

Willie's question startled Nick out of thoughts that held him spellbound. It was just as well. His imagination was treading dangerously close to places he had warned it against venturing. There was no doubt that his body was tempted to follow. And less doubt still that it wasn't wise.

"The music!" He let go the words on the end of a long breath and looked around as if that might somehow conjure the orchestra they needed. The momentary reprieve from Willie's smile did nothing to provide an orchestra. Nor did it ease his conscience or calm his fantasies, and eager to do something before he could convince himself that he'd much rather take hold of Willie and kiss her until her head spun, Nick hummed a few bars of a tune he'd heard at Almack's.

"We shall have to make our own music," he told her. "And now that the music is playing . . ." He hummed the tune again. "We must begin to dance."

He didn't wait a second longer. One more second of standing there close to Willie—but not nearly close enough—and he knew he would not be accountable for what might happen. He swung into the dance.

Caught up in the crook of Somerton's arm and the shimmer of sapphire magic that sparkled in his eyes, Willie felt a bit as if all the air had been sucked out of the room. Afraid she would make a misstep, afraid she wouldn't care if she did, she listened to him count the easy rhythm of the dance.

"One, two, three. One, two, three."

She looked down at his feet and tried to mirror his moves. It would have been difficult enough to follow had she been fully in control of her body or her thoughts. It was nearly impossible with her head whirling and her fantasies soaring out of control. Before they had gone three steps, she stomped on his foot.

"I'm so sorry!" Horrified, Willie pulled to a stop. "You'll think me as ungraceful as Miss Greenlaw and—"

"No matter!" Somerton laughed and buoyed by the sound, she tried again.

"One, two, three. One, two, three." She found herself reciting the chant with him until their voices blended into a chorus that marked the rhythm of their movements.

"That's it. There. Better." He called his encouragement, as pleased as Willie was that she soon got the simple movements straight and that there were no more injuries to his feet. "Now . . ." Carefully, he turned around the corner where the desk met the bookshelves, showing her as he did how such a seemingly difficult movement could be as simple as breathing and as smooth as a whisper with the right partner.

"Look at me, Willie."

"What?" She had been busy watching her feet and automatically, her head came up and she lost count. She tripped and would have tumbled to the floor if not for the steady pressure of his arm around her.

"You need to keep your eyes on me as we dance," he told her, unfazed by the slip up. "We are going to need to chat."

"Surely not . . . one, two, three . . . Not while we're dancing . . . one, two, three . . . I don't know if I can . . . one, two, three . . . talk at all, m'lord . . . one, two, three . . . I'll lose my place in the dance and—"

"Do you trust me?" The question was as serious as the expression that clouded Somerton's face. Or perhaps it was simply a trick of the light and the fact that they were far from the candle now and his face was thrown into shadow.

"I do trust you," she told him. "One, two, three. It is myself I cannot . . . one, two, three . . . trust."

"Stop counting!" There was a ring of command in Somerton's voice that did not quite match the muted light or the graceful movements. But it did get Willie's attention. She swallowed her words.

"Forget that we're dancing," he told her. "Forget about the room and the feel of the carpet beneath your feet and the music and—"

"But, m'lord, there is no music!"

"See?" Even in the dim light, she saw the smile that gleamed in his eyes. "You've forgotten already. Now listen to me, Willie. Close your eyes and forget about it all."

"Close my—" It wasn't the sensible thing to do and Willie feared it did not bode well for Somerton's feet. Or for her heart. Still, his voice was as impossible to resist as taking her next breath might be. Because she had no choice, Willie allowed her eyes to drift shut.

"Now don't think about the dancing. Don't think about anything. Just feel. The rhythm. And the way the air flutters around you. Feel my skin against yours. And the place where my hand . . ." He adjusted his hold a bit, the touch as soft as a whisper, and though it was so light and her nightdress was so voluminous that Willie could not be sure, she could have sworn his thumb skipped up her ribs before it glided back down again.

Somerton's voice was rough and breathless, no doubt from the exertion of spinning around the room. "Do you feel it?"

Willie was tempted to tell him he could not possibly be speaking about what she was feeling. It was just as well the words wouldn't come. She nodded instead and gave herself over to the magic of the dance and when he tightened his hold ever so slightly and spun her around the next corner, she swore her feet did not touch the ground.

Caught up in rhythm and the enchantment, Willie threw back her head and laughed.

He spun her faster then, and she moved through the steps of the dance as if she had known them all her life, graceful yet wild, somehow, as if they were falling through a pitch-black void, with only each other to hold.

Another corner and Somerton held on even tighter. It did not take her long to realize that even after they were out of the turn, he did not loosen his hold.

Willie's heart, already pounding at breakneck speed, skipped a beat. She opened her eyes to find him looking down at her, half his face illuminated by the light of the candle, the other half lost in shadow. Still, there was no mistaking the longing in his eyes. After all, it would have been impossible not to recognize the same emotion that racketed through her.

Willie did not even realize she'd stopped dancing until the scene settled and Somerton was standing in front of her, breathing just as hard as she was.

"Thank you, m'lord." She tried for a tone of voice that was relaxed and casual. Just as any proper young lady at Almack's might have done at the end of a dance. It actually might have worked if Somerton let go of her. He did not, and at the same time Willie realized it and realized she did not care, he tugged her closer.

"I have never danced, m'lord. But I think this is not usual," she said, glancing down to the place where his hand caressed her hip.

"No," he said. "It is not usual."

"And it is not wise."

"No." They both knew it and still, a smile as hot as a winter's fire lit Somerton's face. "It is not wise at all."

"And we'll regret it, I think."

"Not until the heat of it cools and we come to our senses. I suspect that may be a long while from now."

"A very long while."

"Which means—"

"It means you really should kiss me, m'lord." The words were out of Willie's mouth before she could stop them and before she could convince herself that she was far too bold and far too wanton, Somerton was already laughing.

"Is that what you want?" he asked.

"Oh yes, m'lord." It was the truth and there was no use denying it. Not to Somerton. Not to herself. Not any longer. "More than anything."

"You'd best be careful, Willie." He was still smiling but now there was something other than amusement that sparked in his eyes. It was a look that caused a slow crawl of heat to inch through her insides. "A man doesn't take well to such teasing."

"Nor does a woman. And if that's all it was . . ." As if the shadow of the dancers and the imaginary orchestra still lurked where the light of the candle melted into the darkness, she looked over her shoulder.

Almost afraid to ask and find out she'd been wrong about him and about everything she was feeling, she swallowed a breath for courage. "What did you mean it to be?" she asked. "Was it dancing and nothing more?"

"Did it seem to be more?"

"Did you want it to be?"

Somerton shifted from foot to foot. He puffed out a breath of annoyance but whether it was at her brazenness or because she had caught him with his guard down and his own emotions as clear as the newly washed window at her right shoulder, she didn't know.

And she would have sorely liked to.

"You are the one who said you'd never danced, Willie," he told her. "And I—"

"Took full advantage of the fact that I am far too honest for my own good." Sometime while they danced, her shawl had slipped around her shoulders and as if she could as easily restore the tatters of her pride, Willie tugged the shawl back into place. "I hope you realize, m'lord, that I was not serious."

"You mean you don't really want me to kiss you?"

"Exactly." No one could have been more surprised than Willie that the lie escaped her lips so easily. "You were, after all, recounting your evening at Almack's. You were explaining what it is like when a man and a woman are out on the dance floor together. I do hope you understand—"

"That you were simply pretending to be one of the mindless misses who inhabits such a place. Yes." Though he did not look convinced, he nodded. "And you expect me to believe it. Just as you expect me to believe that the night of the dinner party—"

"Nothing happened on the night of the dinner party." It was the truth and if Somerton chose not to see it, there was little Willie could do. "We talked. Nothing more. And may I remind you that I was pretending to be Devonna Markham at the time. Anything you said to me—"

"I would most definitely not have said to her."

"After you met her, perhaps. But before—"

"Before you got me into this ridiculous predicament I find myself in—"

"Oh, no! You are the one who did that. All by yourself. If you were not so free with your money—"

"As free as you are with your tongue?"

"You asked my opinion, m'lord." The words barely made it through her clenched teeth. "I am but offering it. None of this would be happening if it wasn't for the fact that you are sorely in need of money. You would not have gone to Almack's—"

"And you would not have been here waiting for me."

"Which I was certainly not." Just to prove the point, Willie reached for the book she'd been reading. She held it in front of herself like a shield. "If you'd prefer me to stay out of your library—"

"I'd prefer the truth."

"As would I."

"The truth?" Somerton pulled himself up to his full height which, Willie realized now that he was this close, was quite tall, indeed. His eyes narrowed, he stared down his nose at her. "The truth is that I am out searching for a wife I do not want among women I have no wish to meet. On the one hand, I have a host of creditors who as you so ably pointed out to me, are eager to be paid and less than patient. On the other, I have Ravensfield, who is even more eager to make a fortune off my misfortune and show me to the ton for the fool that I am. It is a damned muddle, Willie, and correct me if I am wrong, but none of it happened until you happened into my life."

"Which I would not have done at all if you had been half the gentleman you pretend to be. You are the one who snatched me from the very steps of the church—"

"Which you couldn't wait to be away from!" He had her there and Somerton knew it. He raised his chin, daring her to dispute the claim and when she could not, he growled with triumph. "It's your fault, Willie. All of it. The wife hunt and the wager and the—"

"The dancing? Was that my fault as well?" It was her turn to gloat and with a small, satisfied smile, Willie made sure he realized it. "I was quite content until you happened into the room. You are the one who started talking about falling off logs and dancing and—"

"Kissing?"

"I may have mentioned it." Willie did her best to hold her head high and her chin steady. He didn't need to remind her that she'd been foolish. More than foolish. She'd been reckless enough to confess a secret that should have been held in her heart.

And there was no excuse for that.

Which didn't mean she couldn't try to invent one.

"Surely you could see that my head was spinning from the dance. It is the only reason I spoke so imprudently."

"I thought it was because you were pretending to be a young lady at Almack's."

She hated to be shown for a liar.

Willie gave him a wooden smile. She went on as if he had never spoken. "I was light-headed. Which means I cannot possibly be responsible—"

"For what you really want?"

"For what I might have said."

"Then it's not really what you want."

It wasn't a question and it did not warrant an answer.

Which is just as well since Willie did not know the answer.

Her mind made up, even if her body was still not sure what she did and didn't want, she turned to leave the room. The feel of Somerton's hand on her arm stopped her.

"Be careful what you wish for, Willie," he told her, and before she could think what he meant or what he meant to do, he spun her around and brought his mouth down on hers.

There was nothing tentative about Somerton's kiss. There was nothing gentle about it, either.

His mouth was hot and it fit over Willie's as if it had been made for the task. His lips were hard, demanding. When she did not relax, he deepened the kiss and when she gave herself to the glory of it and tipped her head back, he touched his tongue to hers. She heard the moan from deep in her throat, felt herself falling, and when he snaked an arm around her waist and crushed her to his chest, she could no more resist than she could stop the sudden surge of heat that flooded her body.

As quickly as he took hold of her, Somerton let her go and feeling just as light-headed as she did when she spun around the room cradled in his arms, Willie struggled to catch her breath and keep her feet.

It helped—but only a little—to realize that he looked as stunned as she felt.

They stared at each other for the space of a dozen frantic heartbeats, too astounded to move, too staggered to speak.

And the only thing Willie could think to possibly do was give in to the temptation of another kiss.

As if it were second nature—a nature she would have never have guessed she had—Willie linked her arms around his neck and kissed him.

Somerton responded instantly and fiercely and when he coaxed her mouth open, she welcomed the feel of his tongue against hers, luxuriating in the moment and in the sensations that coursed through her body like liquid fire.

❧ 12 ❧

....

*S*he luxuriated in the sensations still.

Catching herself in the thought, Willie popped open her eyes and glanced around the breakfast room, hoping that Mr. Finch, who was serving, had not noticed that she was sitting at the table with a cockled-brained look on her face and a want-witted smile on her lips.

Fortunately for her and the fantasies that clattered through her brain as they had all night and all that morning—that is, with all the subtlety of a Waterloo cannonball—Mr. Finch's back was turned. It was just as well. He didn't need to see that her cheeks flamed with heat and just to remind herself that no one else must see it, either, and that she must act as if her whole world had not flipped arse over turkey the night before, Willie grabbed her spoon and stirred the cup of tea that was set on the table in front of her.

It would not be so easy, she realized, to keep what

was left of her composure when she was obliged to face
Somerton again.

No sooner had she reminded herself of the fact than
she heard his voice in the passageway outside the breakfast room door.

A spurt of panic shot through Willie's insides and she
cursed her bad fortune and the fact that there was only
one door in the room and no exit by which she could escape except the window. Somerton was never out of bed
this early and though it was always prepared and kept
hot and waiting, he was never down to breakfast because more often than not, he stayed in his chamber late
and had nothing more than coffee in the morning. He
was never up and about at this hour and she had never
thought to have to face him so soon.

At least not until the taste of his lips against hers had
faded.

Willie gave another thought to the window and actually might have made a move in that direction if she
didn't hear the door creak open. Desperate to calm herself and hide the fact that her hands were shaking, she
grabbed for the papers she had set on the table next to
her untouched breakfast plate. She tapped them into a
pile, reordered them and tapped again.

"Good morning, m'lord." When Somerton entered
the room, no one could have been more surprised than
Willie that her greeting came out as evenly as it did.
"You are awake early this morning."

"Thank you, Mr. Finch." Somerton's response was
automatic when Mr. Finch handed him a cup of cof-

fee. He accepted it and took a sip before he turned to Willie, and though his voice was as composed as hers, there was no mistaking that he was no happier encountering her than she was to find him in a place—and at a time—when she thought herself more than safe.

"I had a bit of trouble sleeping," Somerton replied, and it came as no surprise. Willie had had a good deal of trouble sleeping as well. He glanced at the empty chair opposite Willie's. "You don't mind if I join you?"

"It is your breakfast room, m'lord. Your breakfast." She made to push her chair away from the table. "I can leave you in peace if—"

"No. Stay."

Nick slipped into the chair opposite Willie's and wondered what in the world he was going to say to her. He had no illusions. He knew he had done any number of impetuous things in his life. But none of them, as reckless or as daft or as foolish as they might have been, was as reckless or as daft or as foolish as kissing Willie.

And now that he was faced with the aftermath of his action and with the sight of her across the breakfast table from him, he found himself feeling shuttle-headed and at a loss for words.

"I want to . . ." Wondering how best to phrase what he wouldn't have had to say at all if he had a brain in his head and an ounce of self-control the night before, Nick took another sip of his coffee and glanced over at Mr. Finch. His look, apparently, spoke volumes. Mr. Finch excused himself on the pretext of getting more eggs from the kitchen and Nick started all over again.

"I want to thank you. For last night."

It came out wrong. Even though Willie was making notes next to what looked like a list of names on the paper in front of her and did not look up when he spoke, he saw her jaw tense. He set down his cup and scrambled to cover the faux pas.

"I did not mean what you think I meant."

"But you said what I think you said." She glanced up at him for the briefest of moments but she refused to meet his eyes. "You did say it, didn't you?" she asked, and before he could answer, she went back to her list.

"I meant that I wanted to thank you. For coming to your senses last night long before I did. If you had not wished me good night and left the room when you did—"

"What?" Willie's head snapped up and this time, her eyes were wide, her cheeks were touched with a splash of pink that made him think of the roses that grew outside the kitchen door. She must have known she looked a bit like Nick felt, as if the world had tipped on its axis and it was unclear which direction was up and which, down. She shook her head as if to clear it and as if she hadn't said a word at all, went right back to her papers.

And it was just as well.

As much as he'd enjoyed thinking about it all through the night, he didn't relish putting into words what they both knew all too well: If she had not some-how recovered the sanity Nick so clearly had lost and left the library after the second searing kiss they shared, he was sure he would not be looking at her across the breakfast table this morning at all. He'd be studying her from the vantage point of the pillow next to hers.

The thought was enough to send Nick's desires soaring in the most astonishing directions. Because he refused to let her know it, he looked instead at the pile of papers in front of her.

"You're busy this morning."

"Yes, m'lord."

"And deep in thought."

"Yes, m'lord."

"Household business?"

"In a way, m'lord."

"I do wish you would call me Nick." The request was as much a surprise to him as it was apparently to her. Willie looked at him in wonder.

"It is my name." Nick scrubbed a hand over his jaw and winced. Perhaps because he was too on edge to sit still, Rooster O'Reilly had been less than precise with his morning shave. There was a scratch on his cheek and a notch of skin taken out of his chin that had only stopped bleeding before he walked into the breakfast room. "It wouldn't hurt for you to call me by my name."

"It would be improper, m'lord." She didn't need to add that it would not be nearly as improper as everything they had done the night before. "And far too informal."

"It would be pleasant to hear once in a while. My friends all call me Somerton. It is only my family that uses my Christian name and it is, you will agree, far more pleasant to hear it spoken now and again than it is to hear only *m'lord this* and *m'lord that.* It's tedious, don't you know."

"Yes, m'lord—" She caught herself and flinched. "Yes. Nick."

He had never had an opinion one way or another about his name but hearing it from Willie's lips suddenly made Nick think it sounded very good. He offered her a short-lived smile that was of little use. Willie had already gone back her papers.

He was not hungry, but Nick got up and filled a plate. At least if he were wondering what Simon Marquand might have slipped into the food, he wouldn't spend his time wracking his brains with thoughts of how he wished he could get things back to the way they were the night before.

Even before he kissed Willie.

His hand poised over the serving spoon next to a dish of thick-sliced ham, Nick paused. Long before he kissed Willie, last night was quite remarkable.

There was the dreadful tedium of Almack's, of course, but after that . . .

For just a moment, he closed his eyes, reliving the light-as-air feeling of twirling through the library with Willie in his arms.

It was remarkable. She was remarkable, a vision swathed in linen and with that damned fiery hair of hers as sumptuous as silk around her shoulders. A vision with her bare toes peeking out at him.

It wasn't until he realized that he was smiling that Nick knew for certain that he was a madman.

He needed to think of Willie less, not more. And nothing was sure to make him think of her more than thinking of the way she felt in his arms. With her mouth hot against his and her breasts soft against his chest and his fingers itching to nudge aside the ridiculously high neckline of her nightdress and caress the bare skin beneath—

"Eggs, m'lord?"

Mr. Finch arrived just in time to save Nick from himself. Though he was not fond of eggs, he took a large helping. He headed back to the table.

"And what is it, exactly, that you're so busy studying, Willie?" he asked her.

"A list, m—" Her shoulders went back a fraction of an inch. "A list, Nick. A revised list. Of marriageable ladies."

It was not such surprising news.

Which didn't explain why it twisted through his gut.

"You've revised . . ." As if it might help him better see the long list of names she had written down in her precise hand, he tipped his head and leaned forward. "Are you so anxious to get rid of me, then?"

It was a rhetorical question.

At least Nick thought it was.

Which didn't explain why Willie didn't realize it.

She clasped her hands together atop the papers. Her knuckles were whiter even than the lace cloth. She looked at Nick steadily and she didn't need to say a word, he knew what she was thinking because it was exactly what he was thinking about.

About the kiss.

And the touch of skin against skin.

About the scorching heat.

And the desire that even now tingled in the air between them like the charge that is said to ride the sky before a storm.

They both knew that they had to find him a wife as quickly as possible and this time, the urgency had nothing to do with Nick's lack of the blunt or with the fact that Ravensfield was determined to make a great deal of money off Nick's ill fortune.

They had to get Nick married. Fast.

Before it ever happened again.

Because if he ever started kissing Willie again, he knew there was no way he'd be able to stop.

"Nick, you are a sly boots!"

Lynnette Overton, Nick's cousin, was a vivacious girl with mahogany hair and dark eyes that sparkled in the light of the candles that burned around the room. She was a tiny thing with energy enough for any three people twice her size and she twinkled a mischievous smile up at him at the same time she tapped her painted silk fan against his sleeve.

"No one expected you to be bold enough to host another soirée." Lynnette smiled politely to an elderly matron who shuffled by. "The ton is positively agog at your cheek!"

"Agog, perhaps. But not averse to taking advantage of my hospitality." Nick wasn't sure if the realization cheered him or sent his mood plummeting even lower than it had been in the week since the incident in the library with Willie. He paused long enough to greet the Duke and Duchess of Chesney, then turned again to his cousin.

"They pretend to be scandalized," he told her. "All of them. In truth, they are as prurient as those who stop and stare at the scene of an overturned carriage. I can't decide if they are really here to enjoy themselves or if they secretly hope they might be witness to another debacle. Imagine the thrill of seeing the Viscount Somerton further damage his reputation. And the absolute ecstasy of having, firsthand, another few weeks' worth of fuel for the gossip fires."

Lynnette laughed. "At least you can console yourself with the fact that the Markhams are not here!"

"That is something, I suppose."

"And the young lady in question . . ." She craned her neck and tried her best to look over the heads of the guests who were filing into the room and taking their seats in preparation for a performance by Leonardo Pancotti, the famous tenor.

"The young lady is question is Lady Sylvia Moore-Paget." Without trying to look too obvious, Nick tipped his head toward where the young lady was taking her seat in the front row next to her mother, Lady Margaret Moore-Paget. "She is the heiress to the old Earl of Parmenter's estates."

Lynnette pursed her lips. "And that makes her a very wealthy young lady, indeed." Because she was so short, it was difficult for her to see and she cocked her head right and left, trying to catch a glimpse of Lady Sylvia through the crowd. "She looks to be a pleasant enough girl."

"I suppose." It was true. Lady Sylvia had clear skin, a full head of mousy but well-tamed hair and, if what little exposure he'd had to her earlier in the evening meant anything, she was well behaved and well enough interested in Nick to pretend to be interested when he asked her opinion about the weather.

Which didn't explain why just thinking about her made Nick feel as if his shoulders were loaded down with lead weights.

"She seems a bit tall to me."

Lynnette elbowed him in the ribs. "How can you tell when she's seated?"

"Her teeth are not even."

"Are you looking for a wife? Or buying a horse?"

"They say she is used to getting her own way in things and that she can be a termagant when she is crossed."

"Then, my lord, you will simply have to be sure not to cross her." Lynnette let out a laugh as airy as the scent of the lilacs that grew outside the windows. She gave Nick a meaningful look that he pretended he did not notice. "You are clambering for excuses, I think."

"I am clambering for an end to this evening so I can get on with—"

"What?" This time, it was impossible to miss the look his cousin shot his way. Lynnette's eyes were aglow, her brows were raised in curiosity, and for one terrified moment, Nick wondered how much she knew. Or how much, at least, she could guess at. "Are you so anxious to carouse with the Dashers that you would leave your guests?"

It wasn't what Nick feared she might say and he breathed a sigh of relief and glanced around, nodding politely to his guests. There was a sizable crowd gathering, which wasn't at all a surprise. Though this was to be his first-ever performance in London, Leonardo Pancotti's fame had preceded him. He was an opera singer of huge talent, huge appetites and huge proportions— or so Willie had assured Nick when she talked him into hosting this musicale—and he had made a name for himself on the Continent. As a whole, the ton was already passionate about the man and being among those invited to Lord Somerton's to be the first to hear him sing made this quite the most sought-after invitation of the Season.

The entire thing was a stroke of genius on Willie's part and Nick had told her so more than once in the days since she had announced the scheme. In fact, it was, for the most part, the one and only thing they had talked about.

Uncomfortable, Nick twitched his shoulders.

There was a time he and Willie talked about everything: the latest amusements in town, the newest fashions and why they were so ridiculous, the freshest news and the most interesting gossip.

These days, in formal conversations filled with stilted sentences and uncomfortable silences, all they talked about were Italian opera singers.

And all because he'd kissed her.

"Speaking of Signor Pancotti . . ." They weren't but Nick thought it just as well to get his mind on the things it should have been concerned with. And off the one person he could not afford to think about. "Shouldn't he be here by now?"

"He's here right enough. I saw him arrive." Lynnette looked over her shoulder toward the door. "Your Miss Culpepper took him aside to get him settled."

"She is not my Miss Culpepper," Nick told her in no uncertain terms. "And you'd think the man would be settled by now." Again, Nick glanced around, just to be sure his musical guest was not somewhere in the room. If he was, Nick was sure there would be a crowd gathered around. All he saw instead was a room filled with people who were looking excited and just a bit impatient.

It was time to get the performance under way.

"Ladies and gentlemen . . ." At the same time Nick ushered Lynnette to her seat, he raised his voice and the murmurs of conversation in the room settled into a hum of expectation. "I have not had a chance to greet all of you personally as I would have liked but I welcome you now to Somerton House." Because he knew it was expected, he glanced at Lady Sylvia and offered her a smile. She was too engrossed in smoothing a wrinkle from her gown to notice but her mother—who, Nick had heard was more than eager to snag a title for her daughter—sat up a little straighter in her chair. Just to make sure those sitting nearby had not missed the special attention His Lordship paid to her Sylvia.

"I am sure we are all anxious to hear Signor Pancotti." Anxious to turn away from the self-satisfied look on the woman's face, Nick turned toward the door and as if they had rehearsed the introduction as well as the *maestro's* entrance, it snapped open.

Unfortunately, Signor Pancotti was not on the other side of it.

Mr. Finch was, and he waved Nick out into the passageway.

"You'll excuse me one moment," he told his guests and more curious than ever, he ducked out into the hallway and closed the door behind him.

"Problems, sir." Mr. Finch led Nick toward the back of the house and kitchen. "That Pancotti fellow . . ."

Once they were through the kitchen door, he didn't need to say another word.

The scene that greeted Nick was like something out of the last act of *Hamlet*. Bodies littered the kitchen floor. One of them was Clover, who was looking none the worse for wear in spite of the fact that her gown was twisted up around her knees and her hair was a fright. Bess and Marie were on their knees next to her. Madame and Flossie were standing close by, wringing their hands.

Simon Marquand was a few feet away, bent over a second prostrate figure. Because the man was lying face-down, Nick could not easily identify him. At least not until he realized that his initial thought was of a beached whale in knee breeches.

"Signor Pancotti!" Nick hurried into the room. "Good God! You haven't killed him, have you?"

He had not even realized Willie was in the room until she came into his line of sight. She was carrying two wet cloths in one hand and the stump of a broken brandy bottle in the other. She plunked what was left of the bottle down on the table, twisted one of the cloths and handed it to Clover. None too gently, she slapped the other on the back of Signor Pancotti's neck.

"Of course no one's killed Signor Pancotti," she said. "Though those of us who have been unfortunate enough to spend some time with the man were sorely tempted." She nudged the singer with the tip of one shoe and when he did not so much as move, she shook her head in disgust. "What he is," she told Nick, "is royally drunk."

"Drunk?" Now that he had more of a chance to take in the scene, Nick noticed the glass that had rolled to its side on the table next to where Pancotti was lying.

Willie puffed out a breath of annoyance. "He asked for a drink," she explained. "To calm his nerves, or so he said. I brought him a bottle and I tried my best to keep him amused but . . . well . . ."

Madame Brenard grumbled a word Nick couldn't quite hear. " 'E's as full of 'imself as the Channel is of water," she said. "An infuriatin' man. After a while, we all got tired of sittin' 'ere listenin' to 'im go on and on about 'imself."

"So we went to make sure everything was prepared for your guests." Willie took over the telling of the tale. "And when we got back . . ." She looked down at singer and her lips thinned.

"It's my fault, Your Lordship, sir." Clover sniffed back tears and with the help of the other girls, pulled herself to her feet. "I come in a'lookin' for them biscuits what Willie said she was makin' and this 'ere fellow 'ere . . ." Her eyes filled with tears and her words were swamped.

"By that time he was quite drunk," Willie explained. "He took hold of poor Clover and what started—as Clover so aptly describes it—as a bit of a cuddle, got too intimate much too quickly. I happened into the room at just that moment. Seeing that I had no choice . . ." She glanced toward the broken bottle. "I defended Clover the only way I was able."

"And now you can show me to the door," Clover wailed. "For it is all my fault. Old habits die hard, as they say, and I just naturally found myself smilin' at the man. I've ruined everything and—"

"Don't be ridiculous!" Nick stepped over the tenor and took Clover by the shoulders, the better to calm her and keep her attention. "No one's going to sack you for smiling. Make her a cup of tea," he ordered Madame. "Make tea for everyone. Sit down and calm down and—" He looked over his shoulder toward the door and the passageway that led back to the salon where one hundred people were waiting for the night's entertainment. "I will go make Signor Pancotti's excuses and send everyone home."

"Oh no!" As if that was all it took to bring the situation under control, Willie brushed her hands together. Her mind as made up as her expression was determined, she grabbed Nick by the arm, spun him around and headed out of the room with him in tow. Outside in the passageway, she gave him a gentle push. "Get back to your guests," she told him. "There will be entertainment this evening."

"Yes, but Willie, I—"

She was obviously not in the mood for *buts* and the way she looked at him, Nick was thankful there wasn't another brandy bottle at hand.

"Damn it, Nick," she said, "I will not see you humiliated again in front of a houseful of people. I said there will be entertainment and damn it, there will be entertainment. Now, get in there and be the perfect host. I shall take care of the rest."

"What a perfectly charming evening!" Lady Sylvia Moore-Paget was so used to repeating the polite phrases that were expected on occasions such as these that she barely bothered to sound as if she meant it. Her expression as blank as it had been all evening, her intonation so controlled and so terribly polite it made Nick's teeth hurt, she stood out of reach of the evening air that flowed through the open front door on the end of an invigorating breeze and looked Nick over. When she was done, she gave a little toss of her head that he supposed was meant to be flirtatious. It made her look rather as if she were a barnyard chicken, pecking away at the dirt.

"You will be attending our ball next week?" Lady Sylvia's mother accepted her wrap from Mr. Finch, her question to Nick not much of a question at all. Her tone of voice made it clear that if he intended to take his interest in her daughter any further, he would be there.

Fortunately for Nick's belief that the truth was always the best way to deal with a woman—even if it was not always the surest way to her heart—Jem bounded up the front steps at just that moment.

"Carriage is 'ere," Jem told them, poking his thumb over his shoulder. "And you'd best get a move on it, on account of because there's another one behind it and Miss Lynnette is waitin'!"

Lady Sylvia gave a weak laugh that hardly blocked out the choking sounds her mother made. "So clever to have the boy who sang for us this evening pretending to be your footman," Lady Sylvia said. "And acting as if he does not know how to speak to his betters. And the conjurer . . ." She gave a cursory glance to Mr. Finch, who was waiting with Lynnette's Poland mantle. "Lord Somerton is quite awake on every suit, is he not, Mother? He will set the style for the whole ton, if I am not mistaken, and soon we will all have entertainers in our homes who keep the whimsy alive by pretending to be house staff after their performance. It is quite clever, indeed."

"And I am so glad you enjoyed it." Nick bowed over Lady Sylvia's hand and ushered her and her mother to the door and it wasn't until it was closed behind them that he dared let go a sigh of relief.

"Thank God it's over!"

Lynnette emerged from the morning room where she had taken each of the staff aside to give them a silver crown in appreciation for their hard work. "It was quite the most extraordinary evening!" She clapped her hands and swept into the entryway as if she were dancing. "Who could have imagined that your little tiger would have the voice of an absolute angel? And Mr. Finch . . ." She grinned at the butler who, not used to having ladies—gentle or otherwise—offer him so open and honest a smile, blushed to the roots of his hair. "Where on earth did you learn such incredible sleight of hand, Mr. Finch?"

"That is something we will discuss another time." Because he did not wish to go into it, Nick reached for Lynnette's mantle and draped it over her shoulders. "Thank you for acting as my hostess." He kissed her cheek and moved forward to open the door for her. "I could not have done it without you."

"You couldn't have done it without your Miss Culpepper, you mean." Lynnette beamed him a smile over her shoulder and skipped down the steps. "You must be good to her, Nick darling. You don't want to lose her."

When Nick turned from the door, Willie was waiting to speak to him.

"Signor Pancotti is up, finally, and sent back to his lodgings," she told him. "If you'd like me to pack and leave as well—"

"Leave?" He looked a bit like he did when she

punched him in the nose. "Really, Willie! I have had enough drama for one night. I don't need to hear you talking like a perfect block."

"I should have kept a better eye on Signor Pancotti." It was the truth and Willie wasn't ashamed to admit it. "I hold myself responsible. And besides . . ." She glanced away.

If she had been paying more attention, she would have heard Nick come nearer. By the time she realized it, he was standing in front of her. His eyes were soft in the last of the candlelight. His smile was as dazzling.

"What you are going to say is that you never should have bashed the old boy on the head." Nick's laugh tickled through her like the spring air. "I have a secret to share with you, Willie. From what I've heard, I wouldn't have minded a chance to thump the blackguard myself. I had thought to go to the kitchen right now and have a go at him but since he has left . . ." He smiled. It was the first candid smile she'd had from him since the night of Almack's and she found herself a bit weak-kneed under its influence.

"And what of Lady Sylvia?" It was not the most pleasant of subjects, but it was safer than standing there letting his smile play along her skin like liquid sunshine. "She seems . . ." As if she could see past it, Willie looked toward the door where Lady Sylvia and her mother had disappeared only a few minutes earlier. "Pleasant?"

"Are you trying to convince me or yourself?" As if getting rid of the very notion and all remnants of Lady Sylvia's presence, Nick twitched his shoulders.

"She's as rich as Croesus," Willie reminded him.

"And did you watch her?" He walked over to the front window and looked out, and satisfied that his cousin had gotten away safely, he turned the other way and looked toward the open door of the morning room. Bess, Marie, and Flossie were cleaning up; Clover had been sent to bed with a cup of chocolate and a gold half sovereign from Nick that Willie was not supposed to have seen him give her. It hardly made up for the ordeal of having to put up with Signor Pancotti's unwanted advances and she was sure Nick knew that. But it did bring a smile to Clover's face.

"When Mr. Finch put on that most remarkable show of prestidigitation, did you happen to see Lady Sylvia? And by the way—" Nick glanced back to where Willie was standing.

"I checked Mr. Finch's pockets," she assured him. "He didn't make anything disappear that wasn't supposed to disappear and everything that did disappear was returned as it should have been."

Nick seemed surprised, but not by Mr. Finch's uncharacteristic honesty. "I meant, how did you know? That he could do so many remarkable things? Making coins appear as if out of Lynnette's ears. And making Lord Asterleigh's pocket watch disappear, then materialize again. It was astounding!"

"Indeed." Willie smiled and it wasn't until she did that she realized it was the first honest smile she'd offered him since the night of Almack's. It felt good to be back on even terms with Nick, if only for a moment.

The next moment, the thought of everything they'd said and done in the library left her feeling as if she couldn't catch her breath. "Mr. Finch . . ." She shook herself away from the thoughts that threatened to upend her and reached for the candlesnuffer sitting on a nearby table. One by one, she put out the candles in the entryway. "Mr. Finch has been entertaining us with his magic in the kitchen these many weeks. It seemed only natural to share his talents with your guests. Especially when we were so sorely in need of entertainment."

"And Jem?"

"I heard him. Singing in the stables. Though I have never heard Signor Pancotti, I cannot help but think that Jem's voice was much the better choice for an evening of music. He's a sweet child."

"And his talent should be encouraged."

It was all the permission Willie needed to do what she had been meaning to ask Nick for permission to do. There was a church nearby and a boys' choir. Jem would fit in admirably.

She moved on to the candles that burned on a table near the stairway. "I am glad you enjoyed yourself."

"Don't you mean you are glad my guests enjoyed themselves?"

His comment brought her up short. "Of course." Willie swallowed her mortification and scrambled to cover the slip that she feared betrayed the fact that even while they had been dancing around each other and the emotions that had been so raw and recklessly exposed the night he kissed her, he had always been first on her mind.

"I did not want to see your guests disappointed. And Lady Sylvia . . ."

Willie cursed herself. Try as she might, she could not keep her curiosity tamped. "I did so want you to make a good impression on Lady Sylvia. You did, didn't you? Make a good impression on Lady Sylvia?"

"Lady Sylvia—" Nick drew in a deep breath and let it out with a puff of annoyance. "I hate to disappoint you, Willie, but . . ."

The feeling that flooded through her was so far from disappointment, Willie couldn't help but look up and meet Nick's gaze.

"The entire time Lady Sylvia watched Mr. Finch do those astonishing things . . . the entire time she listened to Jem sing . . ." He shook his head. "I know you tried to be careful in your choices of the young ladies I should meet, Willie, but Lady Sylvia . . ."

This time, the tremor that moved over his broad shoulders had more to do with dismissal than annoyance. "The entire time she was here this evening, Lady Sylvia never once smiled."

❧ 13 ❧

"I say, Willie, can you pass me one of those biscuits?" Arthur Hexam pointed across the table with his fork. "Not those!" He pulled a face when she reached for the tray of sweets that had been provided along with their supper baskets. "The ones you made and brought along. You know, those kajoo . . . whatever!"

"Kaju badam." Smiling, Willie passed him the plate. "I am glad you like them."

"Like them!" Palliston whisked two biscuits off the plate when it made its way by him. "When it comes to your biscuits, Willie, Hexam here is an absolute nickninny. He acts as if he's never tasted biscuits before."

"And you do not?" Not to be outdone, when the plate finally made its way to him, Hexam took three biscuits. Biting into the first one, he tipped back his head and breathed a sigh of perfect contentment. "You are an artist, Willie. No mistake about that. And you say you have others?"

Willie lifted the basket she'd brought along and nudged back the cloth that covered it, just so they could see inside. "Nankhatai," she said, pointing. "You will like these as well, I think. Though they are meant as a sweet. Which means—"

"They should be saved for after dinner." Before Hexam could protect them, Latimer whisked the biscuits off the table in front of him.

A good-natured brawl erupted between the friends and watching it, Willie sat back and smiled. Hexam, Palliston, and Latimer reminded her a great deal of her brothers.

Except that they never spouted Scripture, never lectured about morality, and never preached against the evils of drink.

Which made them quite a bit more entertaining than her brothers had ever been.

If only she could come to feel the same way about Nick.

The thought snuck up unawares and feeling suddenly self-conscious, Willie got up and busied herself with making sure everything was ready for supper. The table was set, the dishes were in place, the silver gleamed in the light of the candles. It didn't stop her from arranging and rearranging things.

"You're supposed to be a guest here. Not a servant."

Lynnette Overton entered the supper box and immediately put a hand on Willie's arm to stop her. "You are supposed to be enjoying yourself," she reminded Willie.

"I am!" It was the truth and Willie was not about to

deny it. She glanced around at the scene of classical Rome painted on the wall of the supper box and out the entryway to where the fashionable paraded by in the light of globe lamps set along the outside walk. "I never thought to ever come to Vauxhall," she told Lynnette. "And I am so happy you invited me to accompany you and—"

"It is I who am happy." Lynnette gave her arm a friendly squeeze. She looked over to where Hexam, Palliston, and Latimer were finally settling down and seeing that their hair was mussed and their neckcloths were askew, she laughed. "You wouldn't have me spend the evening by myself with the likes of the Dashers, would you? They are a rowdy lot." She did not look the least put out by the fact. "I am grateful you could join us."

"And I am grateful you invited me." Willie glanced toward the doorway. "It's just that—"

"Don't pay it any mind." Lynnette patted her arm, though how she could have possibly known what Willie was about to say was a mystery.

Rather than try to fathom it and so that she wouldn't be expected to explain, she glanced again at the door. "Is Nick . . ." She swallowed the name and horror-struck, looked at Lynnette out of the corner of her eye and when she saw that Lynnette did not look the least bit put out at the familiarity she had used so freely, she went right on. "Is Lord Somerton on his way?" she asked. "Has he met with Lady Catherine yet?"

"Last I saw them, they were chatting together like fast friends." Though a meeting with Lady Catherine Sutcliffe was the exact reason for this visit to Vauxhall Gardens, Lynnette did not look especially pleased. She wrinkled her nose. "She's a beautiful thing," she confided to Willie, her voice low. "Hair as dark as coal. Eyes like fire. I hear her personality is just as fierce."

"Which should make her quite attractive to your cousin."

"Yes, it should." Lynnette looked no more pleased by this admission than she did by the fact that Nick and Lady Catherine had yet to join them for supper because they were strolling the Grand Walk.

Or perhaps they were together in the privacy of the Dark Walk.

It was best not to think of such things, and Willie knew it. But knowing a thing was right and doing it was not always easy. In spite of how she tried not to, she couldn't help but picture Nick arm in arm with Lady Catherine on the narrow, dark pathway that was oftentimes called Lovers' Walk.

At the same time her stomach bunched she reminded herself she was being foolish.

After all, she was the one who'd convinced Nick that Lady Catherine just might be right for him. She was the one who explained all she could find out about the lady's background, including her wealth. She was the one who pointed out that Lady Catherine was a little older than the other women on Willie's list and that, perhaps, that might mean that Nick and Lady Catherine had more in common. And though she had not failed to mention that Lady Catherine was a widow, she had not bothered to bring up all that it might mean. Having been married, the lady must be worldly-wise and more experienced than the other women Nick had met. The sort of experience Lady Catherine must have learned in her marriage bed might be even more pertinent than was the state of her financial affairs.

And another thing Willie knew it best not to think about.

On paper, she reminded herself, it was an ideal match, and rather than stand there like a cabbage head and worry that they had taken to each other, she should be happy. After a string of what might charitably be called courting disasters, perhaps Lady Catherine was the one.

The right one.

The one Nick was destined to marry.

"They are suited by temperament, I think." As if she had been reading Willie's mind, Lynnette slid her a look. "Much as you and Nick are."

"A fact that is certainly not true. And if it were true, then it is certainly not relevant." Willie smoothed the skirt of her gown, the better to hide the fact that discussing such things made her tremble like a leaf. "Lady Catherine was not my first choice because of it. Though I have little experience in such matters, I hear that two people of like character may be instantly attracted but that the attraction may not last. And a marriage, I think, is meant to last a good long time."

"You should be a philosopher, Willie!" Hexam overheard their conversation and called out his encouragement. "Yours is certainly a most original viewpoint."

"You sound like Somerton's doting aunt," Latimer added.

Lynnette laughed. "And tonight, you are supposed to be nothing but a friend." She tugged Willie toward the table. "Come. We can wait only so long," she said, her laughter as light as the frothy concoction of a dress she wore. "Unless Mr. Hexam is planning on keeping it all to himself, perhaps he could pour us a glass of wine."

"Indeed!" Hexam did the honors. He poured for each of them and when he was done and the drinks were passed, he raised his glass. "To Miss Lynnette," he said, smiling at her. "And to Willie," he added, jumping to his feet and lifting his glass in her direction. "The best biscuit maker this side of Delhi."

"And the best organizer on the planet!" Latimer said.

"And the best thing that ever happened to our friend Somerton!" Palliston added.

"How terribly amusing!"

The husky voice from the doorway made them all turn just as Nick stepped into the supper box. He had the most striking woman Willie had ever seen on his arm.

Lady Catherine Sutcliffe was as dark-haired and as dark-eyed as Lynnette had said. What Lynnette had not mentioned was Lady Catherine's high cheekbones, or her Cupid's-bow lips. She had not said that Lady Catherine had eyes the color of the heart of a candle flame or skin that was as clear as daylight and as pure as alabaster. She had not reported that her gown was impeccable or that her figure rivaled Madame Brenard's in its fullness and sensuality.

And if she had, would Willie have discouraged a meeting between Nick and Lady Catherine?

She pushed the thought out of her mind and realized that she, like all the others, was staring.

It was a reaction that, apparently, Lady Catherine was more than used to. Her supremely confident gaze skipped over the men one by one. They had been introduced earlier in the evening and now, she nodded to Lynnette. Finally, she let her gaze rest on Willie and though Willie had no doubt that Lady Catherine was as passionate as Lynnette said she was, she could not help but notice that the lady's eyes were as cold as the diamonds she wore in her ears and at her throat.

"You must be . . ." Lady Catherine paused for the briefest of moments, as if offering a chance for someone to correct her. "Willie?" She looked Willie up and down and for the first time since Nick had proposed it, Willie wished she had accepted his offer of a new gown for the night's festivities. At the time, it seemed an unwarranted extravagance and even though he'd sent for a modiste who had come to Somerton House with an army of assistants and a great many fabrics to choose from, she had firmly refused.

Of course, that was before she knew her neat but simple gown would be looked on by Lady Catherine as if were no more than a frightful scrap. No sooner had the look touched Willie, the message loud and clear, than Lady Catherine turned to Nick with a smile and wound her arm through his. "I do confess, I am baffled. What is it your friend here said? That Willie is the best thing that's ever happened to you? Whatever did he mean, Nick dear?"

The familiarity of her words grated on Willie's nerves. It did not, however, seem to take Nick aback in the least. He conveyed Lady Catherine to the table and when she was seated in the chair to the left of Willie's, he took the chair on Lady Catherine's other side. "Palliston is right," he said, glancing down the table and offering Willie a smile that was not nearly as heated as the look he gave Lady Catherine. "Willie is my majordomo, so to speak. Part steward, part housekeeper, part taskmaster."

"A servant. How terribly progressive of you. Lawd, Nick . . ." Lady Catherine put a hand on his sleeve. "You'd best be careful or people will be calling you a Whig!"

It was not an especially amusing jest.

Which didn't explain why Nick laughed.

Or why he didn't move away when Lady Catherine slid her hand from his sleeve. From there, when she thought no one could see, she put it on his knee.

What was it Madame had once told her? That men liked their women bold? Nick certainly seemed to. In spite of the fact that they were in so public a venue, he warmed to Lady Catherine like a farm dog to a winter fire and because the very thought and all it meant made Willie's cheeks flame, she turned in her chair so that neither Lady Catherine nor Nick might notice.

Thankfully, she was able to spend the rest of the meal in nearly complete silence. Lady Catherine had stories to tell and she told them with gusto: stories about her travels on the Continent and beyond that made the Dashers—

including Nick—smile and ask questions and tell stories of their own.

Stories about parties at her magnificent home in Richmond and country weekends at her vast estates in Northumberland and galas at her splendid houses in town and in Bath that made the Dashers—including Nick—wonder out loud at the woman's vigor and at the fact that one woman alone could manage so prodigious and demanding a social schedule.

Stories about her marriage to a much older man, who she hinted had far less vigorous appetites than her own and did not mind when she found other outlets for them that made the Dashers—including Nick—laugh out loud and nod knowingly and smile like loons.

Stories that bored Willie nearly to death.

She caught herself in the thought just as the dinner dishes were being whisked away and shook herself out of the daze that had held her in its mind-numbing clutches for the better part of an hour. She was just in time to see Lady Catherine turn to Lynnette.

"They say your cousin is involved in—of all things— a marriage wager. It cannot be true." She gave a pretty pout that she did not bother to waste on Lynnette but turned full on Nick. "Pray tell, m'lord, you would not be so cruel as that, would you? There will be women by the dozens with broken hearts if word goes around that you are searching for a wife."

"The wager is Ravensfield's doing," Nick explained. "And the man is, as you may have heard, absolutely mad."

"Does that mean you are not looking for a wife?"

Willie did not have to see the expression on Lady Catherine's face to know exactly how she looked when she asked the question. Lynnette was sitting directly across from Lady Catherine and Willie saw her roll her eyes.

"I may be looking for a wife." Nick was not usually so coy and something about his tone of voice made Willie turn to him. She found him staring into Lady Catherine's eyes as if they were the only two people in the room.

And she suddenly found herself feeling as if her heart had been snapped in two.

Before she could remind herself that it was rag-mannered in the extreme, Willie grabbed for the plate that held her biscuits and poked it under Lady Catherine's nose.

"Kaju badam?" she offered. "Nankhatai?"

"Kaju . . ." Lady Catherine's upper lip curled just enough to expose her evenly spaced teeth. She looked from the biscuits to Willie and as if that were all the answer she need give, she turned back to Nick. "Oh Nick, darling, you aren't really falling prey to all that prattle about the mysteries of the heathen countries, are you?" There was enough of a lilt in Lady Catherine's voice to tell him she knew it was impossible but she had to ask nonetheless. "Indian food? It's positively passé."

"It's Willie's speciality." If Nick heard the edge of acid in Lady Catherine's voice, he did not show it. Then again, it may have been hard for a man to hear anything at all when the woman sitting next to him was skimming her hand along his thigh.

Rather than watch, Willie stood abruptly. The quick movement was too much for the plate of biscuits and they rained down on Lady Catherine's head and into her lap and into the deep décolletage of her dress.

Across the table, Lynnette pressed her hands to her mouth, choking back a mumbled sound that might have been indignation. Or laughter. Latimer, Hexam, and Palliston automatically leapt to their feet to help and their hands were already stretched to where a couple of the biscuits had disappeared into the pillowy softness between Lady Catherine's breasts when they realized their mistake.

"I am so sorry." Though it was true enough about the biscuits, Willie wasn't the least bit sorry that Lady Catherine was so surprised, she stopped caressing Nick's thigh. Before her expression betrayed her, she stooped to pick up the biscuits scattered around Lady Catherine's chair. Nick offered Lady Catherine a hand to help her to her feet and when she stood, biscuits and crumbs rained down on Willie's head along with a look she could feel from Lady Catherine. One that fairly bored through her back.

Nick took charge effortlessly. "Willie is a wizard when it comes to Indian cooking but unfortunately, it looks as if you won't have a chance to find that out tonight."

"Unfortunately." Lady Catherine's voice was no warmer than the look that met Willie when she stood. But though it was as cold as ice, it didn't last long. The next second, Lady Catherine turned and put a hand on Nick's arm. "I hear the fireworks here are the product of wizards, as well." She lifted her chin, aimed a sleek smile at Nick and wound her arm through his. "Why don't you take me now to see them, Nick darling."

She had not thought to see Nick until the next day.

If then.

Which was the reason Willie was immensely surprised to turn from where she'd been watching the fireworks display and find him standing behind her.

It was just as surprising to see that he was alone.

"Lady Catherine—"

"She's gone." As if it were all the explanation he needed, Nick twitched his broad shoulders. "Off in her carriage and headed toward home last I saw her. Though if it was her splendid home in London, the magnificent one in Richmond, or the impressive one in Bath, she did not bother to say."

His sarcasm was not lost on Willie, she simply didn't care to acknowledge it. She had spent nearly an hour *ooh-ing* and *ahh-ing* with the rest of the crowd, pretending to be interested in the pyrotechnics when all she could think about was Nick and Lady Catherine and what fireworks would erupt between them once he accompanied her home and they were alone together.

She should have been feeling relief at the realization that the lady in question was gone and that apparently, Nick was not especially bothered by the fact.

Which did not keep her from seething with anger

and resentment. Whether she was angry and resentful of Lady Catherine for being so beautiful and so charming and so attractive to Nick, or angry with herself for reacting so to the realization, she did not know. She only knew that her stomach was tied in knots, that her heart ached, and that she felt hollow and alone.

She did not like the feeling.

"Home you say?" Try as she might, Willie could not quite make her voice sound as aloof or her words as flippant as every amusing syllable that fell from Lady Catherine's beautifully shaped lips. "And you, sir, are not headed there with her?"

The last of the sparks of the Catherine wheel spinning wildly somewhere on their right glowed in Nick's eyes when he looked down at her. "Did you think I would be with her?"

As serious as the question was, Willie could not help herself. She barked out a laugh. "Lady Catherine certainly did."

"Yes, she did." Nick expression was unreadable. "She asked me to accompany her."

"But you refused?"

He did not answer but turned from the display and offered Willie his arm. She knew it wasn't wise to allow herself such close contact, but she also knew it was impossible to ignore the offer. She put her hand on his arm and fell into step beside him.

They made their way in silence for some time toward the place where Lynnette and Nick's friends had gone for refreshments and she assured them she would meet them after the fireworks show. All the while, Nick greeted those of his acquaintance whom he knew, tipping his tall top hat to the ladies, smiling and nodding to the gentlemen and taking no notice whatsoever when each and every one of them looked at Willie with a question in their eyes. The longer he pretended they had nothing to discuss, the more sure Willie was that they did.

They were almost to the Grand Walk that ran the length of Vauxhall when she could no longer contain herself.

"You cannot keep doing this, you know," she told him.

He glanced at her. "Doing what?"

"Rejecting marriage partners."

"Possible marriage partners," he corrected her.

"Possible marriage partners," she conceded. "You cannot keep rejecting possible marriage partners."

He stopped and untangled her arm from his so that he could face her. "Did you ever think that rather, they are rejecting me? In droves, I might add, which is not an especially pleasant thing to have to admit."

"Don't be ridiculous." Willie waited for him to declare that he was exaggerating or perhaps fabricating the story altogether; he simply looked at her levelly.

As confused as she was confounded by the look, she threw her hands in the air and walked away. "They cannot be rejecting you. In droves or otherwise. It's impossible."

The last sound she expected to hear from Nick was a

laugh. He caught her up and walked beside her. "And what makes you think that?"

"Because . . ." It was impossible to tell him what he should have already known. What she knew all too well. What she felt in every inch of her body. And every ounce of her being. What pounded through her heart with each staggered beat it took when he was anywhere nearby.

That no woman in her right mind could reject Nick.

Willie decided she could not even try to explain. It was too personal a thing to confess and besides, they were in too public a place. "It just is," she told him instead. "It's simply impossible and you know it."

"Do you mean that you can't imagine any woman who would dare refuse me? Do you think my title that attractive?"

"Your title?" It was her turn to laugh. "I suppose there are those who would think so."

"But you are not one of them?"

Willie shook her head, amazed. There was no surer proof of the gulf that existed between her world and his than this. The very fact that he did not realize it only made the gulf seem wider.

"A title is only important to those who think it might be within reach," she told him. "To the rest of us—"

"It is irrelevant. Yes. I was afraid so." Nick brows dropped low over his eyes. "It isn't easy to think that most of the population finds one extraneous."

He was so serious, Willie had to smile. "Not as extraneous as simply beyond expectation. A title is impressive, surely. As are vast estates and splendid homes and—" Before he could hear the acid in her voice, she swallowed the rest of what she might have said to parrot Lady Catherine. "But, don't you see? It is all a world apart from everyday existence."

"Which doesn't explain why I've yet to find a woman to scoop up my title and me along with it."

"No, it doesn't." It was her point exactly and she didn't understand why he did not see it. "Which means, I do believe, that you are the one delaying the inevitable."

"Only if you think of my marriage as inevitable." He sighed because, of course, he knew it was inevitable, too. "Perhaps there's something wrong with me." He couldn't be serious and yet Nick looked sincere enough. "What do you suppose it is, Willie? Is my personality that dreadful?"

She thought back to the first night she'd met him, the preposterous wager the Dashers had made with the Blades and the even more preposterous way they had gone about winning it.

"Not usually," she told him and when he looked cut to the quick she added, "There are times you are charming and thoughtful and even kind."

"Well, thank you." He didn't look especially pleased by the compliment. "Then perhaps it's the way I look," he suggested. "Am I too tall?"

She took the measure of him, looking up from the tips of the boots Rooster O'Reilly had shined to within an inch of their lives, all the way to the top of Nick's hat.

"You are taller than some," she said. "But not so tall as others."

"Too fat then?"

"Hardly."

"Too much a dandy?"

She need only look around to know the answer to that question. Compared to some of the bejeweled, bedazzling fops who paraded the grounds of Vauxhall, Nick was positively somber.

"You are well dressed and most of the time, well behaved. You are not too tall and I can't think I've ever heard a man say as much about himself in the first place. You are not too fat. What you are is a terrible procrastinator. You know you must get this over with. You must find a wife with a healthy income or find yourself in terrible straits."

"Is it the color of my eyes, then?" He took a step closer and caught Willie's gaze.

"The color of your eyes . . ." Willie heaved a sigh of impatience. She was trying her best to reason with the man. The least he could do is try to be reasonable in return. Instead, he was teasing. She could see as much in his eyes and in the tiny smile that played around his mouth. Rather than think about either, she untied and retied the ribbons of her bonnet.

"The color of your eyes is fine," she told him.

"How do you know? You haven't looked."

She adjusted the loops of the bow at the same time she gave him a little *harrumph* of displeasure. "I do not need to look." It might graciously be called an under-

statement. What he did not need to know is that his eyes
and the way they sparked when he laughed tickled her
dreams and her imagination. He did not need to know
that she could close her eyes and see the color. Or that
even when he was gone from a room, she could feel the
way he sometimes looked at her. And the heat that
erupted each and every place his gaze alighted.

Willie looked down at the tips of her shoes. "Your
eyes are blue," she said.

"How blue?"

He was an exasperating man and just to let him
know, she snapped her gaze to his.

"Ah, that's better!" Before she could move out of his
reach, he cupped her chin in his hand. He was wearing
gloves of the softest kid and the leather caressed her skin
like a whisper. "Now, Willie, look." He tipped her chin
up a fraction of an inch. "Is it my eyes, do you think? Is
it the shape or the color that makes the ladies reject
me?"

"The color of your eyes is perfect," she told him. She
wished only that her words were so perfect. They
sounded as if they came from very far away, even to her.

Nick, apparently, did not notice. As quickly as he
reached for her, he dropped his hand and whisked his
tall top hat off. He scrubbed a hand through his hair.
"Then perhaps it's my hair. Wrong style. Wrong length.
Wrong color there, too, perhaps."

"Your hair . . ." She had no intention of doing it but
when he ran his hand through his hair, he mussed it terribly. She smoothed an errant curl back from his fore-

head and imagined how it might feel if her gloves were off. "Your hair is quite pleasing."

Before she could lower her hand to her side, he caught it in his and pressed it to his chest. His heart beat strong and hard against her fingertips. "Then perhaps it is my lack of romanticism. It could be that the ladies are not aware that I have a beating heart or that it might positively race. At the right time. With the right woman."

It was positively racing now.

The realization hit Willie like a bolt and uncertain what to say or how to control her own heartbeat—which was racing every bit as wildly as his—she spun away. Her head down, her steps quick and as sure as they could be when her head was spinning and her blood pumping so hard she couldn't hear a thing, she raced into the nearest cross path. Once she was out of sight of the rest of the Vauxhall revelers, she took off running.

"Willie!" Behind her, she heard Nick's voice and she cursed her impulsiveness as well as her bad luck. Of all the places she might have chosen to run, she had picked the Hermit's Walk, the smallest of the Vauxhall paths. She pulled to a stop and glanced to her right and the wilderness that bordered the path.

Even before she could think to escape that way, Nick found her.

"Damn it, Willie. I told you I feared there was something about me that makes women run the other way! You didn't have to prove it."

His jest was met with silence and Nick tried again. "It must be my lack of a romantic heart after all. That is when you decided to run. When you pressed your hand to my chest."

"I am not the one who pressed it there." Willie turned away when she spoke to him and though the movement muffled her voice, it did little to soften the pain that flowed through each of her words.

Before he could stop himself, Nick stepped nearer. "I'm sorry. I didn't mean to upset you."

"I'm not upset."

He might have been convinced if she did not snuffle at the end of the sentence.

"And I never meant to make you cry." He put his hand on her shoulder.

"I'm not crying."

"Yes, I can tell. By all the sniffling." Nick reached for his handkerchief and handed it to her. "I only meant to make you laugh."

When he held the handkerchief over her shoulder, she snatched it out of his hand and swabbed it under her nose. "I know." She sniffed. "It's just that I thought—"

"What?" It wasn't wise to care, yet Nick could not help himself. Whatever was the matter, it was serious. At least to Willie. Which made him care very much.

"I thought that you had gone. With her. And—"

Nick found himself suddenly smiling. "Did it bother you?"

"It's none of my concern."

"That's not what I asked. I asked if it bothered you to think that Lady Catherine and I—"

"She would make you a serviceable wife." Willie blew her nose and wiped it vigorously before she turned to him. "Even Lynnette said as much. You are of the same temperament and the same tastes. You laugh at the same jokes and she is not at all shy about—" She thought better of continuing, then thought again. "She wanted you."

"And I wanted her. At least I wanted to want her." He angled a finger under her chin and tilted her head up. "That is, until I came to my senses and realized she wasn't you."

Willie's eyes widened in astonishment. Her breath caught. She could not have known that so simple a thing made her look more beautiful than ever.

And that Nick wanted her more than he'd ever wanted anything. Or anyone.

She swallowed hard and though he could feel the tremble of emotion that vibrated through her, she did not step away and she did not lower her gaze. "Are you saying—"

"That it's you I want. Yes." The confession was as cleansing as a spring rain and Nick laughed. "It's as simple as that, Willie. I did not go home with Lady Catherine because I wouldn't have enjoyed myself in the least. Not unless it was your eyes I was looking into . . ." He bent and brushed a kiss as light as butterfly wings across her eyes. "And your lips I was kissing . . ." He touched his lips to hers. "And your body . . ." Though he warned himself as he had warned himself a dozen times before—that it wasn't wise to start something that it would be just as foolish to finish—Nick was beyond caring. He pulled Willie closer and trailed a series of slow, deliberate kisses down her neck. He tasted the hollow at the base of her throat and when he heard her moan from deep in her throat and felt her arch her back in response to his touch, he slid his mouth further still, nestling a kiss between her breasts.

"Nick." The name escaped Willie on the end of a sigh. "I—"

"Yes, I know." He kissed his way back up again. Along her neck. Across her jaw. He nibbled the delicate skin of her earlobe and fought for some semblance of control at the same time he wondered about the logistics of a man, and a maid, and a covering of wilderness and darkness.

"Nick, I—"

When he kissed his way back to her lips, Willie put her hands on his shoulders. "I must tell you—"

"What?" He smiled down into her eyes and wondered at the reflection of the man who looked back at him from them. "You're not certain?"

"Oh yes. Very certain, indeed." Willie pulled out of his reach. "That is why tomorrow, I will be leaving your employment."

❧ 14 ❧

Nick wasn't exactly sure when his life started falling apart.

He vaguely remembered a time when things were simple. The town held pleasures for a man who knew where to look and could afford them, and like so many other men of his age and station, he was not averse to seeking them out and making the most of them. There was drink. There were women. There was no end to amusements from gaming to boxing and from the turf to the theater.

He had been content then.

Even though he assured himself it was true, the thought sat on his shoulders like the fog that draped the trees outside and uncomfortable with it, Nick shivered and lifted the glass of claret that stood ready at his elbow.

"If not content, then at least satisfied," he assured himself. "With the gaming. And the boxing. With the wine. With the women."

With the predictability.

And with the very fact that while it was all amusing and diverting and damn good fun, none of it meant much of anything.

Which was exactly the way he'd always liked it.

"Now . . ." Because he could think of no other way to handle the muddle in which he found himself, he drank his claret and hoped for inspiration and when it did not come with the first sip or even with the second, he plunked down his glass.

"Not to your likin', my lord?" Rooster O'Reilly scurried into Nick's dressing room, a clothing brush in one hand and the coat Nick had worn the night before to Vauxhall Gardens in the other. "I can get you something else if you'd rather. A good glass of ale, that's what a man in your state of mind needs."

"My state of mind?" Nick wasn't sure whether to be amused or irritated. "Would you mind telling me, Mr. O'Reilly, exactly what you think that state of mind might be?"

Rooster, apparently, did not recognize irony when he heard it. On his way past, he stopped and perched himself on the edge of the dressing table where Nick sat.

"No doubt about that, sir," he said. "And no doubt about what's causin' it all. Herself is upstairs even now." As if he could see up to where the servants had their rooms, he looked at the ceiling. "She's packin' and no mistake. Boxes and trunks and bags and all. I hear the girls say that she's leavin'. And soon. And while none of them is willin' to venture a guess as to why, or at least none of them is willin' to say what they might think . . ."

Rather than sit there and listen to everything he already knew, Nick scraped back his chair and stood. He walked as far as the window and nudged aside the draperies. Just as he suspected, there was not much to see. Fog shrouded the city as neatly as if it had been wrapped in lamb's wool. Even so, he could make out the shape of the sturdy wagon that was stopped in front of the house. He had not a shred of doubt that Willie had hired it to take her away.

He dropped the drapery back into place and turned, crossing his arms over his chest and leaning back against the wall. "Are you willing to venture a guess?" he asked Rooster.

"No guess needed at all about it. You came home last night lookin' like thunder. And Miss Willie . . . well . . ." Although Nick suspected he'd already come near to wearing a hole through the fabric, Rooster started brushing his coat again. "No mistakin' the way her eyes was red, if you'll forgive me for mentioning it, sir. Between the two of you . . ." Rooster stood and put down the coat. He set his shoulders and planted his feet, much as Nick had seen him do in the ring when he was readying himself to be on the receiving end of a punishing blow.

"Between the two of you, sir, you'll be drivin' us all to drink. Which isn't a bad place for a man to be driven, if you catch my meanin', sir, but in an instance such as this, it isn't the most ideal of solutions to your problem."

"If I have a problem."

Rooster had the good grace not to look at Nick as if he were a madman. "Of course you have a problem and no mistake about that. She's walkin' out on you!"

"Let her walk!" Too edgy to keep still, Nick pushed off from the wall and did a turn around the room. "If that's the way she feels—"

"The way she feels is as plain as the nose on your very own face, if you'll pardon the familiarity, my lord. And as plain as mine." Rooster poked a finger at his misshapen nose. "She's upset and hurt."

"Hurt?" Nick decided then and there that Rooster had no idea what he was talking about. "It was her idea to—"

He pulled back the words before they had a chance to leave his mouth. It was bad enough that the staff was already abuzz over Willie's imminent departure. He didn't need to add to the gossip by letting anyone know what had happened on the Hermit's Walk.

Or that Nick was still stinging from the rejection.

"All I'm sayin' sir, if you'll excuse me sayin' it at all, is that sometimes things on the outside of the boxin' ring ain't so different from things inside. A mill is a mill, whether a man is usin' his morleys . . ." He demonstrated, raising his fists. "Or not. And sometimes, a man has to take it on the chin, if you take my meanin'."

"Even if he ends up with his nose smashed and his gut aching as if a fist had been poked through it?"

"That's the beauty of the thing, sir!" Rooster's grin revealed any number of missing teeth. "Though sometimes he takes a pummelin', there are other times when he can get in a few licks of his own."

"Are you suggesting that I box Willie's ears?"

"Not at all, sir, and if I ever said such a thing—so help me God—my dear, departed mother herself would come back from the grave and give me a lickin' the likes of which I'd never recover from. That's not what I meant at all." Rooster hung Nick's coat in the wardrobe that took up a goodly portion of the wall and went about the room, straightening and tidying.

"What I mean, sir, is that a man has to make a show of things. Even if he loses in the end . . . well . . ." He pulled himself up to his full height—which was not very tall at all—and straightened his shoulders. "Even if he loses in the end, sir, at least then he knows that he's done all he could."

"And I haven't?"

"Beggin' your pardon, sir, but if you had, that there wagon wouldn't be out in the street with them big bruisers tryin' to load it and Jem and Mr. Finch getting in their way sly-like so as they don't realize it's happenin'. Just so they can delay things so that Miss Willie don't walk out on us. And on you, sir."

As much as Nick hated to admit it, he knew Rooster was right. After Willie's pronouncement last night and their return home in complete and completely uncomfortable silence, he had done nothing to try to change her mind.

He hadn't attempted to reason with her because he'd determined that their situation was well beyond reason.

He hadn't tried to argue, either, because he knew that arguing with Willie—about anything—was the surest way to make a man feel as if his nose were up against a brick wall and his determination was getting him nowhere at all except the place that she wanted him to go.

He hadn't endeavored to talk to her because once they were in the house and she had fled up the stairs and he had retreated to his room with a bottle of brandy that soured after the first taste, he had convinced himself that what was done was done. And there wasn't a thing that could change that.

"She was jealous," he said, trying to reason through the thing aloud and hoping that by doing so, he would gain Rooster's support. "There was another woman, you see, and—"

"Of course she was jealous." As if it were a thing even the dimmest Tom-a-Doddle would have understood from the start, Rooster shook his head sadly. "The woman was beautiful, I venture, and as she was probably one of them that Miss Willie has said you might want to marry, she was probably well dressed and wealthy and as able to charm a man as a robin is to sing."

It was as if Rooster had been there.

Nick groaned. "I told Willie that none of it made any difference. That the clothes and the jewels and all the blunt from here to Edinburgh didn't mean a thing. But—"

"But you didn't rightly show her."

Nick defended himself instinctively. "I tried."

"Beggin' your pardon and not for the first time this afternoon, my lord. May I say, sir, that tryin' a man's way and tryin' a woman's way . . . well, they are two different things."

"Which means I should try again."

The thought had not occurred to Nick before now and now that it did, he felt a bit as if a weight had been lifted from his shoulders. "You think I should march up there and—" As quickly as it lifted, the weight descended again. "And what?" he asked Rooster.

Rooster shook his head. "That's what comes from havin' the looks and the title and the money all your life. You've never had to work for a woman like us regular blokes do. And now that you do—"

"Now that I do, I'm not sure which way to turn." Nick glanced down at the dressing table where he'd been seated earlier. Before they left for Vauxhall the night before, Willie had gone over her list of marriageable ladies with him and because there was something unsettling about thinking of her walking around with his future in her pocket, he had asked to keep it. It lay right where he'd left it and he picked it up and read it over quickly. A plan formed and his mood lifted.

"Rooster . . ." On his way to the door, Nick clapped Rooster O'Reilly on the back. "You're a genius!"

"Put down that portmanteau!"

Nick's voice rang through the tiny room like a death knell and startled, Willie had no choice but to listen. Too stunned by his sudden appearance, his tone of voice and the grim expression on his face to do anything else, she set down her bag.

He strode into the room like a coming storm and Clover, Bess, Marie, and Flossie—who had been helping Willie pack at the same time they were trying to convince her to stay—took one look at him and scattered into the passageway like frightened mice. Without even bothering to turn around, Nick reached for the door and slammed it closed. It rattled on its hinges.

"You're not leaving," he told Willie.

"Not—" Except for the black look on his face, she might have been tempted to laugh at the absurdity of the thing. "Of course I am leaving." Her voice sounded especially small in light of the fact that his vibrated through the small confines of her room like cannon fire. "There is a wagon waiting out front that is loaded with my things and I am going—"

"Nowhere." Nick cut off her argument with the sharp movement of one hand. "You are going nowhere, Miss Culpepper. Not for a good long while. Not until I say it is time for you to leave."

"Really?" Not as frightened by his inflated performance as she was simply fascinated by it, Willie stepped back and took stock of the man. "I left my father's custody a good long while ago," she told him. "What makes you think you can act the churl much as he did and that I will listen to you any better than I ever listened to him?"

"What, you ask?" As if it were exactly the question Nick had been waiting for, his eyes gleamed. With a flourish, he whipped a single sheet of paper from his pocket, unfolded it, and dangled it in front of Willie's nose. "This is all I need, I think," he said, and though he sounded eminently pleased with himself, Willie was not exactly sure why. The paper was so close to her eyes, the words on it were no more than a blur.

Carefully, so that he would not get the idea she was trying to renew the kind of soul-searing, mind-numbing, blood-heating contact they had had the night before, Willie reached for his hand and pushed it until the paper was a decipherable distance away. The writing came into focus immediately and she recognized her own hand.

"It is my list," she said.

"Aha!" Pleased, though she could not have said why, Nick whisked the paper away. "That's it exactly," he said, looking mightily satisfied. "And so, of course you see why you cannot leave."

"I certainly do not." Willie crossed her arms and stepped back, her weight against one foot. "If you think you can walk in here and bully me with some—"

"Bully?" Nick's shoulder's went back and he looked down his nose at her. She had not realized until that moment just how aristocratic that nose was or how a man who had been trained since youth in the fine art of being better than those around him might use such a skill so effectively. "If I wanted to bully you, Miss Culpepper," he told her, "you would be well and truly bullied. No. That is not at all what this is about. This is about our bargain."

"Our—"

"Bargain." As if it had some bearing on the matter, he fluttered the paper and her neatly written list. "I rescued you from your father: and in return, you said you would find me a wife."

"And I have tried."

"But you have not succeeded."

"And as you yourself admitted, it is not for any lack of enthusiasm for the project on my part. If you were not so—"

"Obstinate?"

"If that is the word you choose to use, so be it. I thought, rather, that *particular* might be better suited to describe how you've been acting. If you yourself were not so particular, you might have had a dearly beloved by now. Instead, you complain when the women are too tall. And you protest when they are too short. You criticize the ones who are too plump for you and you worry about the ones who are so thin they look as if the next good wind will blow them to Bristol. You don't like the talkative ones and you like less the quiet ones. Lord knows, I have tried my best. I am beginning to think you were right last night, m'lord. Perhaps it is not the ladies at all who are the problem, but you."

She had hoped the mention of the night before would have some effect on him. If he was half as staggered as she had been by the kiss that had shaken her to her soul and the touch that had sent her screaming toward the brink of ecstasy, he would not have been able to stand there and look at her so levelly. If he was half so perceptive as she, he would have been able to see the truth that had been staring her in the face for longer than she cared to remember: Once he had the wife he so badly needed, any relationship between them would be impossible.

There would be nothing left for either one of them. Nothing but regret and heartache and more regret still.

If he saw the truth, if he felt it gnawing away at his heart as she did at hers, he would not have been able to stand there looking as if they were discussing the week's list for the greengrocer.

"You said you'd find me a wife, Willie." He tapped his finger against the list written in her neat hand. "You have failed to deliver."

"I never—"

"You said you would oversee the matter, beginning to end."

"And I have done my best to—"

"You said you would take care of things."

"I cannot." It wasn't until the words were out of her mouth that Willie realized her voice was just as loud as Nick's. "I have done all I can do. You'll have to do the rest yourself."

"No."

It was as simple as that. At least to him.

When Willie made to go around him, he stepped into her path and blocked her way. "You promised, Willie."

"I never said—"

"I won't let Ravensfield get the best of me."

Like the fog outside her window, the truth seeped through Willie and chilled her to the bone. "You only care if you marry because by doing so, Ravensfield will lose a good deal of money."

"Isn't that reason enough?"

"I never thought so."

For just a second, she thought she saw the fire in Nick's eyes fade. She must have been mistaken. The next moment, he was as sure of himself as ever and just as sure that a loud voice and a great deal of bluster was sure to convince her. "One more try." He pointed at the last name on the list and Willie did not have to see it to know which one it was.

"Amelia Morrison. The American heiress."

Nick's eyes lit. "She's in London."

"Americans are not as enamored of titles as some of our families here."

"That's not at all what you told me when you suggested her. You said her father—"

"Was eager to establish some sort of aristocratic ties for his family. Yes." Unfortunately, Willie remembered it well. That would teach her to be so honest.

She turned from Nick and went over to where she'd left her portmanteau. "Will you host another dinner?" she asked him.

"I was thinking of a ball."

"And you want me to—"

"To organize the thing. To take charge. To make sure Jem is scrubbed as clean as a church floor and the girls are on their best behavior and that Simon Marquand doesn't take advantage of the fact that he's a poisoner and—"

"*Alleged* poisoner," Willie corrected him. "And after that?"

"After that . . ." Nick shrugged. "I will consider our bargain to be at an end. If Miss Morrison is as fine a young lady as you reported, then I will have my wife and all will be well."

"And if she is not?"

"If she is not, then you will have tried your damnedest and that will be the end of that. You will be free to leave. Anytime you like. I won't try to stop you."

She apparently didn't need to tell him that she agreed. As if it were just the outcome he expected, he nodded, satisfied, and headed out the door.

He was gone no more than a minute or two when Madame poked her head into the room. "Gladder than I can say to see that they're takin' your things from the wagon."

"I am not at all sure it is a good thing." Willie took off her mantle and draped it over a nearby chair. "I think, rather, that it might be the biggest mistake I have ever made."

"Not bloody likely." Madame laughed. "Believe me, lamb, there will be plenty more missteps in your life. Only . . ." She glanced over her shoulder toward the passageway and the stairway. "Only however did he talk you into it?"

"He didn't talk me into it at all." It was the truth and even though it gave her no satisfaction to admit it, Willie knew she had no choice. She had been sidestepping the truth since the very first moment Nick smiled down into her eyes.

"I talked myself into it," she told Madame. "And only because this is the very last try. Chances are, it won't work any better than the last one. Or the one before. And by then, the time will be up and Ravensfield's ridiculous wager will be at an end and Nick won't feel as if he has to find a wife any time soon and then perhaps—"

"And then perhaps . . . ?" The question glistened in Madame's eyes.

"Perhaps then things can go back to the way they were," Willie admitted. "Perhaps just for a little while longer."

"I hear tonight's menu has a decidedly Eastern flavor!" Outside the ballroom of Somerton House, Arthur Hexam grinned in anticipation. "Indian food. How absolutely marvelous! And how unique! You know . . ." As if sharing a secret, he bent his head closer to Willie's. "They are talking about you from one end of London to the other, Miss Willie."

"Me?" Willie's stomach went cold. Her mouth went dry. She was sure Mr. Hexam was referring to the fact that she was a fool. After all, only a fool would have stayed to orchestrate Nick's last chance with the last woman on this Season's list of appropriate *partis*. Only a fool would have convinced herself that by doing so, she would watch him find fault with this woman as he had found fault with all the others and that because of it, she might somehow change the things that couldn't be changed, alter the things that had happened between them, and redirect the course of his future. A future, which she knew for a fact could not possibly—in any way, shape, or form—include her.

At the same time she told herself it was impossible, she wondered how everyone in town had come to learn what a goosecap she was.

"I don't know what to say." Willie offered Mr. Hexam a smile that, no doubt, looked as wilted as it felt. "Do you mean they are saying I am—"

"They are saying you are the Shakespeare of hostesses! The Isaac Newton of decorators! The Nelson of the culinary arts!"

"Good heavens, Mr. Hexam!" Willie laughed, as much from relief as from Hexam's tendency to embellish. "You shall turn my head!"

"As you have turned the heads of every hostess in town." Palliston joined them, brushing his hands together to get rid of the crumbs that, Willie suspected, had come from the lamb and curry samosas that had already been put out on the tables for the guests to enjoy along with their drinks. "Why just yesterday, Hexam and I—"

"Paid a visit to Lady Catherine." Apparently not willing to be left out, Hexam picked up the telling of the story. "You remember what she said the night we were at Vauxhall. She said Eastern food was—"

"The words were, if I remember correctly, *positively passé*." The tone of Willie's voice told them she had not forgotten. Nor was she likely to.

"That may have been what Lady Catherine said," Hexam's brows slid up his forehead.

"But she does not practice what she preaches," Palliston added. "Because yesterday when we stopped in for dinner—"

"Wouldn't you know it, she served curry!" Hexam grinned, pleased that he'd been the one to deliver the last word. "And she is not the only one. You've started something of a fashion, Willie, though none of what I've had in other homes is nearly as good as yours. And no one else serves those kajoo—"

"There are plenty baked for tonight," Willie assured him, but when he made a move to go in search of them, she stopped him. "They will not be brought out until after dinner."

"Damn!" Hexam's expectant expression dissolved. The next second, he recovered his usual good spirits. "I say, you haven't seen Somerton anywhere about, have you?" he asked.

Today, like every day these past few weeks, Willie had not.

Nor had she spoken to him more than was necessary.

He was staying out late again.

And Willie—who might have been a fool but was not a big enough of one to wait in the library as she had the fateful night he'd first kissed her—was lying awake in her bed until the wee hours to hear his carriage pull up to the door.

He was spending more and more time with the Dashers again, drinking and carousing.

And Willie was missing the easy friendship they had allowed themselves to develop in the days before they were want-witted enough to let their passions get the better of them.

He had directed the planning of tonight's ball.

And Willie was at his side the entire time, wishing every day of it that she had had the courage to leave that foggy afternoon. Dreaming that things might somehow change.

As soon as he declared Miss Amelia Morrison as unsuitable as every other woman he'd met this Season.

The thought brought her back to her senses and it was a good thing, too. She heard Lynnette sweep into the entryway with a greeting to one and all and knew that Nick's other guests would not be far behind.

"I must see what Miss Lynnette is wearing, for she's been talking about nothing but her dress ever since the day Somerton announced this ball." Hexam headed down the stairs.

Never one to be left behind, Palliston hurried after him.

And Willie was left by herself to stand where she could not be seen from the front door and watch the parade of Society's best arrive looking splendid and much in spirits for the night's festivities.

"Has she arrived yet?"

Willie was not surprised when she heard Madame's voice behind her. She had smelled Madame's perfume only a moment earlier.

"I take it you are talking about Miss Amelia Morrison."

"That's the one." Madame leaned over Willie's shoulder and clicked her tongue in critique of the gown the duchess of Nelderly had chosen to wear. "No sign of 'er yet?"

"Not yet." Willie watched the continuing parade.

"And you aren't worried?"

The question was so close to the one Willie had spent so many days asking herself, she could not help but smile. "She will be too tall," she said and when Madame looked at her in wonder, Willie did not even try to explain. "Or she will be too short. She will be too chubby. Or she may be too thin. She will chatter like a loose shutter in a windstorm. Or perhaps she will be of that particularly annoying sort who never speaks a word unless spoken to and even then, does it in tones so quiet, no one can possibly hear."

"Ah!" Madame's eyes lit. "I see what you're getting at, lamb. It's why you stayed, isn't it? You think 'e will not find 'er fit."

"I am sure of it. Even so . . ." Willie's expression sobered.

"Nothing can change. You know that well enough." Madame nodded sagely. "It doesn't mean a woman can't dream."

"Even if her dreams can't possibly come true?"

"Especially then." There was a flurry of excitement down in the entryway and Willie moved forward just a bit for a better look. Because of where she stood, Madame's view was blocked and she moved impatiently from foot to foot behind Willie.

"Well?" Madame strained her neck but short of walking out into the open where every guest could see them, there was no place for Willie to move to allow her a better view. "Is it 'er? Is she 'ere?"

"Yes. It must be." Willie stood on tiptoe.

"Is she too tall?" Madame asked.

"She does not appear to be." Willie looked again, sizing up Amelia Morrison according to Mr. Finch, whose height she was familiar with. "Nor does she look too short."

"Ah, too fat then?"

"Hardly."

"Too thin?"

"Not from the looks of things."

Behind her, Willie heard Madame growl a curse. "What of 'er, then? 'Er 'air? Is it too dark? Too drab? Lookin' as if was made from the tail of an 'orse?"

"Her hair is perfectly styled. It is the very color of Lord Somerton's." Willie watched the way a golden curl of Miss Morrison's head caught the candlelight and gleamed. "She's as golden as a goddess. And she seems to smile a great deal. And quite sincerely." Before she could stop herself, Willie moved forward just as Nick came forward to welcome Miss Morrison and her parents.

"She speaks only when spoken to?"

"Hardly." Willie moved a step nearer the railing. "She seems to have already engaged N— that is, Lord Somerton, in conversation. He's smiling down at her."

"And 'er?" Too impatient to wait any longer, too curious to care who might notice, Madame pushed past

Willie for a better look. "Oooh . . ." One look and Madame's face went pale. "Damn it, but they do look well together."

They did.

And at the same time she realized it, Willie's heart sunk to her slippers and her blood ran cold.

For as well as she had organized the staff and readied the house and prepared herself for tonight, she realized now that all along, she had been counting on one thing and one alone. There would be something about Amelia Morrison. Just like there had been about all the others.

Something Nick could object to.

Willie's breath caught in her throat and the truth choked her.

As carefully as she planned, she had not planned on Amelia Morrison's being perfect.

15

*A*melia Morrison was perfect.

Standing across from the lady herself, a brandy in his hands, the truth hit Nick like one of Rooster O'Reilly's beefy right hooks. Just as Rooster's opponents must have done at such moments, he braced himself, breathless and stunned, while the truth vibrated through skin and tissue, muscle and bone.

Amelia Morrison was as golden as a summer dawn. She had a nose that was slim and turned up just slightly at the end. She had a chin that was as perfectly shaped as that of a marble Roman goddess. Her skin was flawless. Her eyes were a blue that matched Nick's almost perfectly. Her lips were not too full or too thin, her body was nicely rounded and as appealing as her easy smile, her melodious laugh, and the engaging way she had of looking a man directly in his eyes when she spoke to him.

She was not too tall.

Though there was a time or two during the evening that Miss Amelia's father apologized ever so politely for the unfortunate fact, the lady herself knew a thing or two about politics and she was not afraid to express her opinions—always graciously, of course, and never without allowing sufficient time for rebuttal from whoever it was she was talking to and ample opportunity for lively debate.

She was well read and better educated than Nick expected an American to be and as well mannered as any lady of his acquaintance. The Morrisons had distant relatives in London with whom they were staying for the Season and those who were in attendance did nothing but add to the impression Miss Amelia—whom they affectionately called Amy—made with every clever word and every delightful smile.

She painted more than competently with watercolors, they told Nick. She rode exceptionally well and with great vigor. She sang like a lark and played any number of musical instruments. She was, in short, a joy to be around, and—they mentioned it even though they were sure it was not well-bred and His Lordship must know it besides since it was common knowledge about their dear, dear Amy—she was exceedingly plump in the pocket.

He might have been suspicious of such praise if he himself had not been witness to one demonstration after another of the lady's sweet disposition, her kindness and her endearing manner.

Though no one was meant to see it, he noticed that

when she arrived at Somerton House accompanied by her parents, Miss Amelia slipped Jem a crown. A little later in the evening, she did not so much as bat a long and luxurious eyelash when Bess—who was serving drinks—stepped on her foot. In fact, it was Amelia who apologized to Bess for being so much in the way.

It was, all in all, an irresistible package, but Nick knew better than to be swayed. He had met such paragons before and he knew that often, loveliness hid a multitude of sins.

Beautiful women had the propensity for being demure. Generous women had the tendency to be sanctimonious. Women whose relatives called them by sweet little endearments such as Amy were quite often and quite unfortunately, quite boring.

Miss Amelia was none of those things.

She told comical stories and laughed heartily when others said something amusing. She danced as if she'd been born waltzing and did not even once tramp on Nick's feet. When he looked at her across the refreshment room and offered her—briefly and ever so discreetly, of course—the kind of smile he'd learned made timid women tremble with fright and those who were more plucky tremble with anticipation, she did not hesitate to smile back. Openly. Warmly. With just enough heat to let Nick know that if they were stirred at the right time and in the right place and by the right man, Miss Amelia's passions would be every bit as impulsive as her smile.

And just as vigorous as her riding was said to be.

Catching himself in the thought, Nick forced himself back to the matter at hand.

At the moment, that matter was Miss Amelia's father, Samuel Oswald McGlinn Morrison, a man with a bushy head of silver hair, bristling eyebrows, and a jaw like a shovel blade. He had a personality that was every bit as formidable as were his looks and a tenacity that made him famous on both sides of the Atlantic as the driving force behind any number of successful enterprises.

"Delicious!" Morrison wasn't the least bit shy about smiling broadly when he finished one of Willie's Indian biscuits. "You're an incredibly gutsy fellow," he told Nick. "There's not a host I can think of in Boston or New York who would have the imagination to serve a menu the likes of the one you put out for us tonight. My compliments, sir, to your cook."

"My cook is not so much responsible for the menu as is my—" Nick hesitated for a moment, realizing suddenly that he didn't quite know how to refer to Willie. She was not so much his housekeeper as she was his steward, not so much his steward as she was his secretary. Not so much his secretary as she was a matchmaker, an administrator with the organizational powers of an army general, a force of nature.

She was also, he reminded himself, the one and only reason he was standing there now, chatting with Samuel Morrison at the same time he considered Morrison's daughter's attributes, her more-than-pleasing smile and the delightful way she had of looking at him as if he were the only man in the world.

Or at least as if he were the only man who mattered.

He would have been less than human had he not admitted that he liked the feeling. And less than honest with himself if it didn't make him uncomfortable.

"Can't tell you how it would fry their bacon to have me show back up in the States with a title in the family," Samuel Morrison said and when Nick was not quick enough to cover the fact that he had been too deep in his own thoughts to be listening, Morrison laughed.

"Those who said I'd never make anything of myself," he explained. "Those who believe that a poor boy from the streets of Boston can never amount to a hill of beans. That is the beauty of our great country, Your Lordship, meaning no disrespect to your kingdom here. Back home, any man, rich or poor, can make anything of himself, just as I have. And still, there are those who think it means little."

"And yet, you've proved your worth." It seemed enough for Nick, yet Morrison shook his head.

"Want to rub their noses in it," the older man confided. "You know, show them just how wrong they were all these years. And the way I figure it, there's no better way than snagging a title for my beautiful daughter here." Morrison wound his arm through Miss Amelia's. "Now that would show them all, wouldn't it?"

Miss Amelia had the good grace to blush mightily. The color in her cheeks perfectly matched the tiny sprigs of pink roses embroidered on her gown. "You are forgetting, Papa . . ." She gave Morrison's arm an affectionate squeeze at the same time she turned her extraordinary blue gaze full on Nick. "You're forgetting about love."

"Love!" Morrison barked out a laugh that made heads turn. "I will leave that part up to the two of you." He gave Nick a broad wink. "As for me . . . I'm going to look for some more of those incredible biscuits. If you'll excuse me." He bowed and backed away at the same time he took his daughter's hand and placed it in Nick's.

"You must forgive Papa." Watching her father walk away, Amelia smiled. She did not pull her hand away. "He gets so enthusiastic about each of his projects."

"And are you?"

She smiled prettily. "Am I—"

"Enthusiastic?"

She may have been surprised that he was so coming, but she was not put off by it. It was another thing Nick decided he liked about her.

Miss Amelia took a step closer. "Oh yes, my lord, I am very enthusiastic indeed."

It was a good thing, Nick reminded himself. It meant he had found the one thing he had convinced himself did not exist: a woman who didn't exasperate him beyond all measure with her prattling and her chattering and her guffaws like a monkey's. A woman who did not offend his sensibilities with her public attempts at seduction nor one who was likely to turn tail and run the first time he made a move to kiss her.

In short, he had found the perfect woman who would make him a perfect wife.

And damn it to hell and back, it was all Willie's fault.

*　　*　　*

Even before it was over, those in attendance declared that Lord Somerton had done the evening's ball to a cow's thumb. The menu was both exotic and unique—not to mention delicious—and unbeknownst to each other, many of those who wolfed the samosas and devoured the kaju badam harbored secret plans to be just as exotic and just as unique and to serve just such food in their own homes at their own upcoming gatherings. The spirits, as was expected from Lord Somerton's cellar, were high quality and liberally poured and though not one of the guests got foxed except for old Lord Donald Lampert who was—or so they said—in such a state even before he arrived at the front door, there was a great deal of good-natured laughter and even some song before the night was over. The company was top-of-the-trees.

As for the rumors about Lord Somerton and Miss Amelia Morrison that started up even before the first dance of the night?

The talk went from mouth to mouth and from ear to ear as fast as Lord Somerton's great good friend Arthur Hexam ate biscuits, and nearly before the first guest walked out of the door of Somerton House, word of the way Miss Amelia looked at Lord Somerton and the way Lord Somerton smiled at Miss Amelia was already on the tips of a thousand excited tongues. As was the fact that Samuel Morrison had invited His Lordship to visit the family privately the next day.

There could be only one thing he was so anxious to discuss.

It did not take long for the news to reach across town to the Duke of Ravensfield who, though he was occupied with a certain Parisian lady who called herself Gigi even though her given name was Bertha, grumbled a curse. In spite of Gigi's best efforts to keep his mind on other things, the duke himself could not help but think of the amount of money he would lose should the gossip be true.

It took even less time, of course, for the report to make its way to the kitchen of Somerton House.

Bess, who had been serving in the ballroom, could not help but notice that Miss Amelia waltzed more than once with Lord Somerton and that Lord Somerton did not seem to mind the lady's rapt attention at all.

She mentioned it to Clover.

Clover, who was cleaning up the glassware, had heard a crumb of conversation between an elderly dowager and a young buck that was all about the way that even after Lord Somerton delivered her from the dance floor and deposited her back with her mother, Miss Amelia kept her hand on his arm a moment longer than was necessary.

She told Marie.

Marie confirmed the account, for she had seen as much for herself when she peeked into the ballroom after refilling the food on the buffet table in the refreshment room.

Of course, she couldn't wait to tell Flossie the story.

Flossie, always too sensitive both for her former profession and for her own good, instantly turned into a watering pot and could only be soothed by Mr. Finch, who had been spending more and more time with Flossie of late. Luckily, he had come belowstairs for a bit of a respite at just that moment and quite fortuitously, he had a silver flask filled with brandy in his back pocket. Grateful for the nip when they needed it most, they passed the flask from hand to hand, too troubled by all that was going on abovestairs to question where the flask had come from or the fact that it was etched with the coat of arms of the Duke of Horley, one of the guests.

Once her sobs subsided and Madame Brenard was found, Flossie told her what was afoot. Madame did not need to hear it. She had already gotten word from Rooster O'Reilly, who was in the back garden teaching Jem the difference between an uppercut and a right cross while they waited for Lord Somerton's guests to depart.

None of them had the heart to tell Willie.

None of them needed to.

Two hours after the last guest was gone, the news still sat square inside Willie. Right where her heart used to be.

She looked around the ballroom, checking to be sure that everything had been cleaned and put away and when she was sure it was, she extinguished the candles that had been left on the tables around the perimeter of the room. With each little flame she snuffed out, she felt more and more in the dark and as cold as ice even though the June air that wafted in from the open windows was pleasant.

She had only herself to blame and she knew it. Not for what had happened, of course. It was not her fault that Miss Amelia was beautiful. It was not her fault that Nick was attracted to the woman.

It was her fault, she reminded herself, that she was there to see it happen, and for that if for no other reason, she supposed she deserved what she was feeling. The aching that tore at her insides. The blackness that wrapped around her heart.

If she had not been so easily persuaded by Nick's request for help, she would be far from Somerton House by now and she would not know how Amelia Morrison smiled at Nick.

Even if she did still care that Nick smiled back.

"If wishes were horses . . ." Willie's voice fell dead against the silence that filled the house. She'd long since shooed the rest of the staff off to their beds and she walked the empty hallways one last time to make sure everything was in order, convinced now as she was when she sent them away that she'd rather be alone than watch the way they looked at her, their expressions filled with a sympathy they dared not put into words and she dared not let herself hear.

If she had been more impervious to Nick's smile and less susceptible to his charm.

If she had been more realistic and less a fool.

If she could convince herself that she did not love him.

The thought had no sooner settled inside her than she heard a crash from the direction of the library. Curious, Willie hurried to investigate.

She opened the door even as the brandy in the glass Nick had thrown across the room was still dripping down the wall. He didn't look at all surprised to see her.

"I wouldn't have suggested this damned ball in the first place if it wasn't for you." Nick's voice matched the thunderous expression on his face. "If you had a brain in your head—"

"I?" Though she was tempted, Willie didn't make a move to retrieve the pieces of crystal scattered near the point of impact. Neither did she try to sop up the brandy. This was one mess that wasn't her responsibility.

She closed the door behind her and stood with her back to it. "You are the one who insisted on hosting a ball," she reminded him. "You are the one—"

"I wouldn't have needed to." Nick stalked over to where she stood. "If you hadn't threatened to leave."

"Don't be ridiculous." He was being anything but and if Willie needed more proof, she had it instantly. He held her in place, one hand on each of her arms, and frowned down at her. There was no mistaking the anger that simmered in his eyes, but there was another emotion in them as well. One so filled with longing, it took her breath away.

She struggled to find her voice. "My leaving had nothing to do with—"

"Your leaving had everything to do with it." He hauled her nearer. "I only thought of hosting another damned social function to make you stay. I thought if you had some work to do—"

"You thought what?"

His hands slid to her shoulders. "I thought we could figure out what the hell we're going to do," he told her. "I thought we could find some way out of the muddle. I thought I'd make one last attempt at finding a wife and when I didn't—"

It was impossible to stand there with the unspoken words hanging between them. Willie pulled out of his grasp and moved away from his disturbing nearness.

"Even the research I did into the lady's background did not prepare me," she said. "She's all and more than I expected." Willie turned away and went to stand near the desk. "She's lovely."

"And as pleasant as a day in May." She knew he was simply reporting what she'd heard to be true.

"She's as wealthy a wife as you're ever likely to need."

"And as charming as can be."

"She's perfect."

"Hell, Willie, she isn't you."

The most difficult thing she'd ever done was not respond to the emotion that shimmered through Nick's voice. She ached to have him hold her in his arms. She yearned for him to kiss her the way he had at Vauxhall Gardens. Still, she kept her place.

"But you'll ask for her hand nonetheless. And as soon as tomorrow if what I've heard is true." It was not a question, but he owed her an answer. And she owed him the honesty of looking at him when he gave it to her.

Willie turned to face him.

She was just in time to see the stab of regret that sparkled in his eyes as surely as did the light of the fire that flickered in the fireplace. "I have the family name to consider. Family estates. Family honor."

"And she has the blunt to take care of that and more. It will help, I think, that you are well matched."

"A little."

He was trying to make her feel better. She wondered if he knew that she never would. "A lot, I think," she told him. "You are of like mind and that means a great deal. And though I had heard the lady was pretty, I had no idea she was so lovely. Your coloring is remarkably similar. Your children will be beautiful."

A smile came and went over his expression, lighting his eyes for a moment. He stepped closer. "That's funny," he said, "I keep picturing little carrot-headed children." He reached for her and put a hand in her hair, tugging at the pins as he did so that her hair came loose and tumbled around her shoulders. He combed his fingers through it. "I keep imagining a whole troop of them, little boys and little girls with freckled noses." He glided his thumb over her cheeks and nose. He brushed it over her lips. "I keep thinking—"

"Don't."

The single word was enough of a surprise to make him stop. He moved back a step and looked into her eyes. "Don't—"

"Don't think," she said. "Not about anything. Don't let's think about the future, Nick. We both know what you have to do for your family name and for your family honor. But that is tomorrow. And tonight—" Willie pressed her hands to his chest. His heart was beating as fiercely as hers and she let herself enjoy the sensation. Right before she kissed him.

For a moment, he was startled by her brazenness. The next second, all his surprise was forgotten in a rush of desire the likes of which Nick had never felt before. He deepened the kiss and when Willie melted into his arms, he kissed her ear and her neck and the hollow at the base of her throat. He brushed a trail of kisses across the tops of her breasts but unlike the night at Vauxhall Gardens, she did not shy away.

"It's all I'll ever have of you." She looked up at him, her eyes bright with unshed tears. "It isn't enough. It isn't all I want. But—"

"I know." His lips touched hers like a whisper. "It isn't all I want, either, but—"

"Nick . . ." Willie looped her arms around his neck. "We are talking again. We are always talking. And if we're not careful, soon enough we'll talk ourselves out of what we would like most to do."

He tried for a smile that didn't quite make its way past the lump of emotion that blocked his breathing and made his chest feel as if it were being squeezed and because he knew he would never find the words—not when Willie was looking at him with desire sparkling in her eyes and his own longing for her so strong, he could taste it—he lifted her in his arms and carried her to the fire.

Even when he set her on her feet, she kept her arms around his neck. Her fingers feathered through the hair at the nape of his neck, the touch both casual and intimate, and he felt suddenly as callow as a boy and as eager as he'd ever been for anything.

"If you will help me . . ." Turning, Willie scooped her hair off her neck and for a moment, Nick could not think what she wanted him to do. The next second, it hit with all the power of a summer storm.

"You want me to—"

Willie laughed, the sound as warm as the fire that danced in the grate. She glanced at him over her shoulder, her eyes alight. "I want you to undress me, m'lord."

"Willie . . ." Nick could not imagine what was wrong with him. He wanted her more than he wanted his next breath and she, it seemed, was of much the same mind. Still, he hesitated.

Reaching around her, he hooked a finger under her chin and tilted her head so that she was looking at him over her shoulder. "Do you know what you're asking?"

"Oh yes." There was a sparkle in Willie's eyes that had nothing to do with the fire. "Madame has told me, you see. All about it. She says that a man and a woman—"

"It's not what I meant, Willie." Nick's voice warmed with the emotions that flooded him. "When we scooped you up from the front of your father's church we were looking for a virgin and I never thought to be the one who—"

"Would you rather some other man—"

"And that isn't what I meant, either." He could not help himself. He couldn't wait a moment longer. Conversation or no conversation, crossed purposes or not, he had to kiss her. He spun her around and he kissed her slowly and thoroughly enough so that by the time he was done, she was a little more starry-eyed.

And a great deal more determined to carry on.

Willie ruffled Nick's neckcloth, tugging at one end until it loosened. She untied it, pulled it off, tossed it over her shoulder. She would have gone right to work on his coat if he hadn't stopped her, one hand on hers to still it.

"We must talk."

"I don't want to talk. I don't want to do anything but let you kiss me."

"But tomorrow—"

He saw her swallow hard but she did not look away. "Don't you see, that's why it is so important. We have tonight. And it's all we have. And it's all we will ever have. If you don't want—"

"You. I want you." He cupped her chin in his hand and smoothed his thumb back and forth across her jaw until he felt her vibrate with anticipation. "I want you more than my heart, Willie."

Smiling, she turned in his arms. "Then you must help me out of this dress," she told him, and again, she scooped up her hair and bent her head.

For a moment, Nick could do nothing at all but stare at the sweep of her freckled skin. It looked as delicate as porcelain against the black cloth of her gown. Just to be sure she was real—that this was fact and not some fantasy of a mind too long deprived of what it had so long wanted—he skimmed a hand over her skin. He pressed a kiss to the back of her neck and slid his mouth down her spine and still kissing her, he undid the buttons at the back of her gown, one by one. When he was finished, he put his hands on her shoulders and slid them down. The dark dress drifted to her hips, revealing a linen chemise that looked pristine against Willie's rosy skin, and—

"Drawers!" Nick could hardly help himself. He had to smile. It was the only way he could keep his desire for her from choking the breath out of him. He glanced over the linen drawers, at the smooth sweep of her buttocks, and the length of bare leg exposed just below where the drawers buttoned below her knee. "Willie, I would not have thought you as progressive as all that. Imagine!"

She had the good grace to blush but even blushing, she was brazen enough to turn to give him a better look. "Do you like them?" she asked.

"I like you." He skimmed a hand over the back of the drawers and over her nicely rounded backside and when she pulled in a breath and leaned back against him, Nick was lost.

"I like your fiery hair," he whispered close to her ear. He skimmed a hand over the knee-length chemise that topped her drawers. "And your fiery personality. I only wish—"

"Enough!" She pressed a finger to his lips. "We said we wouldn't talk, remember? So if you will allow me, m'lord . . ." She didn't wait for his permission and she didn't ask for his help. As expertly as one of Madame's girls might have done, she undressed him. She worked with exquisite slowness, each touch of her hand, each brush of her breath against his skin designed, or so it seemed, to send him even closer to the brink. It wasn't until she was done that she skimmed a look over him that heated Nick through to his soul.

Willie could not keep her hands from his body a moment longer. "You're a fine specimen of a man," she told him, gliding her hands over his chest and down farther still. And when he hauled in a breath and held it, she could not help but tease him further. She did it with a kiss to his breastbone. And another to the place where his heart pounded so hard, she swore she might be able to hear it if the blood rushing in her ears would allow it. She stood on tiptoe and nipped his earlobe and when he caught her in the crook of his arm and skimmed a hand under her linen chemise and over her bare breasts, she tipped her head and arched her back and wondered that anything could feel so good. Or so right.

When he raised her arms and tugged the chemise over her head, she did not stop him. Nor did she forget a word of the advice Madame had once given her. When she turned again to face him, she gave him little chance to look at her. Instead, she leaned close to Nick until her breasts brushed his bare chest.

"Oh Lord, Willie, you have been learning a thing or two from Madame."

Willie grinned. "Are you telling me that I'm doing this the right way?"

"There is no wrong way. Not with you." He bent and pressed a kiss between her breasts at the same time he loosened her drawers and skimmed them over her hips and when she stepped out of them, he followed the trail his hands had laid over her with a series of fiery kisses.

Willie's yearning grew. A frightening craving pulsed through her until her whole being was focused on the sensations. The flick of his tongue against her skin. The tug of his mouth on her nipple. The touch of his bare skin to hers.

His tongue skimmed the valley between her breasts and Willie moaned. Impatient for more, she shuffled even closer, and he tucked one leg between hers and cupped her from behind and as if it were a pattern, like the steps of the waltz he'd taught her in this very room, she rotated her hips against his.

"Willie . . ." Nick kissed her again. Her lips and her eyelids and her breasts. "Willie, we need to—"

"Yes." She led him to the sofa and when she lay down and pulled him down on top of her, she saw that Nick was smiling.

He moved into her slowly, watching her face, and when she caught her breath and groaned her pleasure, he quickened the pace to a rhythm as steady as the dance.

Faster and faster, the cadence increased until Willie thought she would shatter. She did, finally, with a jolt that made her let go a tiny shriek of pleasure and surprise. Nick thrust against her, harder and faster. The next second his body shuddered and his mouth was on hers, drinking in the breaths she fought for.

Willie held him close and kissed him hard and lost

herself in the taste of him and the warm afterglow of passion.

Once, she'd thought not making love to Nick would be the hardest thing she would ever do in her life.

Now she knew she was wrong.

It wasn't not loving Nick that was difficult, it was loving him.

Especially when she knew that it could never happen again.

❧ 16 ❧

....

"**D**on't be silly!" Nick kissed the tip of Willie's nose. He kissed her cheek and her chin. He nuzzled her neck and he would have slid his mouth down farther still if she had not laughed and squirmed away. Still, he could not be so easily put off. He moved off the sofa and followed her over to where she stood near the fireplace.

"There's no reason to be shy. Madame and Bess and Clover and the rest of them would be as happy as mice in malt to know what we've done." He came up behind her and looped one arm around her waist. He tickled a hand up her ribs and brushed his palm over her breasts and the suggestion that vibrated through his voice was as tempting as his touch. "They would not mind in the least if they found us here in the morning."

"Don't you see? That is exactly the problem. They would not mind what we've done here tonight." Willie's voice skipped and jumped with each ragged breath she took. "They would be very happy for us. But happy people do tend to talk and a careless word to the greengrocer or to one of the girls from the nearby houses who Clover and Bess sometimes spend their idle time with—"

"Let them talk!" Nick gave a throaty laugh. He kissed her shoulder and her arm. He swept aside her hair and kissed the back of her neck. "Then everyone will know what a lucky man I am."

Lucky?

It was such an impossible concept, Willie could do nothing but shake her head. Didn't he realize that word had a way of traveling at a faster clip than any horse of good bottom could run? This word did not need to travel to the Morrisons.

The very thought made her heart squeeze but Willie did not bother to tell Nick as much. He knew the truth as surely as she did.

"You must get to your own room so that Rooster finds you there in the morning," she reminded him, though how she was able to think clearly when her entire being was focused on the way he was swirling his fingers across her bare skin, she was not at all sure. "And I must be getting to my own room."

Nick had other ideas.

He rolled her nipple between two fingers and she pulled in a breath and caught her bottom lip with her teeth.

"Do you still want to scurry up to your own room?" he asked her.

"Yes." Though her mind was made up, Willie's voice was no louder than a whisper.

He slid his hand across her bare stomach, and she leaned back against him and groaned.

"Do you still want me to head off to mine and lie in my own bed, alone and aching for you with every breath I take?"

He made it sound so cruel, even if he was laughing. Even that did not change her answer. She nodded. "Yes."

Chuckling deep in his throat, he pressed himself against her and she realized that he wanted her—again.

"Do you really want to say good night right now, Willie, my love?"

"Yes." It was the wise thing to say, even if it wasn't true.

"And now?" He glided his hand between her legs.

Willie's voice caught on the end of a sound that was pure ecstasy. "Yes!"

"Very well." He made a move to step away and she realized how foolish her protests were.

"No!" she spun to face him and saw that he was laughing.

He moved a step nearer. "You will not send me all alone to my bed?"

"Not yet."

He nuzzled a kiss to her throat and skimmed his hand between her legs. "You will stay awhile and keep me company?"

"Yes." Willie melted into his embrace. "Oh, yes!"

*   *   *

As tempting as it was to give in to Nick's sweet persuasion—and it was very tempting indeed—Willie did
not let herself get distracted. At least not another time.
When they were done, they dressed hurriedly and outside in the passageway at the place where he would turn
to go to his chambers and she would head toward the
back stairway and to her own room, he kissed her gently
and wished her a good night. Reluctant to let go of her,
he held her tight and consoled himself with the fact that
he would see her in just a few short hours.

He toyed with the buttons at the back of her dress,
and she knew if she gave him even the slightest encouragement, he would have her out of the garment again in
less time than it took for her heart to make one crashing
thump against her ribs.

"You'll have breakfast with me?" His voice tickled
against her ear.

"Of course." Willie kissed his cheek and his lips before she hurried away, offering a quick prayer of thanks
as she did. Because the passageway was dark, he could
not possibly have seen that when she told him she
would see him again in the morning, she had her fingers
crossed behind her back.

It was nearly dawn by the time she was ready.

Willie glanced around her room one last time. There
was still much that needed to be packed but that could
not be helped. Right now, there was no time. She would
have to leave her books behind, and the straw bonnet
Lynnette had insisted on buying for her the last time

they shopped in Bond Street together. She would have to leave a great many things behind but she wasn't worried; Madame would see that her things were sent. As soon as Willie contacted her. As soon as she determined what she was going to do and where she was going to go.

Moving quickly and quietly, she finished stowing her most essential possessions in her portmanteau, blew out the single candle she'd used to work by and hurried out of the room.

The sun had not yet climbed over the horizon and the city was shrouded in fog. At least it wasn't raining. Bad enough that she was sneaking out of the house like a thief. Worse yet to have to do it in the rain.

At the bottom of the stairway, Willie looked around one last time. She would miss Somerton House. Over the last months, the place had been more a home to her than any she had ever made with her family. She would miss the counterfeit paintings and the suit of armor that she had suspected all along was more spurious than it was historically important and without question, she would miss the people she worked with. As impossible as it might have seemed the night they arrived at the Church of Imperishable and Divine Justice with mischief in their hearts, she would also miss the Dashers. Especially Mr. Hexam and Mr. Palliston and the duke of Latimer. She would most assuredly miss Lynnette, for they had grown as close as sisters.

She refused to stop and consider how much she would miss Nick.

An errant tear trickled down her cheek and Willie

wiped it away with the back of her hand. Though she did her best not to, she could not keep herself from looking up the stairway toward where she knew Nick was sleeping in his chambers. She had only to ask and she knew he would allow her to stay. She had only to knock at his door, and she knew he would welcome her with open arms and take her into his bed.

She had only to make love with him one more time and she knew she would never have the strength or the courage to leave him again.

Though her body advised otherwise and her heart reminded her that there would never be a place in it for anyone but Nick, her mind was made up. She put on her bonnet and tied it under her chin. She lifted her portmanteau and inched open the door, thinking in spite of herself of the night she'd left her father's church and never looked back. Just like the door of the Church of Divine and Imperishable Justice, the door of Somerton House creaked, the sound as loud as rifle shot in the morning quiet.

She held her breath and a minute passed, and when there was no sign of Mr. Finch or Jem or Madame—who, in spite of the fact that she snored rather heavily, swore that she slept as lightly as a feather—Willie slipped out of the house and closed the door behind her. The morning air was damp and cold and she pulled her mantle closer around herself. The fog was as thick as Simon Marquand's pea soup and narrowing her eyes the better to try and see through it, Willie started down the stairs.

She was almost all the way to the pavement when a

shape stepped out from behind the shrubs that bordered the stairway.

It was impossible to see the man's face but there was no mistaking who it was. Even in fog as thick as herrings, she would have recognized the long, greasy hair anywhere. The drab clothing. The two eyes that shone out at her through the gray morning mist, as cold and colorless as a dead cod.

"A bit early to be out and about, wouldn't you say, Miss Culpepper?"

Willie sucked in a breath of surprise. She had not thought to meet anyone this early in the morning.

Most especially she had not thought—now or ever— to see the Reverend Childress Smithe.

"Word has it you'll be headin' out early this mornin', my lord. Could it be you'll be payin' a certain sort of special call on a certain special young lady?"

Nick had to give Rooster O'Reilly credit. What the man lacked in subtlety, he made up for in enthusiasm. He bustled around Nick's dressing room, getting his master's things ready for the day, and if he noticed that the clothes Nick had worn to the ball the night before were not so much neatly put aside as they were dropped where he'd left them when he returned to his room, he neither commented nor criticized.

"Am I right in thinkin' you'll be wantin' your buff trousers, sir? And the brown coat, I'm thinkin' for an occasion such as this. You'll cut a fine dash when you speak to the young lady's father."

"Her father? I wouldn't speak to her bloody father if he were the last—" Nick caught himself at the brink of giving the Reverend Mr. Hannibal Culpepper the dressing down he so soundly deserved. It took him a moment to realize it was not the father—or the young lady— Rooster had in mind.

He forgave Rooster the blunder. But only because there was no way Rooster could have known about the remarkable events of the night before. More to the point, Nick was feeling particularly enthusiastic himself. He could hardly fault a man for being lively and inquisitive when it felt as if a whole new world had opened to him.

Thanks to Willie.

"Is Miss Culpepper . . ." Nick wondered if Rooster noticed the way his voice warmed over the name. "Is she down to breakfast yet?"

"I doubt it, my lord. It is a bit early, you'll be beggin' my pardon for mentionin' it. Even for the likes of Willie." He glanced out the window at the sky, which was just beginning to brighten behind a batting of fog. "Beggin' your pardon again, sir, but a person can't help but wonder, if you know what I mean, Your Lordship, sir. It's not exactly like yourself to be up and about at this hour."

"It isn't, is it?" Grinning, Nick reached for the cup of coffee that Rooster had brought up on a silver tray. Every morning, Rooster brought up a cup of coffee. Most mornings, it had long gone cold by the time Nick was awake enough to drink it. He took a drink now and surprised at how good it tasted, he nodded his approval.

"Damn, but it's good when it's hot! It looks as if I've been missing a great deal by spending so many of my mornings abed. Are things always this splendid at this time of day?"

Rooster looked uncertainly out the window. "It's not exactly splendid, if you get my drift, Your Lordship, sir. Soupy, more like it. And not promisin' to be the most glorious of days."

"Ah, that's where you're wrong." Nick reached for his buff trousers and stepped into them. He shrugged into his shirt and though he tried not to think of how he'd shrugged out of just such a shirt only a few short hours earlier and how Willie had helped him do it and all that had happened after, he could not keep himself from smiling.

"Not the brown," he said when Rooster presented the coat. "The green, I think. The better to contrast with that damned flaming hair of hers."

Rooster's eyes clouded with confusion. "But, sir. She's golden-haired and—" His mouth dropped open and a look of absolute astonishment crossed his face. It was followed immediately by a smile as wide as the Thames. "Are you tellin' me, sir—"

"It's exactly what I'm telling you." Nick gave him a friendly slap on the back. "It's a new day, Rooster! And I am a new man."

Rooster's eyes sparkled. "And the lady, sir?"

"The lady," Nick said, heading for the door, "is meeting me downstairs for breakfast."

* * *

At eight, Nick checked the clock on the mantel in the breakfast room for the fourth time in as many minutes. Willie was usually down to breakfast by now and impatient to see her, impatient to talk to her, and just as damned impatient to send Mr. Finch on some fool's errand as soon as Willie walked into the room so that he might kiss her silly, he drummed his fingers against the tabletop and downed another cup of coffee. In his mind, he played over any number of scenarios that might explain her absence but as they presented themselves—each more imaginative and impossible than the last—he silenced them with a healthy dose of logic.

Today was not a usual day. Hadn't he told Rooster as much? He should not expect Willie to act in a usual way. Especially considering the fact that she might be feeling just a bit shy.

As if he needed any confirmation of the theory, Nick thought of everything they'd done the night before. In light of it, it was impossible to keep a bolt of desire from streaking through him.

Though he'd never thought about it before, he suspected it could not be easy for a woman to face a man over the breakfast table when only a few short hours before they had faced each other with nothing between them at all and delighted so completely in each other's bodies, that he tingled still, just from thinking of it. Willie had made him feel things even the most skilled bit of muslin he'd ever been with had not made him feel.

Still, he must not forget that as bold and as intelligent

and as astonishing as Willie was, she was also inexperienced. He must be patient and not fault her for being bashful.

At nine o'clock he convinced himself that he had simply been too enthusiastic with his affections the night before. Poor, sweet Willie! She must be exhausted.

By ten, the eggs on the sideboard were cold in spite of the fact that Nick had asked Mr. Finch to replace them not once but twice, just so they were sure to be hot and ready when Willie arrived. Nick finished yet another cup of coffee and paced the length of the room.

By eleven, he was sure that he was an utter nod-cock. Of course Willie was in no hurry to come down to breakfast! He was usually not out of bed as early as this and she knew it. He suspected she had taken advantage of the opportunity. She would be down in a moment.

By noon, he was long past waiting.

"Madame!" Nick need not have bellowed. Sensing that something was amiss, Madame was waiting right outside the door to the breakfast room.

"Sir?"

"Has anyone looked in on Willie?" he asked.

His question must have been something of a surprise. Madame stepped back and took stock of him. "Willie? You mean you ain't callin' for your carriage? To go over to see—"

"Willie." Nick reined in his growing impatience. "Has anyone seen her this morning?"

"Not that I know of, sir. I thought she must be up and about somewhere and—"

Nick excused himself around Madame and took the stairs two at a time.

He didn't bother to knock. Let the staff talk if they so wished. He was long out of patience. He pushed open the door to Willie's room and stopped frozen in his tracks. Across the room, the wardrobe door was open. Willie's clothes were gone.

Behind him, he heard Madame choke out a sob. Not one to be patient herself, she pushed past him and looked around. " 'Er portmanteau is missin'," she said. "As are 'er slippers. And 'er best black gown. And—"

By the time Madame turned again to the doorway, Nick was already halfway to the front door.

"Jem!" Nick's voice echoed through the house and though he was outside stationed at the bottom of the stairway where he would be ready if it happened that someone came to call, Jem heard Nick well enough. He suspected that every man, woman, and child between Somerton House and St. Paul's heard.

At the sound of his master's booming voice, the boy's eyes widened and his lower lip trembled. Though he was, for all intents and purposes, working, Jem was not one to spend too much time being too little active. Under the watching eye of Bob—a scruffy stray dog that was lounging contentedly thanks to the plate of eggs Jem had fed him earlier—Jem had been teaching a tiger named Malcolm who worked nearby to roll dice. With the assistance of a pair of fulhams that always came up to Jem's advantage, he had also been winning steadily.

When the front door flew open, Jem stuffed the loaded dice into his pocket. He had no need to warn Malcolm away. One look at the expression on Lord Somerton's face and Malcolm dove behind the shrubbery where, more days than not, Bob slept on the blankets Jem had pinched from Lord Somerton's linen cupboard. Thinking he had been found out—about the eggs, the blanket, and Bob—Jem urged the dog into hiding with Malcolm and tossed the plate into the shrubbery with them.

By the time Nick made it to the bottom of the stairway—with Madame, Mr. Finch, Rooster O'Reilly, and every other servant of the household trailing behind—Jem was ready. Scrawny shoulders squared even if they were not steady, he turned to face his fate. "M'lord?"

If Nick was not so concerned about Willie, he might have commented on the corner of woolen blanket he saw sticking out from the bushes. The one that looked all too familiar. He might have mentioned—in the kindest way possible, of course—that there was a large brown and black monstrosity of an animal who looked to be licking eggs from one of the porcelain plates adorned with the Pryce family crest.

He was in too much of a hurry to care.

"Willie," he said and though he did not explain that he was looking for her or why, Jem apparently caught the drift.

"Ain't seen 'er." Jem scraped one finger under his nose and looked up and down the pavement as if by doing so, he might make Willie appear. "Not since last night anyways," he elaborated. "When we was cleanin' up, sir. From that there ball."

"I know she was here then." Nick wasn't sure if the feeling that clutched his insides was panic or heartbreak. He wasn't sure he wanted to know. He did know that he had to fight to keep his voice even and calm so as not to upset the staff. He might have had a good deal more incentive to do it if not for the fact that Bess and Marie were already crying, Flossie was twisting her white apron into knots worthy of Rooster's neckcloths, and Clover was holding her breath and clasping both hands to her mouth, sure that her son was about to receive a sound drubbing, all because of a dog she'd told the boy to be rid of days before.

"It's after the ball I'm talking about," Nick told Jem. "After say, three or so this morning."

It was a bit of information none of them had been aware of before now and Nick knew exactly how they'd construe it. The ball had ended early, just after one. Willie had sent the staff to bed soon after when the most pressing of the cleanup was finished. If Lord Somerton knew of Willie's whereabouts up until three in the morning . . .

As if they'd choreographed the move as neatly as the steps of a contredanse, Nick heard a collective, thunderstruck gasp and felt each and every gaze of each and every one of his servants drill into his back. He heard Simon Marquand cough politely and saw out of the corner of his eye the way Mr. Finch elbowed Madame. He couldn't fail to miss the way Madame grinned like the cat's uncle.

"Excuse me, sir."

At the sound of a voice from somewhere near the stairway, Nick turned, grateful for the interruption before any of his staff could interrogate him. He found a head—and the shoulders that belonged to it—peeking out from between two yews. "Is it the nice young lady you're lookin' for?" the boy asked. "The one what 'as all that flamin' red 'air?"

Nick's hopes surged. "That's the one," he told the boy. "Come out here. Come on." He had not meant to call the dog out with the boy but apparently thinking the command was aimed at him, the creature came trotting along. It parked itself at Nick's feet, its tail wagging.

"Good heavens!" Though he was a firm believer in everything Beau Brummel had ever said about the virtues of cleanliness and the benefits of plenty of hot water and much soap, Nick was not one to be finicky. Still, even he could not stand so close to the dog without wrinkling his nose. "I say, sir . . ." He turned to Jem, who had thought to make a clean getaway and was just about to duck behind Clover's skirts when Nick caught him by the scruff of the neck. "Does this animal belong to you?"

Jem's eyes were as round as saucers. His voice was breathless. "Couldn't be, could it, sir?" The smile he tried for wilted on contact with Nick's frown. "Ain't supposed to have no animals, my lord, sir."

"And are those same animals you ain't supposed to have supposed to be eating from the family china?"

"Ain't supposed . . ." Jem swallowed hard. "Ain't supposed to, sir."

"Then I suggest you take this animal that ain't supposed to be here and ain't supposed to be eating my breakfast from my dishes and see to it that he is scrubbed until he is squeaky. That way, the rest of us will be able to breathe freely and concentrate on the problem at hand."

"Yes, sir." Jem didn't wait to be told a second time. He called to the dog and together, they disappeared toward the back of the house.

"Now . . ." Nick turned his attention back to the urchin in the shrubbery. "Did you say you saw Willie? When, sir? And what was she doing?"

Seeing that Jem had not caught hell for his acquaintance with Bob, the boy ventured out of his hiding place. "It was early, sir." He scuffed his boots against the pavement. "Just as the sun was comin' up. What little sun we can see today, what with the fog and all. I was waitin' for my master to get in." He pointed toward the home across the way where he was employed. "And I seen a carriage pull up. I wouldn't have thought nothin' of it, sir, except for the fellow what got out of it. All dressed in black, 'e was. Like a regular vision of Death."

"Ravensfield?" It did not seem possible, yet Nick turned the thought over in his head. If Ravensfield had some prank in mind and intended to make Willie a part of it . . .

He stopped himself just short of calling for his carriage so that he might head over to Ravensfield's and beat some sense into the man. But only because he had yet to get the full story.

"Was it a gentleman?" he asked the boy. "Tall? Fine clothing? A crack carriage?"

"He was tall, right enough." Thinking, the boy squeezed his eyes shut. "And a real spindle-shanks, if you get my meanin', my lord. Thin as a yard of pump water, 'e was. And 'air down to 'ere." The boy pointed to his shoulders.

"Not Ravensfield," Nick mumbled to himself. And yet the description sounded familiar enough. The truth hit with all the force of a fist to the stomach.

"Reverend Smithe?" He looked to Madame for confirmation but he needed not a word from her. The worried look in her eyes spoke volumes.

New urgency in his voice, Nick turned back to the boy. "What did they do, Willie and this man?" he asked. "And which way did they go?"

"Willie didn't do nothin', sir. On my honor, she didn't. Just said something to the man and then 'e like put his arm around 'er, sir, and walked 'er over to that there carriage. 'E got into the carriage with 'er, sir, and last I seen them . . ." He pointed down the street. "They was 'eaded that way."

It wasn't nearly all Nick needed to know but it was enough. At the same time he reached into his pocket for a coin for the boy, he gathered his household staff around him to plan his strategy.

....

*R*ooster O'Reilly stopped in at Jackson's Rooms in Bond Street that afternoon and later, at the Daffy Club. Though none of them anticipated that the search for Willie would end in violence, it would have been shortsighted to begin it without knowing that reinforcements were in the wings should they be needed. Rooster knew a great many people and most of them were brawny, brave, and threw a hell of a punch. As he was quick to point out, a few of them owed him favors. By the time he returned to Somerton House, there were a dozen burly men with him, all of whom pledged their assistance in exchange for a meal in the kitchen and a few bottles from the cellar to quench the thirst that would, no doubt, come from waiting.

Five Fingers Finch had friends of his own and he put the network into action as soon as he arrived at the East End pub where many of them spent their days. He returned with no news to report—and smelling as if he'd bathed in ale—but he did his best to cheer Nick by reminding him it was early days yet; like the Polite World, the criminal classes had a rumor mill all its own. If there was mischief in the works, one of his associates would get wind of it soon enough.

Madame and the girls were busy, too. They left Clover behind to supervise Bob's washing up and went out to canvass the neighborhood, talking to everyone they knew and many they did not in hopes of finding someone who'd seen more or heard more than Malcolm had reported. A tweenie by the name of Susan who worked in a home farther up the road would talk to no one but Madame and only in private. Susan, it seemed, had crept out of the house early for an assignation with a young man. Though she and her swain had been busy themselves and thus disinclined to watch the goings-on around them, Susan had seen both Willie and Childress Smithe. Her story verified Malcolm's.

All the while, Nick did not sit idle. It would have been impossible and besides, there were facets of the investigation only he could manage. After all, it would not have been nearly as effective to send an emissary to the Church of Divine and Imperishable Justice. As it was, the unexpected appearance of the Viscount Somerton was enough to draw Ebenezer and Amabel Miller's attention away from the hymn they were in the process of rehearsing—and butchering—when he wrenched open the door and marched into the church.

He was prepared to bribe them if that's what it took

to gain their cooperation. It happened that he needn't
have bothered.

The fact that Nick was chafing at the bit and looked
as if he could bite through bricks was enough to convince the Millers that it was in their best interest to tell
him all they knew.

Unfortunately, what they knew did little to calm
Nick's worst fears.

"India, you say?" Arthur Hexam had poured himself
a drink the moment he strode into Somerton House. It
went down nicely on top of the drink he'd poured at
home to calm his nerves as soon as he received Nick's
message that Willie was missing. Finished with the one
drink, he reached for the bottle that Palliston had been
kind enough to bring along when they traipsed up to
the third floor. "Well, there's some comfort in that, I
suppose. At least they are not headed to Gretna Green."

Some comfort, yes.

It was small.

There was a drink on the floor next to Nick, too, but
though Palliston had plunked it down just a few minutes earlier, he'd completely forgotten its existence.
Thoughts of India, Gretna Green, and the incredible experience of making love to Willie swirled through his
head and produced nothing but more anxiety to add to
the disquiet that had been plaguing him since the moment he realized Willie was gone. He was on his hands
and knees, his head poked into a little-used cupboard
tucked beneath an even less-used stairway. There was a
mountain of discarded odds and ends in the cupboard,

all of it coated with dust, and Nick's clothes were streaked with dirt, his hair was disheveled, his face was caked with grime.

He supposed that had he been feeling more inclined to sit and do nothing and less inclined to be restless enough to wear the carpet away from pacing it, he might have listened to his friends who told him what he was doing was a job for one of the servants. He didn't. Searching through the library, the box room, the butler's pantry and—with the help of Madame and the girls— every one of the bedchambers, gave him something to do.

Something besides worrying. Something besides wondering where Willie was. And if she was safe. And if—as the Millers had hinted must be true, for surely no man of the cloth could be so wicked as to force a woman to do otherwise—Willie herself had contacted Reverend Smithe and arranged to meet him, that she had gone with him willingly.

A veneer of dirt was a small price to pay in exchange for trying to get his mind off the blame he could not help but place squarely on his own shoulders. One moment, he wondered if his too-ardent demonstration of his affections had caused Willie to panic and if her panic made her run. The next, he questioned whether he had, instead, simply not done enough to make her happy and keep her where she belonged.

"And you're sure they said Willie and this Smithe fellow would be leaving from Dover?" Latimer's question broke through Nick's brown study. He paced back and forth behind Nick, sounding no more calm than Nick felt. "What if they lied? This Mr. and Mrs. Miller . . . what if they lied? What if they are in league with this awful Smithe person and they were told to lie to you should you come inquiring about Willie?"

Nick didn't bother to acknowledge the questions. He was in the process of picking through a trunk that looked to be promising. It was filled with household account books from his father's days. After what he'd learned from Rawdon Farleigh when he tried to sell what he thought were the family treasures, he suspected there was nothing inside the ledgers but red ink. He burrowed his hand beneath the books and felt the edges of a wooden box.

Encouraged, Nick dug out the box and backed out of the cupboard. He didn't bother to get up off the floor but held the box in his lap and snapped it open.

Just as he remembered seeing when he was a lad, his father's dueling pistols were still inside.

A smile on his face as deadly as the barking irons in the wooden box, Nick pulled himself to his feet and tucked the pistols into the waistband of his trousers. "Something tells me they knew I was not in the mood to be lied to," he told his friends and without waiting for them to comment, he hurried downstairs.

There was a flurry of activity in the entryway, which was devilishly inconvenient. Eager to get to the bit of cavalry known as Midnight that had been saddled and waited outside for him, Nick hurried down the last few steps. He did not even bother to look at the man he sidestepped around on his way to the door.

"Lord Somerton?"

He was tempted not to answer the man's befuddled-sounding inquiry. He might not have if he did not recognize the voice and if that recognition did not spark a memory in him.

Good lord, he'd forgotten!

"Mr. Morrison!" Nick stopped and turned to Samuel Morrison who, looking him over and noting the dust, the dirt, the grime—and the pistols—could not help but stand back and stare in wonder.

"Good to see you, Morrison," Nick said, his words as quick as the move he made to leave the house. "Stop in again. Another time, perhaps. Then we can—"

"But Lord Somerton, you said you would call today."

Dismayed at his lack of manners, Nick stopped long enough to grab the bag of food Simon Marquand had prepared for him to take on his journey. "I . . ." He scraped a hand through his hair and a shower of dust sprinkled the shoulders of his coat. He wiped off the front of his jacket and dirt fell around his feet like snowflakes. "I hope you will offer my apologies to Miss Amelia. We have had something of a household emergency, you see. If you would allow me to call upon her another day . . ."

He didn't wait for Morrison to answer. He didn't need to. If Morrison was any less interested in snagging a viscount for his daughter than he had been the night before, he would not have made the trip to Somerton House.

His words dangling in the air behind him along with the memory of the confused expression on Samuel Morrison's face, Nick hurried out the door. The others would follow behind in his carriage and Latimer's. He didn't wait to see them off or to offer any last minute instructions. He grabbed the reins that Jem tossed to him, hopped onto Midnight and headed for Dover.

To say that the King's Head was not the most elegant establishment in Dover was, in Willie's opinion, not so much an underestimation as it was simply a complete miscoloring of the truth. The furniture, being old, was far too massive for the small proportions of the rooms. There wasn't an inch to move, much less to breathe. The ale in the public room was not only warm but bitter as well. The mutton dished up by a serving wench with fleshy arms and—even this early in the morning—rings of sweat on her shabby dress, was stringy, greasy, and just this side of being ice cold. The air was heavy with the smoke that poured from a chimney with a bad downdraft.

The place smelled of years of unwashed bodies and she had no doubt that upstairs in the rooms that were let to the unwary, travelers were packed three or more to beds not large enough to accommodate even one in comfort.

She was glad she would be gone from the place soon enough and gladder still that when she was, she would be rid of the Reverend Childress Smithe.

"You're not eating." Smithe looked across the pocked and pitted table at her, pointing toward her nearly untouched plate of food with the tip of his fork. "How can you not be hungry, woman? We have been on the road all these many hours with little to eat and drink. Any normal woman—"

"Any normal woman would be less than delighted, both because of the quality of the food and the cleanliness of this place." She did not bother to add that watching the Reverend Smithe shovel food into his mouth and chew with it open did little to add to the ambience. Nor did the fact that he had a dribble of fat on his chin. "It's not that I don't appreciate—"

"Appreciate?" Smithe did not so much laugh as he did bray. Like a donkey. He washed down a mouthful of food with a swallow of ale, wiped his mouth with his sleeve and reached across the table to spear the lump of mutton from her plate and claim it as his own. "You'll learn to appreciate me, right enough, missy. Far better than you ever appreciated your sainted father, I'd venture."

"I think not." Willie folded her hands on the table in front of her. She had been reluctant to discuss the details of her plan with Smithe on their trip from London. They had been crammed with six unfortunate others on the top of a stagecoach and the wind whipping around them from a phalanx of ill-boding clouds as well as their proximity to strangers who had no need to know Willie's business had made explanations not only challenging but awkward. Besides, she thought what she had to say was better delivered in private. Especially since Smithe seemed, for reasons she couldn't fathom, to think that his unexpected arrival at Somerton House was more of a delightful surprise than it was a rather distasteful shock.

"As I was in the middle of saying before you were so rude to interrupt me, Mr. Smithe, I appreciate the fact that you were willing to accompany me this far. I must make it perfectly clear, though, that I have no intention of going any farther. At least not with you."

"What?" Smithe's mouth fell open. Which was not a particularly pretty sight considering that it was filled with half-chewed mutton. He swallowed it down in one gulp and slammed his knife against the table. "Are you telling me you ain't grateful?"

"Grateful?" The word had not occurred to Willie. "I am glad things worked out the way they did and that you happened by—"

"Happened by? You think so?" Smithe's throaty laugh caused a shiver to skitter up Willie's spine. "You think I just happened to be passing by at that hour of the morning? That in all of the city of London, I just happened to find you?"

Now that Willie thought about it, it did seem unlikely. "I suspect," she told him, "that you left Glasgow and were passing through London on your way to Dover and from there, to the mission in India. I suppose the Millers had something to do with you knowing where I was. If they were true to form—and I have no doubt that they were, since small-minded, self-righteous, iron-bound dogmatists are no more likely to suddenly become charitable than leopards are to change their spots—they probably said something about how wicked I was and how I was, no doubt, living a depraved life at Somerton House. They probably failed to mention—since they did not know it, of course, and if they did, they would not have bothered in any case not being as concerned with the truth as they are with the outward appearance of morality—that being in Lord Somerton's employ was much the best thing that has ever happened to me in my entire life."

It was the truth, and as much as Willie knew the memory would make her heart ache for as long as it lasted—and that it would last for as long as she had breath—she was glad for everything that had happened in the time she'd spent with Nick.

"Well, if it was so good to be in Lord Somerton's employ, why were you leaving?"

She had not expected so perceptive a question from a man who was anything but and answering him, she forced herself to keep her gaze on Smithe's. If she did not, she was certain that he would sense that she was not so much lying as she was telling him half the truth. She hardly cared what he thought of her, she simply was not yet ready to admit to herself how very much she cared for Nick. If she did, the pain of leaving him would be more than she could bear.

"I had a purpose for working with Lord Somerton. That of finding him a wife." She congratulated herself for her even tone and level gaze. And if she pulled her hands into her lap and clutched them together until her knuckles were white? Smithe would never know and it was good practice. She would need to learn to live the rest of her life missing Nick. She might as well get started.

"He has found a suitable match and it is thanks to me, I am glad to say. My business with him is over. It was time for me to leave."

Smithe sat up, his eyes glittering. "Time for you to repent, more like. Time for you to learn to regret the error of your ways. Turning your back on your dear father . . . risking your reputation and your future . . . You are lucky, miss, that I returned to London and heard the truth of all that was happening from the faithful Millers. You are luckier still that I have not changed my mind. About you." As if he were conferring an especially superb honor, he sat up straight and tall. As if he would never let her forget that he had done her the favor, his eyes glittered in the dull light. "If you change your ways and repent your sins, I am willing to forgive you. You may come with me to India. I will still allow you to be my wife."

The thought of giving herself to Smithe as she had to Nick was enough to bring a sting of tears to Willie's eyes. "I hardly need your forgiveness." She stood. "Nor am I interested in going to India. With you or with anyone else. I am most especially not interested in becoming your wife. In fact, I'm leaving. Now." She glanced around for her portmanteau, which had not only her possessions but also her money in it. It was nowhere to be found.

Smithe stood and though she expected him to be angry, he looked more tired than anything else. His shoulders slumped. His eyes lost the sheen of annoyance that usually was their only spark of life. "I am sorry you have changed your mind about me, Miss Culpepper," he said. "I fear it is because you have turned toward wicked ways. I warned your father it would happen but . . ." He sighed. "Apparently even his righteous and formidable influence was not enough to save you from your own sinful tendencies."

He looked through the smoky air toward the stairway. "I thought you would want to freshen up before we boarded the ship that is waiting for us in the harbor. I had your bag taken up to a room. Go. Get it. And leave. I cannot find it in myself to regret the loss of a woman so depraved."

First he was insightful and now considerate. The transformation was nearly enough to make Willie feel sorry for him.

Nearly.

Before he could change his mind and start a to-do that she would be only too happy to finish, Willie hurried away in search of her traveling bag.

Though there was custom in the public rooms, there weren't many travelers who had paid for a private room and most of the ones she looked into were empty. The King's Head had been built into a small space, its floors stacked one upon the other and it took Willie a while to trudge from the first floor to the second, from the second to the third, and finally from the third to the fourth.

She might have known Smithe would have secured for her the smallest room in the most out-of-the-way corner of the inn. She finally found her portmanteau in a cheerless room at the end of a long and narrow hallway. Her traveling bag was tucked up between a narrow bed and a battered table. The sky was more threatening than ever and the only light in the room came from the single window opposite the bed. Even so, Willie could not fail to notice that Smithe's bags were also there.

At the same time she realized that Smithe had lied about paying for a room for her use alone, she knew she had to get away from the place, and as fast as possible.

But by that time, it was already too late.

Behind her, she heard the sound of a stealthy footfall. She turned around just in time to see Smithe already in the room with her. And he already had the door locked behind him.

The last time Nick had climbed a vine-covered trellis up a vertical stone wall toward a window where a single candle flickered behind a thin gauze of drapery was the fateful night he burst in on the young widow—and each and every one of the Blades—at the Duke of Weyne's country home. That night, the entire escapade had been blurred with a haze of claret fumes and enhanced by the enthusiastic encouragement of friends who were no more able to see through the cloud of spirits than he was.

Nick had been so foxed as to be fearless. He had been so fearless as to not care a fig when his foot slipped, or his knuckles scraped the wall just behind the vines, or a bit of trellis snapped off in his hand. So fearless—and so thoroughly foxed—that it was all a lark. He laughed along with his friends, even when he dangled high above the ground and grappled for the nearest handhold that might save him from crashing down to the cobblestones where they stood with their faces upturned, their mouths open, their claret bottles poised as if they were waiting to see if they would be toasting Nick's success. Or drinking to his all-too-brief life.

This time, he was stone cold sober and he wasn't laughing.

Inch by careful inch, Nick climbed a vine-covered trellis up a vertical stone wall toward a window where a single candle flickered behind a thin gauze of drapery. He was halfway to his goal when his foot slipped at the same time a bit of trellis snapped off in his hand and he dangled high above the ground and looked down to where his friends stood far below on the cobblestones, their faces upturned, their mouths open, their claret bottles poised. Much to his astonishment he found that he didn't care a fig. Not about his scraped and bleeding knuckles. Or the fact that he had to struggle to find another handhold. Not even about his all-too-brief life.

Damn it, he didn't care about anything except Willie and the fact that she was up in the room where that single candle flickered behind the threadbare draperies and the grimy window.

That, and the gut-wrenching fact that had been confirmed only a short while earlier by the innkeeper: Willie was with the Reverend Childress Smithe.

Nick's stomach clenched but he paid it no mind. He didn't have the luxury. It was late in the afternoon and the sky threatened rain and it was not easy to see through the gloom. Still, he managed to find the growing end of one of the vines and he looped it around his hand, again and again. Using it like a rope and hoping it was secure, he hoisted himself up an inch or two, his arm muscles straining, until he found a slat of trellis where the wood wasn't rotted. His feet solidly planted again, he looked up at the window, still ten feet above his head, and wondered as he had wondered every minute of every hour he'd spent searching for Willie, if she was safe.

Dover was a sizable place and this day like every day, it was packed like herrings in a barrel with travelers. Even with the help of a number of young men he hired from the stables where he'd left his horse, it took Nick hours to locate Willie, so long that the carriages that had followed him out of London and had taken so much longer over the roads than he did, were already in town. As planned, he met his friends at an establishment considerably finer than the King's Head and from there, they plotted a line of attack and began the campaign.

Thanks to a well-placed shilling or two provided by the Reverend Smithe, the proprietor of the King's Head—a man of dark disposition and equally sinister reputation—was reluctant to bother the man of the cloth and the woman he thought to be the reverend's missus. A little of Nick's friendly persuasion convinced him otherwise. It helped, no doubt, that he had Rooster and his toughs with him as well as Latimer, Hexam, and Palliston—who were nearly as worried about Willie as Nick was himself—and Mr. Finch, Simon Marquand, and Madame, who, after the breakneck trip, were in no mood at all to be kept longer from Willie and were not reluctant to let the world know it in explicit terms.

"No answer to my knock," the landlord informed them when he returned to the cramped and dirty space he had the nerve to call a public room. "And the door, sir, it is certainly locked."

A certain edginess had taken up residence in Nick's stomach the moment he realized Willie was missing. With the landlord's words, the tension had turned to dread.

Even he was not sure what worried him more. Was he afraid that Willie was a prisoner? Or more afraid that the truth might be uglier still? Though he tried a dozen ways to understand it and failed miserably each time, he would have been a fool not to consider the possibility that she had gone with Childress willingly and that even now, they were planning the marriage Willie's father had arranged. Perhaps even now, they were sealing the bond between them much as Nick and Willie had done when he thought their feelings for each other solid and even more unshakable than—

Another slat snapped, this one beneath Nick's left foot. He would have plummeted to the ground if not for the fact that his right foot was planted firmly. That, and the sheer force of a will that made it impossible for him to believe that Willie could ever agree to a match with Smithe.

Which meant she needed Nick's help.

The thought burned through him like fire and fueled by it, he made his way slowly up the wall. When he slipped again, he heard a collective gasp from the people gathered below in the inn's dank stable yard. He paid them no mind. His eyes on the prize, his fingers just inches from the stone sill that bordered the window, he paused to catch his breath and let his screaming muscles rest.

He heard the sounds of a struggle before he saw the shadows that twitched behind the curtain.

A man's voice raised in anger. A woman's, just as angry but not as out of control, steely as a blade and so willful as to twist around his heart as surely as his hand was coiled through the greenery. The sounds of the voices were followed by a crash of furniture. And Willie's muffled cry.

Nick covered the last few feet of his climb in one push. At the same time he propped one knee on the window ledge, he banged his fist into the spot where the two window panes closed against each other. They were meant to swing outward and did not oblige. He wasn't about to let that stop him.

Another punch and Nick was through the window. He landed on his feet and pulled one of the pistols out just in time to see Willie standing over the prostrate form of Reverend Smithe. She had a knife in her hands.

"I've killed him, I think." She was in too much shock to look surprised to see Nick. Her eyes glittering, her breath catching over every lungful of air she struggled to take in, she glanced from him down to where Smithe lay in heap on the floor.

Nick thought it impolite to smile while another was suffering but he could hardly help himself. He grinned like a Cheshire cat at the same time he poked Smithe's ribs with the toe of one boot. "Only if a dead man squeals like a stuck pig," he said.

It was, apparently, one small detail Willie had been too distressed to notice. Now that it was pointed out to her that Smithe was not dead but was, in fact, both moaning and thrashing while he clutched what looked to be no more than a small wound to the side of his neck, she backed away from him.

"He said there was a ship," she explained, her voice breathless and hard to hear over Smithe's winging. "And that once we were on it, the captain would marry us. He brought a knife up from when he ate his meal." She looked at the knife in her hands and seeing that it was red with Smithe's blood, she tossed it onto the bed.

It seemed that ridding herself of the knife also rid Willie of all her fears. Of course, the sight of Nick had something to do with that as well. A rush of relief tore through her and she threw herself into his arms.

"Oh, Nick!" She didn't even realize she was crying until she heard her words tear in two. "I knew you would come. Or at least I hoped it. I did. It's just that . . ." She swallowed hard and looked to where Smithe lay. "I couldn't wait any longer. Once we were on the ship—"

"You did exactly the right thing." He held her tight

and smoothed a hand over her hair, which had been mussed considerably in her struggle with Smithe. He kissed her cheek and her nose and, for not nearly long enough, her lips. He might have gone right on kissing her if the door to the room had not crashed inward.

Hexam, Latimer, and Palliston piled into the room followed by Madame, Rooster, Mr. Finch, and Simon Marquand. There were at least a half dozen young men out in the passageway who Willie did not recognize. They all looked as happy to see her as she was to see them.

"Miss Willie . . ." It was Arthur Hexam who made the first move. Because the room was small, there wasn't much space. He hopped over Smithe and oblivious to the fact that Nick's arm was around Willie, he dropped to one knee and grabbed her hand. "I hardly care if you've been compromised," Hexam said. "You are the finest baker this side of Asia, Miss Culpepper, and I would be most glad if you would agree to be my—"

"Oh, no!" Palliston stepped between Hexam and Willie, appropriating her hand as he did. "The last thing you need is to listen to Hexam's prattle," he said. "Miss Culpepper, I would be most honored if you would listen to my suit and agree to be my—"

"It's ludicrous, I think you'll agree." Not to be outdone, Latimer hopped over the bed and insinuated himself between Palliston and Willie. "They are but unlicked cubs," he said, glancing at his friends and smiling his superiority, "and cannot possibly know the tug of true sentiment to their hearts. Miss Willie, if you would but say yes to me, I—"

"Gentlemen!" Willie had no doubt it was meant to be a solemn occasion, no more than she doubted that though they were conveyed away by their emotions, the three Dashers before her were entirely serious. Still, she could not help but laugh. "I am grateful. Truly." She sniffed and when Nick's handkerchief was suddenly in front of her eyes, she snatched it from his fingers and smiled her gratitude. She wiped it delicately under her nose. "I do not think, really, that this is the time for such talk. I have, after all, just rebuffed one proposal." She looked down at Smithe and clicked her tongue. The injury she'd done him was no more than a scratch and yet the man carried on so! Disgusted as much by Smithe's hen-heartedness as she was by his person, she shook her head and turned her attention back to the Dashers.

She was just in time to see Mr. Hexam's expression fall. And Palliston's cloud. And Latimer's grow even more earnest.

"Perhaps we should be rid of Reverend Smithe before we worry about anything else," Nick suggested, and Willie was grateful for it. He stowed his pistol and at his signal, Simon Marquand and Mr. Finch each grabbed one of Smithe's arms. None too gently—for his face was to the floor and his nose, being prominent, was in no small amount of peril—they dragged him out into the passageway where they turned him over to the young men who were well muscled enough to make sure the good reverend knew of their displeasure. If the bumping sounds they heard meant anything, the Reverend

Smithe was on his way down the stairs and well into learning a lesson.

Though Hexam, Palliston, and Latimer looked reluctant to follow, Madame waved them on. She gave Willie a wink and bustled down the passageway after them. But not before she closed the door behind her.

"Oh, Nick!" Willie put a hand to each of his cheeks and kissed him hard, her whole heart so tangled up in relief and the affection she had for Nick that she found she could barely breathe. "I'm happier than I can say that you came for me."

"I would not have had to come for you if you had not run away."

His words were not so harsh as they were simply true and, guilty, Willie moved back a step. "I couldn't stay," she said. New tears sprang to her eyes. "If anyone found out about us—"

"Anyone?" A look of confusion darkened Nick's handsome face. "You mean—"

"The Morrisons, of course. If I stayed and we were tempted again—" She couldn't bear it if he looked at her tenderly and she turned away and moved as far from him as the little room allowed. "If I stayed, it might have jeopardized your marriage to Miss Morrison. You have . . ." She was almost afraid to ask and yet she knew she had no choice. She had to know the truth. "You've talked to Mr. Morrison?"

He nodded. "Right before I left town."

She wasn't sure what else she expected him to say. In that part of her made whole and wild from the taste of his lips and the heat of his lovemaking, she imagined that he would pull her into his arms. That he would toss her onto the bed and, even as Madame and the rest of them waited in the dingy little room downstairs, that he would take her again and make her his own.

Instead, he didn't say a word. He didn't move. And Willie knew her dreams were nothing but fantasy. And false, as illusion often is.

Clutching her hands at her waist, she turned back to him. "Thank you," she said, her voice husky with emotion she dared not reveal. "Thank you for coming for me. I'm sorry I inconvenienced you. You must convey my regret to Mr. Hexam and Mr. Palliston and—"

"You mean you're not going to take any one of them up on his offer of marriage?"

He meant it as a jest but Willie didn't feel like smiling. "No." She shook her head. "Give them my apologies, please. If there's anything I can do to make it up to you—"

"There is one thing." Nick linked his hands behind his back. His knuckles were scraped and he winced a bit but still, he maintained the pose. He was tall and the ceiling in the little room was low. His shoulders were wide and the size of the room was hardly enough to hold the two of them. Even with his cheeks scratched and his clothes dirty and a straggling sprig of ivy trailing from the spot where it had been wound around one of his buttons, he looked more imposing than ever.

And Willie loved him very much.

"I will do anything," she said and she knew in her

heart that it was true. There wasn't a thing she could ever refuse him. "Anything you ask."

"Good." Nick moved toward the door, his movements as brisk and precise as his words. "Then you'll come back to London with me now. It is nearly the end of June and I have an engagement to announce, Miss Culpepper. Damn it, you're the one who got me into this thing. You're going to be at my side when I go through with it."

❧ 18 ❧

....

$\mathcal{I}$f she had not been so weary from her adventure and Nick had not been so insistent on announcing his engagement no later than the night they arrived back in London, Willie might have been tempted to leave again.

As it was, she simply did not have the energy. And she certainly did not have the heart. Right after he bundled Willie into his carriage along with Madame, Mr. Finch, and Simon Marquand, Nick headed back to town on his horse. But while her companions dozed, Willie could find no peace. It was hard to sleep when she was so busy wondering what she might have done differently. And how she ever could have let herself fall in love with a man who was so far out of her reach.

Upon their return to Somerton House, Nick was nowhere to be found. Lynnette arrived as if by magic and while Willie bathed and went to her room to rest, Lynnette took over the household with characteristic energy. By the time Willie woke and dressed in the white and silver gown Lynnette had brought along with her and persisted in badgering her about until she agreed to wear it for the occasion, things were well in hand.

Though Madame and the rest of them must be no more well refreshed than Willie, they had managed, somehow, to put a shine on the house and prepare it for their guests. When Willie walked downstairs, candles gleamed from every sconce and holder. Flowers spilled from the vases that had been arranged on every table. A delicious smell wafted from the kitchen.

And Willie thought that perhaps—if not for the presence of the awful Reverend Smithe, who she heard had been tossed quite unceremoniously onto a ship and told never to set foot in England again—it might be good to be anywhere other than Somerton House, even on a ship and heading toward India. It was preferable to standing at Nick's side when he told the world that he had chosen the beautiful, the charming, the elegant, the perfectly perfect Miss Amelia Morrison as his wife.

It was very quiet.

Willie must have noticed it earlier but her head was so filled with thoughts and her heart so heavy, she did not realize it. There was no sign of Jem or Mr. Finch near the front door, no sign of Madame or the girls bustling back and forth as surely they must do before a great number of people could be welcomed into the house.

As loath as she was to have any hand in it, Willie knew she could not leave it to chance for the night be a success. Nick deserved better than that. She turned and headed into the salon to make sure things were ready.

Though there were instruments ready near one corner of the room, there was no sign of musicians. Though there were buffet tables set up along the far wall and though they were filled with fresh fruit and huge hams and an assortment of sweets the likes of which she had never seen before, there was no sign of the servants who might have brought them there.

Curious, Willie decided to head into the kitchen. She had not made her way farther than the door when it snapped open and Nick walked into the room.

He shone like sunlight in the glow of a hundred candles, his hair as golden as a sunrise, his buff trousers clean and neatly pressed, his blue kerseymere coat bringing out the color of his eyes. Willie's heart squeezed at the very sight of him.

Nick did not look the least surprised to see her or to see that she was alone. He did look surprised to see her wearing Lynnette's white muslin dress.

The gown was no more than a whisper, a confection with short, puffed sleeves and a low neckline. The fabric was shot through with silver threads that caught the light. Looking at Nick, she could have sworn the shimmer of it was reflected in his eyes.

For a moment, he did nothing but stand with his back to the closed door. It looked as if he wanted to say something and for that same moment, Willie's breath caught over the expectation that clamored through her insides like a horse at full gallop. The next second, he swallowed down his words and Willie reminded herself that expectations were a waste of her time. She shook herself out of her daydreams and when she did, Nick pushed away from the door, anxious to get things started.

"Are we ready?" he asked.

"It appears so." Willie glanced around the room. "The food is here but your guests are not. And the staff—"

"The staff is waiting outside." Nick glanced over his shoulder at the door. "I asked if I might have a private word with you before they came in."

"I do not think that's wise." Willie made a move to get around him but he sidestepped and blocked her way. "There's nothing we can say to each other. Not anymore."

"Do you really think so?" The hint of a smile shone in Nick's eyes. "I was going to mention that we're just in time with all this. Tomorrow is the last day of June, after all, and Ravensfield's wager is set to run its course. If I wait until July or later to marry, Ravensfield will come off much the richer. And it will be all my fault. The blackguard will never let me hear the end of it."

"Tomorrow?" The word settled inside Willie, more frightening even than the awareness that assailed her when she realized the Reverend Smithe meant to kidnap her and make her his wife. "You mean to wed so soon as that?"

"Of course." Nick looked at her as if she were mad. "Why wait? As a matter of fact, I've already arranged for a special license and puffed it off to the papers. If you say no now, all the world will know that you are a jilt and that I was not man enough to make you happy."

Willie heard the words, she simply could not comprehend them. Her heart stopped, then started again with enough of a jolt that she was certain Nick heard it.

"And you are saying—"

"I am saying what I should have said before you took it into your head to leave. What I've known for so long but was too blind to see. I can't live without you, Willie, my darling. That's why I am asking. Pleading, really." He took her hand in his. "Be my wife."

"But the money!"

"Damn the money." Laughing, he kissed the little furrow of confusion between her brows, smoothing it away with the heat of his lips. "Damn the money and damn the family name. What good is it to have a family name at all when you don't have the family you want? What I want, now as always, is you, Miss Culpepper."

"And how will we live?"

Nick kissed her cheek and the tip of her ear. He glided a series of kisses across her collarbone. "On love, I think," he whispered.

Willie's heart swelled.

Her head suggested otherwise.

She pulled back enough to look Nick in the eye. "If you want to marry me tomorrow just so that the Duke of Ravensfield loses his wager . . ."

Nick had the good grace to look contrite. "Damn Ravensfield and his wager," he said. "There is one way to prove to you that I am sincere. I will elaborate later. I will also . . ." He bent to press a kiss to her throat. "Should you allow me, I will also like to demonstrate just how in love with you I am."

There were no words sufficient to convey her answer so Willie did not even try to find them. Instead, she showed Nick and when she was done kissing him thoroughly enough to let him know that she would happily let him demonstrate his feelings for her as soon as they were alone together again, they opened the door and invited their staff inside for the engagement celebration.

July 1, 1816

Though the Dashers insisted otherwise, Nick and Willie had their way. The wedding was small and quiet. The Duke of Latimer stood as groomsman and Lynnette as bridesmaid. The pews at the front of the church were packed cheek to jowl and just as Willie predicted, Madame cried copiously. She could not help but notice that Clover, Bess, Marie, and Flossie did their share of sniffling, too.

Willie wore a wreath of pink roses around her head which—or so Nick claimed—was the perfect match to the color that rose in her cheeks the night before when he found that wonderful, ticklish spot just below her navel that was as smooth as silk and tasted—or so he said—like peaches.

They had not had time to plan much of a going away but they determined that after a wedding breakfast prepared by Simon Marquand and a celebration attended by the cream of the Polite World as well as—scandalously enough—Nick's household staff, they might spend some time at one of his country houses.

They would be forced to sell the house sooner rather than later and as Nick so rightly pointed out, they may as well make some use of it before the time came.

The ceremony was appropriately solemn, even if the groom could not help but smile the entire time, and the wishes of the guests rose up like the sound of the church bells that clanged overhead when Nick and Willie turned to walk down the aisle.

Near the back of the church, a figure cloaked in black stepped from the shadows and into the aisle and they stopped, surprised.

"I couldn't wait to convey my congratulations." The Duke of Ravensfield bowed over Willie's hand and clasped Nick's in hearty good wishes. "I had not thought to ever see you look so happy, Somerton. And I certainly had not thought that it would be because you were an April gentleman."

"I must say, you are looking uncommonly contented yourself, Your Grace." Nick put an arm around Willie's shoulders. "Could that have anything to do with the fact that you made a great deal of money thanks to me? After all, I did not marry in the allotted time."

Ravensfield's grin widened. "A great deal of money, indeed." Still smiling, he pulled a thick packet from inside his greatcoat and handed it to Willie. "And I hope, ma'am, that you will accept a portion of my winnings as my bride gift. There was a great deal of wagering, you see. I've won so much that I confess, I nearly feel guilty. I thought I might share as it were. It's the least I can do for the couple who helped make me even richer than I was when I started out." Before either of them could say a thing, he bowed and hurried out of the church.

"Nick!" Willie did not need to open the packet to know it contained a great deal of money. It was very heavy. "Nick, do you think—"

"That it's enough to keep us out of the suds for a while? Certainly." Nick looked at the packet and at the retreating back of the Duke of Ravensfield in wonder. "Ravensfield!" He called to the man, but he didn't stop. He hurried toward his waiting carriage. Side by side, Willie and Nick dashed down the church steps.

"Ravensfield!" Nick called out again and this time, the duke, who had already climbed into a phaeton and had the reins in hand, had no choice but to stop. He waited, looking none too pleased with the fact that his generosity was not only being acknowledged but might be publicly proclaimed.

Nick realized it as surely as did Willie and he moved to put an end to the duke's discomfort. "Don't worry, Your Grace," he said, "I'm not going to thank you. On the contrary, I was going to point out that you were wrong."

They were on even footing again and looking relieved, Ravensfield lifted his eyebrows, waiting for more.

Though Willie suspected he was tempted, Nick did not make him wait long. "You remember," he told the duke. "Back when you said there were things I took too seriously, but love wasn't one of them. This is very serious." The look and smile Nick cast on her warmed Willie through to her bones. Her fingers still twined in his, Nick raised her hand and kissed it. "You may have won your wager, Your Grace, but I have won the love of my life. Something tells me I have gotten much the best part of the bargain. Perhaps someday I may be in a position to return the favor."

Ravensfield's glance slid to where Nick and Willie's hands were entwined and for the first time in as long as Willie had known him, the arrogant expression he wore like a second skin faded from his face. The smile that touched his lips and his eyes was genuine enough. As was the chuckle that rumbled from deep in his throat.

"I wish you a lifetime of happiness," Ravensfield said. "Both of you. But I sincerely hope you will do nothing to speed me to the place you find yourself. Life as a married man?" A shiver snaked over the duke's shoulders. "It's unthinkable!" He tipped his hat and drove on.

"Who would have thought!" A smile on her face, Willie watched him leave. "Between the generosity of His Grace and my biscuits—"

She had not meant to mention it so early in her marriage when her new husband might not be so keen to think of his wife in trade. Now that the cat was out of the bag, so to speak, there was no use trying to shove it back inside.

"I'm selling them," Willie said, laughing at the expression of sheer wonderment on Nick's face. "We're making them by the dozens and we have more and more orders every day. A good many of them from your friend Mr. Hexam!"

"Willie, you're a genius."

"Yes, I am." She laughed and stood on tiptoe to kiss Nick. "And a lucky woman, as well."

"No luckier than I am, my love." Nick kissed her most thoroughly and might have gone right on kissing her had they not been interrupted by Bob who, unbeknownst to them, had been a guest at the back of the church. Sensing the merriment of the crowd that gathered around Nick and Willie, the dog barked its approval and laughing, Nick put an arm around Willie's shoulder.

"Are you ready?" he asked.

"Do you mean for a lifetime of moments such as this?" She beamed up at her husband and didn't need to say another word, for he knew the truth as surely as she did. She had never been more sure of anything in her life.

Visit the
Simon & Schuster Web site:
www.SimonSays.com

and sign up for our
mystery e-mail updates!

Keep up on the latest
new releases, author appearances,
news, chats, special offers, and more!
We'll deliver the information
right to your inbox — if it's new,
you'll know about it.